"You're really beautiful," Dallas said, before he could stop himself.

"Come on." Allie wiggled on her stool, made uncomfortable by the attention. "You don't have to feed me lines just because we're stuck here."

"What lines?" Dallas stood, and moved around the table, so he was standing right in front of her. Allie craned her neck up to meet his eyes. "I told you, I only tell the truth."

He moved in closer, and she tilted her chin up to meet his. She didn't inch away, but sat very still.

His lips brushed hers, ever so gently. She didn't push him away, or cry out. Instead, she wrapped her hand around the fabric of his shirt and pulled him closer. She spread her knees and instantly he was between them, her arms around his neck, nothing separating them but thin fabric.

She tasted like tequila and something even more delicious, and though he tried, he couldn't get enough of her mouth. Her tongue met his in a little dance, and he felt as if, despite all the many women he'd kissed before in his life, she might as well have been the only one who mattered.

Dear Reader,

Aloha! *Her Hawaiian Homecoming* is my first book in the Heart of Hawaii miniseries, and I'm very excited to introduce you to the place I love most in the world. Like my main character, Allie, I grew up in a mixed-race family, part Japanese and part English. I was fortunate to take many trips to Hawaii growing up, and it was one of the few places I truly felt at home. I fell in love with the one-of-a-kind lava-rock beaches, the gorgeous tropical flowers growing wild, the welcoming people and their amazing aloha spirit.

Hawaii is a place where cultures often collide, and that's what happens when Allie Osaka, who's been running from Hawaii most of her life, comes home to find a cowboy from the mainland has taken over her family's coffee plantation. As they fight each other to figure out who's going to decide the fate of the Kona Coffee Estate, sparks fly.

I hope you enjoy their story—and this little escape to the Big Island—as much as I loved writing it. Our fiftieth state is a magical place, and it's no wonder so many honeymooners escape there every year. Love blooms right alongside those gorgeous birds of paradise.

Here's wishing you tons of warm sunshine, love and happiness.

Mahalo!

Cara Lockwood

CARA LOCKWOOD

Her Hawaiian Homecoming

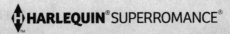

HARLEQUIN® SUPERROMANCE®

Recycling programs
for this product may
not exist in your area.

ISBN-13: 978-0-373-60911-6

Her Hawaiian Homecoming

Copyright © 2015 by Cara Lockwood

Printed in U.S.A.

™ www.Harlequin.com

Cara Lockwood is a *USA TODAY* bestselling author of eleven novels, including *I Do (But I Don't)*, which was made into a Lifetime Original movie. She's written the Bard Academy series for young adults, and has had her work translated into several languages. Born and raised in Dallas, Cara lives near Chicago with her two beautiful daughters. When she's not writing, she keeps busy running 5K races for charity, kayaking and scuba diving. Find out more about her at caralockwood.com or follow her on Twitter, @caralockwood.

Books by Cara Lockwood

**COSMO RED-HOT READS
FROM HARLEQUIN**

Boys and Toys

Visit the Author Profile page at Harlequin.com

Dedicated to Allen Rebouche,
my knight in cowboy boots.

PROLOGUE

THE BITTER, UNSEASONABLE, cold March wind whipped across Lake Michigan, whirling flakes of snow outside the high-rise condo in Chicago as Allie Osaka tore into one of dozens of boxes, all marked with the names of high-end stores.

She felt giddy as she dug into yet another wedding gift. Would it be the fancy coffeemaker? That crystal bowl she loved so much? She slipped her hands into the foam packing peanuts and pulled out two beautiful champagne flutes from her fiancé's uncle. She held them up to the light, admiring their sleek, yet delicate, design, and then carefully put them aside, marking down the item and name on her notepad for the thank-you she'd be writing later. The wedding would be in less than a month, but already they'd been swamped with presents.

She always loved staying over at Jason's swank Loop condo with the breathtaking views of the massive lake, but now it was even more special, because every Sunday morning felt like Christmas: waking up to piles of gifts just waiting to be opened, each representing some new glimpse of their future life together. The pie plates she'd use on their next Thanksgiving or the coffee mugs they'd use daily. She felt suddenly grateful for Jason's large family. It had been just her and her mom for nearly as long as she could remember. Her grandmother lived in Hawaii, but other than that, no aunts or uncles, and just a few distant cousins she didn't know well. Allie worried a little about how lopsided the bride's side of the church would be, but Jason promised he'd have his family fill out the seats. That was Jason: thoughtful to a fault.

Allie whipped her jet-black hair over one shoulder and pulled another in the stack of boxes toward her as Jason wandered out of the bedroom after he'd gotten dressed.

"Are you starting without me?" Jason protested as he headed to the kitchen, grabbing a mug from the cabinet. He poured himself a cup of coffee. He'd thrown on a pair of jeans and a T-shirt, the uniform she loved him in more than his usual work attire of tailored suits.

"I warned you I would if you kept on that iPad of yours."

"Fair enough." Jason was always busy scrolling through something or another on his tablet, usually related to his job. Allie had gotten up and dressed more than an hour before while he'd lain in bed, scrolling through emails. "I had to confirm my Boston trip this week."

Jason traveled a lot, an expectation of working for a capital start-up firm, scouring the country for the next big thing.

"Uncle Mort got us flutes," she said, nodding to the delicate stemmed glasses as she cut into the next box.

"Good ol' Uncle Mort." Jason padded over to Allie and gave her a peck on the top of her head. "Good nearly afternoon, beautiful," he said, brown eyes sparkling as he grinned, sipping at the steaming cup. Allie beamed back up at him, and she felt so happy.

She curled a strand of her shiny black hair behind her ear as she noticed the box in front of her had no return address, only black marker with Jason's name and address on the front. Probably someone who didn't choose to buy something online, Allie thought. Like maybe one of Jason's great-aunts. She glanced at Jason, who stood staring out the floor-to-ceiling windows at the snow.

She tore open the box and dug through wadded-up tissue paper. The minute she touched the coiled-up leather buried beneath, she knew something was wrong. This wasn't anything she'd asked for. She pulled out the packing material and stared, dumbfounded, at the contents: a thick leather whip, a spiked dog collar and…a leather harness…and a frilly black lace thong?

Her first instinct was to laugh, a loud, braying bark, and to hold it up to Jason so they could both shake their heads at whichever of their friends had thought *this* was an appropriate wedding gift. Probably his best man, Stephen. All some elaborate joke. But something stopped her, a tickling doubt, a small pinprick of dread in the pit of her stomach.

She reached for the envelope neatly folded in the back. It had *Jason* scribbled in a feminine loop on the front. It must be some joke. Yes, something they'd laugh about at the wedding, a story they'd retell over and over again. *Remember when...*

But then she pulled the card out and read,

Jason,

You told me no more texts or emails because you didn't want that bland little fiancée of yours to see them, but you didn't say anything about snail mail. I've been a bad girl and need another spanking. I expect to be punished severely when you're in Boston this week. Just like last time.

Xoxo,
Lisa

Lisa? As in Lisa Holly, Jason's contact for the Boston project? *That* Lisa?

Allie's heart pounded beneath her wool sweater, blood rushing loud in her ears. Fear and dread seized her. She wanted to run before her brain put together the clues before her. She wanted to close her eyes and hit Reverse, losing herself in the warm, safe bubble of her wedding plans.

"Wow, it looks miserable out there," Jason said, his back still to her as he watched the snowflakes whirl. "Let's not go anywhere today, all right, babe? Let's stay right here and hibernate."

Jason's voice sounded muffled and far off, as if he was on the other side of a wall. *Just like last time.* Allie read the words once more. Her mind whirled. When was the last time Jason had been in Boston? Just a week ago.

Allie felt light-headed and sick, suddenly.

Bland little fiancée.

Was that what she was?

Allie blinked three more times, as if somehow she could make the words disappear from the page. They didn't. And something else sat in the envelope. She tugged out a photo: Lisa, she presumed, a pale, freckled redhead, clad only in the spiked dog collar and a black thong, her pink nipples erect. Oh, God. She wore the same collar and thong sitting in the box before her. She wanted to fold it all up and pretend she'd never found it. But she had. Maybe there was still some way this could be made right. Maybe Jason could somehow explain this. She knew he couldn't, but part of her still hoped.

"Jason?" Allie's voice sounded strange to her own ears. Eerily calm as she held up the photo in her hand. "What is this?"

Jason turned, mug in hand, expecting, no doubt, to see some harmless kitchen gadget. When he saw the photo, all the blood drained from his face. That expression told Allie everything she needed to know: it wasn't a prank. It was true. All of it was true. He'd been sleeping with this woman— no, *spanking* her. For God knows how long. His Boston project had been going on for... God, more than a year.

"Allie... I..." Jason put down his mug and stepped toward her. Allie jumped to her feet, hands up.

In that moment, Allie felt like such a fool. "I trusted you," she said, and realized how dumb she sounded for saying it. What about her life had told her that trusting people ever worked out? They always found a way to disappoint. "How long?"

"What?"

"How long have you been...into this?" Allie held up the coiled whip.

"Allie, it's... I don't know, it just sort of happened."

"How *long*?" Allie's voice rose, her blood rushing in her ears.

She glared at him and saw he was tempted to lie.

"I don't know. A year, maybe more." Jason's shoulders slumped. "I always wanted to tell you, Allie. I just never knew how."

Jason had proposed to her six months ago, smack in the middle of whatever twisted stuff he was doing with Lisa Holly.

"Who else?" Allie demanded, suddenly imagining an army of women wearing dog collars and handcuffs marching through his bedroom. "Besides Lisa." If there was one thing Allie knew about betrayal, it was that it never happened just once.

"Allie, knowing that isn't going to help you."

"So *more* than just Lisa, then." Her suspicions were confirmed. Did it matter how many others? A steel wall came down then; she could almost hear the clang of metal encasing her heart. *I never should've unlocked that gate to begin with. I should've known this would happen. My fault. It won't happen again.*

Jason grabbed her shoulders. She shrugged him off.

"Don't touch me," she warned him.

"You never wanted to…experiment with me." Now he was going to make it *her* fault. Allie felt like laughing and crying all at the same time. "You know, I tried asking." Jason frowned.

"I told you I didn't want to play *Fifty Shades of Grey*," she snapped, and she meant it. Nothing about pain and sex went together, in her opinion. "I told you that wasn't my thing. If that's what you want, you need to be with someone else."

"Allie…"

"If I was too…too…*bland* for you, why did you propose?"

"Because I love you, Allie. Because…because my family loves you. Because…you had smarts, looks and everything I needed in a wife…"

"Except a twisted streak."

Bland. Bland. Bland. She couldn't get the word out of her head.

"Come on, Allie. This doesn't have to be a thing. It's not like I love Lisa Holly, or…any of the others. It's just something I like to do. A hobby." Jason rubbed his brown shaggy hair with a frustrated swipe of his hand.

"Are you *serious*?" Allie couldn't believe her ears. Was he telling her that him sleeping… spanking…and God knows what else with other women was *a hobby*?

"Golf is a hobby, Jason. *This*—" she held up the photo with shaking hands "—is *not* a hobby. This is—"

"You don't have to make this into anything."

Jason took another step toward her. She took one more back. He wasn't getting near her. Not now, maybe not ever. "Actually, it's good you know. We should start off the marriage being honest with one another. I've been wanting to ask you for a long time about an open marriage. I was going to wait at least until after the honeymoon to bring it up, but now this is much better. Now we can talk about it."

Open marriage? Allie felt the room spin. She'd thought all the grenades had exploded, but here Jason had somehow detonated another one. She wanted to laugh. He thought she'd agree to that. He clearly didn't know her at all.

"God…" Allie thought about calling off all the wedding plans, about losing the deposits they'd put down, about going public with the fact the wedding was off. "This is so complicated." Allie felt her whole world caving in, everything she thought she knew turned upside down.

"When you think about it, it's actually very simple." Jason had the nerve to smile. She wanted to slap it off his face. Nothing about this seemed wrong to him at all. He actually looked *philosophical*. Not the least bit contrite. The man felt zero guilt about anything he'd done. That realization sliced through Allie like a cold wind. "We're on much better footing now that you understand my needs. We'll have an even stronger marriage because of it. This will be better than before. You'll see."

"No." Allie had been a fool to trust him once. She wasn't about to trust him again. Allie stalked over to his front door, grabbed her coat and stomped her feet into her Sorel snow boots.

"Allie, don't make this such a big deal. We can talk about it. Think about how great this is for you. You can sleep with any man you want. I can do what you don't like with someone else. We'll both be happy. You'll see. We can talk about it."

"Nothing to talk about," she said as she felt the tears burn behind her eyes. She didn't want him to see her cry. He'd played her for a fool, but she'd manage to hold on to her last shred of dignity.

"Allie…"

"Go to hell, Jason," she muttered as she spared one last glance at the stacks of beautiful wedding gifts. She'd never get to use them. She'd never have the life she thought of with Jason, or the big, warm, loving family she'd always wanted. Allie rushed outside, half expecting Jason to follow, but he didn't. She flew into the first open elevator, jamming the main-floor button. By the time she ran across the lobby, her vision was blurry with tears as she burst through the revolving doors into the frigid Chicago air. She exhaled sharp breaths in cold, white clouds as she half ran, half stumbled down the sidewalk, nearly careening into people as she went. She felt as if she was breaking apart, her heart splintering like broken ice.

Her phone blared an incoming call in her pocket. She fumbled for it, hoping that, somehow, Jason would make this all right. He'd beg to have her back, see the error in his ways, tell her he'd been a fool. Maybe she could learn to forgive him if he really was sorry. She couldn't believe she was even considering it, but at that moment, the pain hurt too much. She just wanted it to go away.

"Allie?" her mother's voice came through the line, sounding thick with tears. "I have some bad news."

Allie felt numb. *What now? What could possibly make this day any worse?*

"Allie, honey, Grandma Osaka died."

CHAPTER ONE

A month later

DALLAS MCCORMICK CROUCHED near the rainwater tank on the Kona Coffee Estate, where one of the pipes had sprung a leak. The warm Hawaiian sun beamed down on him as he whipped off his T-shirt to help himself cool off. From his vantage point, the property sloped on a rising hillside, where he could just see the sparkling blue of the Pacific Ocean framed by green palm trees.

Perspiration dripped down his back as he grabbed a wrench from his trusty red metal toolbox. He tipped up his straw cowboy hat to get a better look at the problem: a leaky pipe leading to the holding tank. Misuko—Misu to those who knew her—might be dead, God rest her soul, but he still had a job to do on the plantation.

"You gonna stare at that pipe all day or fix it?" The voice belonged to Kai Brady, the dark-haired thirtyish pro surfer and Big Island living legend. He'd walked over from the house next door, which belonged to his aunt Kaimana, and where he'd grown up. Now he lived in a luxury condo near the beach, where the biggest breaks of the island rolled in daily. He still competed, carried a few endorsement deals and managed to find some other businesses to keep himself busy.

Dallas stood, and the two old friends clasped hands, a big grin spreading on Dallas's face.

"Why aren't you out surfing?"

"Already been," Kai admitted, and smiled. "Started at five, done by ten. If you don't watch the sun rise over the ocean, what's the point?"

"Indeed." Dallas laughed. "And who's running the coffee shop?"

"Jesse, naturally." Hula Coffee was one of his side businesses, a coffee shop in nearby Kailua-Kona he ran with his half sister, Jesse. "It's slow. You know the tourists don't get up till eleven." Kai shrugged. His eyes were covered by mirrored sunglasses, and he wore his thick black hair short and spiky. Kai, a quarter Hawaiian, a quarter Japanese and half Irish, was slimmer than Dallas, but nearly as tall. He was all wiry, tanned muscle.

"Aunt Kaimana told me to come check on you. She's worried, now that you own this place."

"*Half* this place," Dallas corrected. He still couldn't quite believe Misu had put him in her will. She'd been like family to him, but still. He wasn't, technically, related. Where he came from in West Texas, only blood mattered. "The other half goes to her granddaughter."

"Kaimana says she should've left it all to you. She's worried about the festival."

"It's still seven months away!" Dallas exclaimed. Granted, the Kona Coffee Festival and Competition every fall was a district-wide event. Anyone who grew coffee on the Big Island participated, and winners got bragging rights all year round. The Kona Coffee Estate had lost out the past three years to Hawaiian Queen Coffee, but Dallas was hoping to change that this year with a new roaster and renewed determination. It had been Misu's greatest wish to win.

Linus the goat, Misu's old "organic lawnmower," as she used to call her, ambled up then. She brayed and looked at the two men, but neither had snacks for her.

"Never too early to start strategizing. That's what Kaimana says." Kai shrugged. "And forget the competition. The shop needs your coffee. It's the favorite house brew." Hula Roast bought half the coffee produced on the estate. Without Hula Coffee, the Kona Coffee Estate would've gone bankrupt years ago. But people here on the Big Island looked out for one another. Tourists came and went, but locals were forever.

"I'm worried the granddaughter may want to sell. I can't break up the estate. Not if I want it to work." The roasting barn was on her side of the middle-line marker, which ran east to west across the property. He'd have to cough up tens of thousands to replace those buildings, and he'd have to give up prime coffee-growing land to build the barn, which he didn't want to do but would if he had to. Coffee growing had seeped into his blood. Learning how to grow something as special as Kona coffee—a kind grown nowhere else on earth—had been a revelation. He'd finally found work he was proud of doing. The Kona Coffee Estate became the home he'd always wished he'd had growing up, and nothing scared him more than losing it.

The tall coffee trees stood, some branches heavy with sweet-smelling white flowers and others teaming with green coffee berries. When they turned red, it would be time to harvest. Kai kicked a toe in the dirt. He shifted uncomfortably. Clearly, he had something on his mind other than coffee.

"I saw Jennifer yesterday," he said at last. "She came into the shop."

Dallas's spine stiffened. He didn't want to hear about Jennifer.

"Yeah?" Dallas tried to keep his voice neutral, but failed. Even at the very mention of her, his blood pressure shot up, and he had to fight the urge to ball his hands into fists. His ex's name had become a fighting word.

"Kayla was with her. She's growing big. Like waist high now. She's going to start kindergarten in the fall. She asked about you."

The words felt like poison darts aimed at his back. "I don't want to talk about them." Dallas set his mouth in a thin line, feeling every bit of raging emotion running through his chest. Kai meant well, he knew it, but he couldn't talk about Jennifer and Kayla. Not now. Maybe not ever. It was bad enough he saw Jennifer's beaming face on all those real estate billboards from here to Hilo, now featuring *Jennifer Thomas*, Hawaii reality show star. He didn't need any more bitter reminders.

"I've got to get this pipe fixed." Dallas turned away from Kai, angrily clamping the wrench onto the pipe and giving it a twist.

"Hey, man. I know it's not my business. You guys were so happy… I just… I mean, I've heard the rumors…"

"And you believe them?" Dallas wouldn't be surprised. The Big Island might be the largest in the Hawaii chain, but it was still just like one big floating small town. No local got to keep secrets.

"Of course not." Kai sounded offended. "After all you've done for me—for Jesse? Are you seriously asking me that question?"

Dallas felt rightfully put in his place.

"The rumors do make you sound like a real asshole," Kai continued. "You should just tell me the real story, so I can set the record straight. You know I've had my share of women troubles." Being one of the wealthiest and most famous surfers in the world came with a price: an endless parade of hot, gold-digging model girlfriends who made his life miserable.

Even though he knew Kai would understand the deal with Jennifer, would more than understand, he'd *relate*, he still couldn't tell. Wouldn't.

Kai looked at Dallas for a long time, waiting for an answer. Dallas focused on the pipe, twisting it hard.

"Not going to happen." Dallas met Kai's gaze, a stubborn set to his chin, the brim of his cowboy hat throwing a shadow across his face. He looked away first, assessing his plumbing handiwork. "There, all done." He dropped the tool back into his box and snapped the metal lid shut.

"Fine," Kai said. "Aunt Kaimana says you shouldn't leave crap like that bottled up inside. It'll cause cancer."

"Oh? Is that an old Hawaiian proverb?"

"With her, everything is a Hawaiian proverb," Kai said and grinned. "She's sticking up for you, by the way. She says there are at least two sides to every story."

"Aunt Kaimana is a wise woman." That was

all Dallas planned to say about what happened with Jennifer.

"Uh-huh. By the way, Jesse said she doesn't care if you get back with Jennifer or not, but that you shouldn't be single."

"Why not?"

"She says it's tacky to be a tourist attraction. If you keep sleeping with all the girls on spring break, then she's going to start printing up brochures."

Dallas felt a reluctant chuckle pop up in his throat. Jesse would do it, too. She was not the kind of woman to make an idle threat.

"I don't sleep with college kids," Dallas corrected. "I like women with more experience. Besides, I hardly ever take them home." He had drinks with tourists, and once, *only once*, he'd hooked up with one, but by and large, he usually just drove them home and tucked their drunk, slurring selves safely into their hotel beds—fully clothed. He thought about the marketing executive last weekend who'd been so intent on learning all about the aloha spirit until she'd had her fourth mai tai.

"You don't take them to your house because you probably hang out at *their* resort. Easier to sneak out in the morning."

Dallas said nothing. If Kai wanted to believe he was getting laid every weekend, then he'd just leave it at that.

Kai shook his head, his mirrored sunglasses catching the light of the sun. "Aren't you too old to be chasing tourists? *I* am, and I'm a year younger than you."

"Tourists are safer than locals." Dallas swiped at the sweat on his neck.

"Why? Because they don't stick around?" Kai cocked an eyebrow, but Dallas just half shrugged one shoulder. The truth was, the locals had heard all the rumors, and he knew for sure that plenty of them believed the lies Jennifer spread.

Kai laughed and gave his friend a hard shove. "You're not in your twenties anymore. You need to evolve, man."

"I tried evolving. It didn't work for me." Dallas thought about Jennifer again, and he felt a cold, hard pit in his stomach. "Anyway, I've got to clean up before Misu's granddaughter gets here. What's her name? Alani, I think."

"You mean Allie." Kai whistled and shook his head. "I haven't seen that girl in years."

"You know her?"

"Yeah, we grew up as neighbors, went to kindergarten together. She moved to the mainland for third grade. She liked mangos. That's what I remember. And she was a super tomboy, climbed every tree we had."

"Misu has a picture of her as a girl on her refrigerator." In that grainy old photo, Allie was a slim, lanky thing, her dark, nearly black hair in a high ponytail, standing next to Misu, who had on a big straw-brimmed hat. Misu kept the picture on a magnetic frame on her refrigerator. "Still doesn't explain why she missed Misu's funeral."

"Hey, don't be so hard on her. I'm sure she had her reasons. She had it really rough when she was little. There was a bad car accident. Her dad died. It was a miracle she survived. Anyway, she and her mom moved to the mainland after that."

"He died?" Dallas knew how that felt. His father had passed on when he was just nineteen. But as a kid of…what, eight? That must've been rough.

The sound of tires on the gravel driveway interrupted the conversation, and both men turned, staring at the path, half hidden by the tall, treelike coffee plants growing in thick rows together. A small, compact white rental car gently nosed its way up the drive. Allie, Dallas assumed.

Linus the goat ambled around the corner, and the driver, skittish, veered hard right—too sharply. The tiny compact tire went off the driveway into the ruts on the side of the road with a hard thump, and splattered the trunks of the coffee trees with mud. Dallas straightened his hat as he walked out to save the damsel in distress.

That was when she opened the door and got out to inspect the stuck wheel.

This was no gangly preadolescent girl, like the one in the dated photo on Misu's fridge. This was a full-blown woman, late twenties, with long, lean legs in formfitting jeans, and thick raven-black hair that fell long and straight past her shoulders. She did look like Misu's kin, had the same chin and pronounced cheekbones. But she was clearly an ethnic mix: not wholly Japanese, but not wholly something else, either. She had flawless olive skin and dark eyes, her thick lashes magnified by mascara. Her thin, just-defined arms that jutted from her short-sleeved T-shirt showed just how fit she was. She had a sweater wrapped around her tiny waist, a wool remnant from Chicago, no doubt, as were her high-heeled leather ankle boots. She flicked a long, shiny strand of hair from her eyes, and as she inspected the damage, the muddied wheel sank three inches into the dark muck. If she were out on the main road, at least three cars would've stopped, men stumbling over themselves trying to help her.

"Wow, that is *not* the Allie I remember," Kai said, voice low.

Dallas didn't like the way Kai said that, and suddenly he felt like calling dibs, as if they were at a bar.

She hadn't seen them yet. Dallas wondered what she would do now. A gorgeous girl like that probably wasn't used to fending for herself. No doubt, she'd be on the phone instantly, asking for help.

Instead, she looked at the wheel, and then, without missing a beat, ducked inside the car to put the gearshift in Neutral. She walked around the car in her sexy but decidedly impractical heels, the black leather boot soles sinking into the mud as she went. She put two perfectly manicured hands on the back bumper and gave it her best push. He had to admire her spirit, even if the effort was futile. She probably couldn't have weighed more than a hundred and ten pounds. One of her boots slipped, but she caught herself on the bumper.

"*That's* the Allie I remember," Kai said. "Never afraid of a little dirt." Kai stepped forward. "Allie!" he called, drawing her attention. The woman's head whipped up, and she squinted. "It's Kai! Remember me? Kai Brady?"

"Kai," Allie repeated, slowly at first and then once more, recognition dawning. "The boy who'd always steal my mango candy."

Kai laughed. "Guilty," he said, and wrapped his old friend in a hug.

"You've grown up!"

"So have you." Kai backed away. Dallas found he couldn't take his eyes off Allie. He'd seen his share of pretty girls, but something about her was just…striking. Flawless skin, a heart-shaped mouth and perfect cheekbones. Her big dark eyes turned to study him, and he felt rooted to the spot. "Uh…" She paused, her eyes flicking down to his bare chest, and it was then he remembered he'd forgotten to put his shirt back on. Where were his manners?

"This is Dallas," Kai said. "He's a good guy, once you get past the cowboy act."

"It's no act," Dallas drawled, glad he could interrupt the little reunion. He wanted more of Allie's attention. "I was raised on a ranch in Texas. I'd offer to shake your hand, but mine are…" He opened his palms to show the dirt from the water tank pipes.

"So you're *Dallas*." She said his name in a guarded way, which made him think they might have gotten off on the wrong foot, probably because he was nonfamily included in the will. His own father didn't believe in giving out land to anyone but family and he had a very narrow definition of what that meant. He couldn't blame her for thinking the same.

"Can we give you a hand?" Dallas asked.

"That would be great," Allie said, but she looked at Kai. Dallas tried not to take offense as he rounded the back of the car. Still, he had to wonder, was there something between them? He watched the two carefully, but saw nothing hint-ing at sexual tension. She looked at him like a long-lost brother. *Good*.

"We've got this," Kai assured her.

"Go on and get in and ease on to the gas when I tell you," Dallas said.

Allie left her post at the back bumper and wobbled her way to the driver's seat, her heels covered in mud. He watched the firm bend of her rear as she ducked into the car.

Dallas grabbed a huge leaf that hung near his head from a nearby banana tree and put it in front of the back tire for a little grip. Kai stood at the other side of the bumper.

"Okay, ready… Give it some gas." Dallas put his shoulder into the back of the car and heaved with all his might. Kai did the same. Allie revved the engine, the wheel spinning and flicking serious mud all over his favorite pair of Wranglers. He gritted his teeth and pushed harder, digging his worn cowboy boots into the mud for leverage. On this push, the car gave a little. He leaned in, and the car broke free of the rut, rolled over the leaf and on to the main driveway again. Kai gave a whoop.

"Teamwork!" he said, and gave Dallas a high five.

She paused on the road, and he jogged up beside her driver's-side window. She gave him a sparkling smile, showing even white teeth and a dimple in her right cheek. Right then, he could see a little of Misu in her, in the childlike glee of her expression. *This is what it looked like when her guard came down*, he thought. He felt a little light-headed. He wanted to reach straight into that front seat and kiss this girl on the lips.

This was not going to do at all. He couldn't be lusting after Misu's granddaughter, for heaven's sake. It wouldn't be right. Misu wasn't here to give her blessing, and besides, Allie still had serious questions to answer.

"Thanks, Dallas," she said now, smiling even more broadly. Her dazzling smile made him forget just what those questions were. "Where should I park?"

Dallas realized the only real pressing question on his mind right at this moment was what that tight little body looked like without clothes on. Kai nudged him, hard. He ignored his friend.

"Uh…right there," he said, pointing to a spot near the water tank, recovering himself, even as he tried to get his dirty thoughts under control. "Misu's house is the yellow one there." She nodded and rolled up the window, maneuvering the car to the spot.

"I thought you didn't like locals," Kai murmured at his shoulder.

"I don't." Dallas watched her brake lights flash. "She's not a local."

"Allie is like a little sister to me. Just like *ohana*. Family." Kai studied his friend. "Careful, Dallas. Don't look so relieved. She's not someone you play with. You get me?"

"I thought you said you didn't believe the rumors."

"I don't. But what I know as fact is that you haven't been yourself since Jennifer."

That was the understatement of the year. Before Jennifer, he would've never spent his time babysitting drunk tourists. But a lot of things had changed since then.

"Dallas, I mean it," Kai grumbled, voice low. "You have to promise me you'll stay away from Allie." Kai held Dallas by the upper arm, his grip a little tighter than it should have been.

"Kai, come on."

"Dallas. I'm asking you. As a friend. Do not play with that girl unless you plan on marrying her. And even then… Just don't mess around."

"I…" Dallas watched Allie hop out of the car, her lean form tight as she made her way to the trunk.

"Dallas?"

"Fine, Kai. Okay, I promise." Allie bent over the back of the open trunk, showing her perfectly rounded assets at the best possible angle. Dallas instantly regretted his promise.

"I'll get that," he said, offering to carry the bag.

"You don't have to." Allie looked at him suspiciously, clutching the suitcase tightly.

"*I'll* take that," Kai said, moving between them, and Allie handed Kai the bag, who took it up the porch steps and avoided Dallas's eyes. He hadn't seen Kai so protective of someone since, well, his sister, Jesse. Kai wasn't kidding about her being family. He followed Kai up the porch and slipped the key into Misu's lock.

"I've got to go check on Jesse at the coffee shop," Kai said. "It was good to see you, Allie. Though I'm really sorry about Misu."

A shadow of sadness passed across her face. "Thanks, Kai." Allie smiled warmly at him, and Dallas felt a little tinge of jealousy. He wanted all of Allie's smiles.

"You remember Jesse?"

Allie's eyes lit up. "Of course! She hated pink!"

"That's her, and she still does." Kai grinned. "Jesse still lives next door with Auntie. We'll have you over for dinner sometime soon." Kai backed off the porch. "Or come for a free cup of coffee at Hula's. And if *this guy* gives you any trouble, you call me." Kai pointed his house key at Dallas, a warning.

"I won't be trouble," Dallas promised.

"You'd better not be." Kai wasn't kidding. Kai was normally a lighthearted, easygoing guy, and when he got serious, which was hardly ever, Dallas paid attention.

"I'd love to come over for dinner and see Jesse. Good to see you, Kai." Allie waved. Dallas had left Misu's place exactly as it had been when she'd gone into the hospital after her sudden and devastating heart attack. All of her furniture and most of her clothes were still here. The simple overstuffed white linen couch she loved sat in the middle of the living room, draped with the pink-and-yellow Hawaiian-breadfruit quilt. The kitchen was dated but clean, its white-tiled floor and older appliances ready for use, and the breakfast nook nearby, which acted as her dining room. Little had changed in twenty years. Dallas knew Allie had been here once. That photograph had been taken right on Misu's porch, so she'd been here then anyway. Her house would've looked much the same.

Allie went straight to the kitchen, running her finger along the old yellow countertop, stopping at the refrigerator. She plucked the photo of her and Misu from the freezer door and stared at it, running a finger over Misu's face.

"She was a good woman," Dallas felt the need to say.

"She was," Allie agreed, her voice sounding far away. She put the photo back and blinked as she looked around the room. She gave the small house a quick tour. "Where's the bathroom?"

"Don't you remember?" he asked her.

Allie shook her head.

"It's outside," he said.

"Outside?" she echoed.

ALLIE STOOD AND stared at her only working shower.

It was *outside*, in a cabana with walls but *no roof.* She plopped down her bag and stared.

How on earth had *this* little tidbit about her grandmother's house escaped her? She used to live here when she was little, that much she remembered. But how old had she been? Seven? Eight? That was before… Well, before the car accident, before she and her mom moved to the mainland, where it had been just the two of them against the world. Of course, with her mom working two jobs, it had pretty much been Allie all on her own. Allie preferred it that way, actually. Anytime she depended on anyone—like Jason— they failed her.

"So if you want to talk about the estate, I'd be happy to…" Dallas stood by her, lingering near the door. Allie did not turn to look at him. If she did, she'd stare at his muscled chest, and she didn't want to do that. She didn't have time for guys who looked as if they belonged in a sexy-cowboy calendar. She had sworn off men this time, possibly for good. The fact that she was very aware of his every movement made her feel jumpy and anxious. Her mind might want to be done with men, but clearly her body wasn't. It had other ideas about what she ought to do with Dallas McCormick.

"I just want to shower."

"Oh…sure." Dallas paused, as if waiting for her to invite him in. She nearly barked a laugh out loud. With abs like that, and those crystal-blue eyes, he was probably used to women throwing themselves at him all the time. *Well, not this one, buddy.*

"I'd like some privacy." Allie was proud that she made it sound official.

"Sure thing, ma'am." Dallas grinned, unoffended, and then tipped his hat at her as he backed out of the cabana. The door slapped shut behind him, and Allie moved to secure the bolt. With Dallas and his broad, chiseled chest out of the room, Allie felt as though she could breathe for the first time. She stared up to where the ceiling should be but saw only blue sky dotted with fluffy white clouds.

"How are you supposed to take a shower when it's raining?" she muttered to herself.

Allie whipped up her thick jet-black hair off

her neck, panting in the Hawaiian humidity as sticky sweat trickled down the nape of her neck.

All she remembered from her childhood at Grandma Misu's were endless afternoons building sand castles on the pristine white beach about a mile away, and of Misu's sticky sweet homemade mochi rice cakes and mouthwatering teriyaki chicken. She had fond memories of Misu, but hadn't seen her grandmother in years. Money had always been tight growing up. She and her mom had barely made rent, much less managed to scrape together enough for two plane tickets to Hawaii. But if Allie was honest, since her father died, she'd been in no hurry to come back. For everyone else, Hawaii might be paradise, but for her, it represented just bad memories.

Still, Allie felt a pang of guilt; she should've come for her grandmother's funeral. But it had all been too overwhelming—dealing with Jason and the called-off wedding. She'd been in no shape to travel anyway. She hadn't been able to get out of bed, much less book a flight.

Jason was just one more person she couldn't depend on, Allie thought. She tried her best not to slide into a pity party: girl loses her dad in a car accident at age eight, is left with a hardly there, working-two-jobs single mom and then a string of unreliable boyfriends…and now Jason. She hated feeling sorry for herself, but sometimes it beckoned like a warm, cuddly robe. Sometimes she just wanted to slip into it for a little while.

She kept coming back to the single fact that she should've known Jason would do this. He'd been her first really serious relationship, but she'd had plenty of short-term boyfriends who'd disappointed in various ways. How could she have been so blind?

Denial. It was probably how she'd spent two years with Jason and never even had an inkling about his penchant for S and M. Granted, he'd been bossy and controlling most of their relationship: always wanting to be the one to decide where they ate, what they did on weekends and even weighing in on what she wore. Sometimes it had grated, but most of the time she'd been fine with just going along. Happy to do what made him happy. He'd always been decidedly in control in the bedroom, but he'd never *hit* her, not once.

She'd thought she knew him better than anyone, but it turned out she didn't know him at all.

Just because she didn't like being beaten like a piñata during sex, she thought bitterly. She was sorry, but she liked pleasure with her sex, *not* pain. Why did that make her boring?

She blinked fast. No more pity party. *That's quite enough of that, Allie.* She should look at the bright side—now she was back on her own. *I'll never have my heart broken again, because there's no way I'm letting anyone within a five-block radius of it.* Allie was officially done with men.

CHAPTER TWO

STANDING IN THE HOT, open-aired shower, Allie
fanned herself. Jet-lagged and sweaty, all she
wanted to do was get clean, change into some
shorts and track down the nearest real estate
agent. She'd use the money to travel the world
by herself. She didn't know where she'd go, but
she'd figure it out.

She glanced up at the blue sky and blinked.

No roof? Who did that? She wondered if anyone would buy a place with an outdoor bathroom.
Allie sighed and turned the knobs of the shower,
half expecting them not to work. Water sputtered
out, and surprisingly, it felt warm, but then again,
the air was a balmy eighty-two degrees. Everything would feel warm, even at room temperature. Allie shrugged out of her too-hot jeans,
T-shirt and wool sweater and stepped into the
warm shower, letting the water rinse over her. She
exhaled. *Remember the positives*, she thought.
*You're not stuck in subzero weather in that bliz-
zard you left back home, and once the property
is sold, you can travel for a year.* That was all she

had to do: keep moving. People couldn't disappoint you if you didn't let them.

Allie rinsed her hair in the warm water and sighed, almost forgetting about the lack of roof when a bright red blur zoomed past her, practically thumping her head.

She jumped, startled, until she saw the intruder: a small, brilliant red bird with black-trimmed feathers, its beak thin and scooped downward. It looked as if a cardinal had mated with a hummingbird, a species she'd never seen before. *Definitely not in Chicago anymore*, she thought. The bird cocked its head to one side and eyed her.

Allie felt like jumping out of the shower and running back to the house, but instead, she shook the shower curtain and the bird flew away.

Wonder what he was doing in here anyway, she thought, rinsing off. She shut down the water and stepped out, reaching for a fluffy white towel. She grabbed one from a hook and wrapped it around her chest, tucking it under her armpits, and then she wrapped her head up in a towel, turban-style, and looked at herself in the foggy mirror. She swiped at it with one hand, wondering what that brown stripe was along the top of her head towel, and that was when she realized the brown stripe was *moving*.

It was a centipede—a huge, disgusting, hundred-leg brown centipede, nearly a foot long and thicker than her thumb.

Allie did what any reasonable city girl would do: she screamed.

She flicked her head downward, and in the same instant, bounced against the thin door and tumbled outside, barely keeping the small light-weight towel wrapped around her as the turban fell to the ground. In her panic, Allie couldn't see where the centipede went. Was it tangled in her hair? Running down her back?

It was a friggin' monster, that was all she knew. She'd never seen a bug that big in Chicago. Ever.

Then she saw the horrible insect crawling in the black lava dirt. She felt relief: it wasn't on her! And yet she felt complete terror as she realized the huge bug was headed straight for her bare toes, its huge menacing back pincher stinger wagging as it went.

She hopped on one foot, squealing, unable to help herself as she looked around for a weapon—a stone, a stick, anything. She couldn't step on the thing with her bare foot.

That was when a square-toed brown cowboy boot crunched it for her, mashing it into the dirt.

"Got it, ma'am," Dallas drawled, an amused smile on his face as the thing twisted and turned under his boot. He ground it farther into the dust.

Allie had never felt so relieved and so embarrassed at the same time. Her wet hair hung in strands down her shoulders, black mud caked her once-clean toes. She clutched the towel more tightly around her chest, but it did no good. She might as well have been wearing a washcloth.

"Th-thanks," she managed, trying to regain her composure. He'd put on a T-shirt, she noticed, wondering fleetingly about whether the Cheeseburger in Paradise was a real restaurant. It clung to his muscular chest, stretched and near popping as if his pecs were planning an escape. He was handsome, even she had to admit. He had golden hair, worn shaggy, with natural highlights from the sun. His age was hard to place, but midthirties, Allie guessed. She felt drawn to him, and immediately shut down the urge.

"Those things are nasty. Sting hurts worse than a yellow jacket. Want me to check for any more?"

"More?" Allie's voice came out as a squeak of fear. She hadn't even considered there'd be another one of those creatures.

"Sometimes they travel in pairs," Dallas drawled, and Allie was unable to tell whether he was teasing or not. "I'll check."

"Okay." Allie stood very still as Dallas made a slow sweep, walking so close to her she could catch the faded scent of some earthy aftershave. He just grazed her shoulder as he glided behind her, and she was more than aware she was standing almost naked in front of him. He seemed to be taking his time, she thought, and doing more looking at her skin than for bugs. She felt suddenly shy.

No one has seen me naked since....Jason. She shifted on her bare feet, very aware of Dallas's eyes on her.

"You're all clear," he said at last, stepping away from her, eyes still on her bare knees.

"Good," Allie said, her face still flushed. "Uh...thanks."

"Anytime, ma'am." Dallas grinned, a big, white smile that made the pit of her stomach feel fuzzy.

"I've...uh...got to get dressed. The Realtor's coming..."

"The who?" Dallas snapped to attention, his demeanor immediately changing from affable country boy to guarded cowboy.

"Realtor. I took the liberty of inviting Jennifer Thomas. I've heard she's the best on the island. I saw her on that show...*Hawaii Living*?"

Dallas looked suddenly pale, as if he'd seen a ghost, but Allie kept going.

"She said she might even want to put the property on the show when I talked to her on the phone..."

"I don't want her here." Dallas's voice was a grunt.

Allie, surprised, shifted on one bare foot to another, conscious of the sticky dirt beneath her bare toes. "Oh, well… I don't know if I can cancel with such late notice. Her assistant was very clear…"

"She *can't* come here. She—" Dallas seemed to lose the ability to speak "—just *can't*."

"But…" Allie didn't get to finish her sentence. Dallas had turned and was stalking away from her, his back taut with anger, his boots making rivets in the mud.

HOURS LATER, DALLAS still felt hot with anger. He couldn't believe Allie had invited his ex straight to his doorstep. Might as well just let loose the rest of the lions and tigers and bears.

Jennifer would be more bloodthirsty than all of them. Dallas was arguing with Jennifer's assistant on the phone that afternoon when he heard a roar near the driveway and realized he'd have to tell the woman to her face just how unwelcome she was. He walked out of his front door and down the path of coffee trees toward Misu's place, carrying a bundle of papers rolled up and sticking out of the back pocket of his jeans. He made it to the clearing in time to see the goat skitter away at the sight of Jennifer's cherry-red convertible BMW. Smart goat. Jennifer was the kind of woman who didn't mind running over anything in her path. Dallas still had the tire tread on his back to prove it.

He frowned as he watched her step out of her sports car, wearing her usual uniform of over-priced designer clothes, which clung tightly to her curves, her too-short skirt inching up her thigh as she slammed the car door with a *thunk*. She met his gaze over the car roof and smiled just slightly, triumph on her face as she flicked a long, curving strand of blond hair off her shoulder. *She must love that Allie invited her here, must be relishing every minute*, he thought.

He glanced in the backseat and saw it was empty, save for Kayla's pink-and-green striped booster seat. She'd be at day care anyhow. He felt a pinch in his chest as he saw her small white stuffed bear. Mr. Cuddles, he remembered. She used to be inconsolable without him. He felt the urge to run it over to her at day care, but then felt a dull ache in his rib cage when he realized that wasn't his job anymore. Hadn't been for nearly a year. Jennifer had made sure of that.

He watched as she vigorously shook Allie's hand, his stomach tightening into knots. He didn't know if he wanted to shout or run, but his whole body felt as if it was on fire. The two women standing there looked like yin and yang: complete opposites, dark and light. Jennifer was a walking Barbie doll, clad all in pastels and wearing high-heeled wedge sandals. Allie had on flip-flops and hiking shorts, not wearing a bit of makeup and looking all the prettier for it. Even angry at Allie, Dallas felt a strong pull to her. Seeing Jennifer standing so close to her made Dallas want to step between them, if only to protect Allie from being eaten alive.

He couldn't believe that once upon a time, Jennifer had shared his bed. She'd been as aggressive there as she was everywhere else in her life. And just as selfish, he thought. It would serve her right if he told the whole island the truth of what had happened between them. Except that they both knew why he wouldn't do that. It wasn't just Jennifer after all. There was Kayla, and Dallas wasn't about to do anything that would hurt that sweet, innocent girl. Jennifer knew it, too. Counted on it.

"Jennifer." Dallas's voice was stern. Jennifer glanced up, worry flickering across her face for a split second. She knew what she'd done, and the honesty of guilt showed in her eyes for the briefest of moments before she quickly buried it beneath a disingenuous smile. *That's right*, Dallas thought. *Just pretend nothing happened.*

"Dallas," she purred, and then threw her arms around him as if they were old friends. He staggered back a step, completely taken off guard. The woman had the nerve to *touch* him? "Good to see you again."

Allie's eyes widened, as she glanced from Dallas to Jennifer and back again.

"You two know each other?"

"Oh, we're *old* friends."

Dallas firmly unclasped her hands from his neck and stepped backward. "No, we're not."

Jennifer flipped her blond hair from her shoulder, not bothering to register the protest. "I was so surprised when Allie here told me you were selling that I wanted to come *right* over." Jennifer ignored Dallas's hot glare.

"I'm not selling."

Jennifer swayed a little, unsteady on her feet. "But Allie said…"

"Allie doesn't speak for me." Dallas set his lips in a thin, determined line.

"You don't want to sell?" Now it was Allie's turn to look dumbfounded.

"Well…I thought it was too good to be true." Jennifer considered Allie and Dallas.

"Now's the part where you tell Allie the bad news," Dallas said. He hated being so close to Jennifer and hated that Allie had brought her here, but the fact was, he would enjoy this next part.

"What bad news?" Allie had no idea what was about to hit her.

"I'm sure you've already considered the problem of selling only Allie's half." Dallas tucked his thumbs through his belt loops. Jennifer suddenly looked uneasy.

"What problem is that?" Allie's voice was sharp.

"*My* half has the seaside views that the tourists want." Dallas nodded toward his side of the property, which sloped downward. Allie's house would have a seaside view, except it was completely obscured by tall coffee trees, dotted with white flowers. Dallas, on the other hand, had a house closest to the beach, nothing on three sides but sparkling blue Pacific Ocean. "Plus, *I* have indoor plumbing."

"You *what*?" Allie's face bunched up in anger.

He took a second to enjoy it. Wasn't his fault that Misu had turned him down when he'd offered to build a bathroom to her cabin when he was doing the same for his.

"And then there's the volcano," Dallas continued, unable to help himself. "Technically, your half of the estate is in Lava Zone Three. I'm in four."

"I know about the volcano. But what are the zones?" Allie's gaze roamed from Dallas to Jennifer and back again.

"It means that you're in a more hazardous zone than Dallas is." Jennifer picked invisible lint from her shirt. "Your house is more likely to be wiped out by a lava flow."

"What?" Allie grew pale.

"The divider line pretty much goes right

through the property." Dallas pointed from one end of the land, drawing an invisible line with his finger straight across the ground. "Because of that, and the lack of a seaside view and plumbing, your half will fetch less than *half* of what mine will if you're selling to developers. If we sold our shares together and split the profit, you'd make far more. Isn't that right, Jennifer?"

"Well…" His ex tried to hedge, but even as slick as she was, she couldn't sidestep this fact. "Dallas is mostly right."

"Mostly right?" Allie looked as if she was going to explode. Her dark eyes sparked like steel striking flint. "How much difference are we talking about?"

"Well, realistically…" Jennifer hesitated, biting her lower lip.

"Spit it out."

"The real value is the land *and* the Kona coffee on it. If you took that away, as well as the seaside views… You've got a pretty small house and a coffee-processing facility, but only a very small share of the actual Kona crop, so it wouldn't be a workable plantation. You'd have to sell it strictly as a residence, and with the lava zone issue and no plumbing…about half as much as we talked about on the phone."

Allie couldn't hide her disappointment, and Dallas saw it clearly on her face. Too greedy, Dallas thought. That was the problem with Allie and every other gorgeous woman he'd ever met. Too damn greedy. Maybe she and Jennifer had more in common than he thought.

"And you can't even get that," Dallas said. "According to the will, Allie can't even sell her half without getting permission from Aunt Kaimana first."

"What? I don't remember that in the will," Allie protested.

"Page three, section E," Dallas said, pulling the will from his back pocket. He'd unrolled a photocopy of the will and began to read it aloud.

Jennifer and Allie listened with interest.

"'If the land is to be divided and then sold, it is the will of Misuko Osaka that Kaimana Mahi'ai oversee the division and issue written approval of the final sale before official transfer can be made to both parties. No sale will take place unless approved by Ms. Mahi'ai.'"

"Wait—Kai's aunt? What does Kai's aunt have to do with my grandma's estate?" Confusion flickered across Allie's face.

Jennifer's eyes narrowed. "You didn't tell me this was a clause in the will." She turned to Allie, her brow wrinkled in frustration.

"I didn't know," Allie confessed, having clearly missed that part. She took the will from Dallas's hands and scoured the wording.

Jennifer sighed, annoyed. "Well, this is a waste of my time, then." Her cheery manner disappeared, and she turned away from Allie.

"Wait—where are you going?"

"Call me *after* you talk to Kaimana," Jennifer said, slipping on her designer sunglasses as she walked back to her BMW. "That is, *if* she'll talk to you."

"Wait!" Allie called.

"Don't bother." Dallas narrowed his eyes as they both watched Jennifer roar back out of the driveway.

"The lawyer didn't read that clause over the phone," Allie said.

"Nope, he didn't." Dallas grinned.

"But *you* knew it was there all along." Allie turned on Dallas, her eyes flashing. He didn't know how she did it, but she managed to look diabolically sexy when she was mad. Dallas had to admit, maybe he didn't mind pushing her buttons. "You couldn't have mentioned it to me before?"

"Me?" A harsh laugh escaped Dallas. "If you were the one who wanted to strip the land and sell it to no-good resort developers for a quick buck, then you should've read the fine print. You had a copy of the will."

"Yeah, but…that's not fair." Allie balled up the photocopy of the will in her hands.

"Oh, really? What else do you call looting your grandmother's property?"

"I'm not looting!" Allie looked mad enough to spit.

"That's right. Not on my watch you're not," Dallas warned, taking another step closer. "You'll have to go through me first."

"You aren't even family." Allie's face turned beet red as anger strangled her words. "What gives you the right…"

"Misu gave me the right. I'm part of this, too, whether you like it or not. She split the land between us for a reason. You haven't been acting like family! You don't know the first thing about your grandmother. You haven't even visited, not once in the five years I've been here. Maybe if you'd come, even once, you'd see the land is worth keeping. But you didn't bother!"

His words found their mark, better even than he thought they would. Allie suddenly looked as if she might slap him straight across the face.

"You don't know what you're talking about," she ground out, eyes blazing, hands balled into fists at her sides.

"I know you didn't come to her funeral. What kind of granddaughter does that?"

Allie looked stricken, as if he'd slapped *her* right across the face. The pain was evident, and Dallas was surprised to see it. He hadn't thought

Allie cared, one way or another. Now, seeing her face, he realized he was wrong. But it was too late to take back what he'd said. The words hung between them like a barbed-wire fence.

Allie said nothing, just turned her back on him and stalked away. He almost called out to her, but something in the way she rigidly moved away from him stopped him cold.

CHAPTER THREE

ALLIE FURIOUSLY SWIPED at the tears on her face. *She* wasn't the one who'd abandoned her grandmother. When had *Grandma Misu* visited, even once, in the twenty years Allie and her mother had struggled on the mainland, moving from one job to the next? What had her grandmother ever done for her besides the annual birthday and Christmas cards she got every year, sometimes weeks late because they were sent to an old address?

Sure, she felt bad about missing the funeral. She should've gone, should've somehow managed the heroic strength to put aside her heartbreak over Jason and just shown up, but, honestly, she'd never asked her grandmother for this land. She had never asked her grandmother for anything. How could she? She lived an ocean away in a different time zone. She knew her grandmother loved her, knew that she hadn't been swimming in cash, but still. Part of Allie felt as if it was just one more person who wasn't there when she needed them most.

Long ago, before Allie's father died, Allie had been the apple of Misu's eye. That was what she remembered—a doting grandmother who sewed her clothes and played endless rounds of doll tea parties on her breezy veranda. But the car crash had changed all that.

Allie still remembered the screech of tires, the sudden crack of metal and glass like a clap of thunder ripping apart the sky. The car accident had taken her father's life and altered hers forever. One of the therapists she'd seen once had called it survivor's guilt. But Allie thought they should just speak plainly: the accident had been her fault. She knew the truth. Her mother knew it. Grandma Misu knew it. If Allie hadn't been in the backseat of the car that day, her father would still be alive. She'd been the reason he'd swerved into the other lane. Allie wouldn't have spent a childhood moving from town to town, her mother chasing whatever low-paying job she could find.

After the accident, everything had changed. Grandma Misu changed. Her only son, dead. She wouldn't get out of bed. Couldn't even hug Allie goodbye that morning she and her mother left.

Allie blinked fast, pushing away the memory. Dallas had it all wrong. Allie hadn't abandoned her grandmother; her grandmother had left her first. Not that she blamed her. Allie had paid the price for the car accident: she'd grown up largely alone.

It was why she'd fallen so hard for Jason. He had a huge family, and they all lived near him in Chicago. When she'd met them, a big Irish clan that got together every Fourth of July and nearly every other holiday, she felt like at last, she was part of a family. A real family. If she was honest with herself, she missed Jason's sisters and cousins and aunts and uncles even more than she missed him.

She sat on one of the bamboo chairs on her grandmother's porch, staring off toward the rooftop of Kaimana's house, just visible above the coffee trees in the distance. She'd have to go talk to the woman sometime. She hadn't seen Kai's aunt in nearly twenty years. She'd been her grandmother's best friend. She held the paper in her hand, the release paper she'd dug out of her copy of the will, the one Kaimana would have to sign to let Allie sell. She'd love to see Dallas's face after she managed to get it signed.

She thought about Dallas and then felt a flash of anger once more. She had no idea how he'd wormed his way into her grandmother's good graces, but Allie didn't trust him, and it had nothing to do with Jason or her dislike of men at the moment. Dallas was up to no good.

Allie pulled herself to her feet. It was time to

talk to Kaimana, see if she'd be open to getting this over with quickly.

She walked down the path of coffee trees and marveled at the bright coffee berries hanging from the branches. Many had turned from green to orange. The breeze brought the smell of the ocean and the raw scent of leaves in the sun. A red bird flew by, landing on a nearby branch. A bright orange, almost red, berry fell to the dirt near Allie's feet, and she was overcome with a sudden memory of her and Kai playing tag in the thick foliage. She'd nearly collided with her father's ladder, where he had climbed up high, basket dangling from his forearm as he picked coffee cherries. He'd smiled down at her, a berry dropping from his nearly full container.

"Careful, I don't want a broken leg, now," he'd warned her, half teasing, a twinkle in his eye as he grinned, showing off the big dimple in his left cheek.

Allie stopped, the memory vivid as it washed over her. She thought she'd long since cataloged every last image she had of her father. But this one was new. She held the hard berry between her fingers and rolled it, just like she'd done when she was five. She stood awhile in the same spot, waiting for something more to come to her, but it didn't. That was what memories of her father were like: fleeting.

Like all the men in her life, she mused, thinking about Jason. *No pity party, Allie. No time for that.*

She glanced at the nearly red cherry in her hand and studied it.

How did it become that brown split bean she'd seen in countless bags of coffee lining store shelves?

She had no idea. Allie liked coffee, okay, as long as it was loaded up with enough sugar and cream that she could barely even taste the coffee bean. Never even had a cup of Kona that she remembered. Funny, she thought. Her father had loved coffee, claimed no other coffee on earth rivaled the richness of Kona. The dark, fertile soil made by the volcano made it so good, he'd said.

She'd never learned to drink coffee straight like he did. Hers was always laden with vanilla syrups and milk, mocha or caramel drizzle. She rolled the red berry between her finger and thumb, thinking as she walked.

The cool breeze coming down from the mountain caressed her bare shoulder. Clouds rolled in off the hillside from seemingly nowhere. A big raindrop splashed in the black dirt in front of her. Odd, she thought, since to the south the sky was a clear blue. Guess it was a tropical shower. She hurried her pace and came to an open clearing, where a bright blue house stood. Where Kai had grown up. It had been painted since she'd been there last, and the porch furniture was different, but she was surprised by how familiar it seemed. She remembered the big mango tree sprouting up in the yard. She and Kai would climb it daily and see who could pick the fruit from the highest branches.

Another raindrop fell, followed by several others, plunking hard in the nearly black lava soil. She barely made it the hundred or so feet to the porch, before the rain came down in sheets, blanketing the rows of Kona coffee trees behind her in warm tropical rain. She shook raindrops from her hair as she eyed the front door. Bright pink-and-white tropical flowers grew near the porch. A huge bird of paradise rose up from the edge of the porch step, a magnificent flower growing like an ordinary marigold.

She rapped hard on the door. Seconds later, a heavyset woman with warm eyes and thick black hair, a silver streak running through it, opened the screen door. Allie recognized the familiar smile. She wore her same old flowered muumuu with a shiny dark macadamia-nut necklace. Besides the streaks of gray in her hair, she had aged little in twenty years.

"Aloha," she said in greeting.

"Aloha." Allie smiled. "I'm Allie Osaka. Misu Osaka's granddaughter? Remember me?"

"Aah… Uh… *Ōlelo Hawai'i 'oe?*"

Allie blinked at the woman. Was she speaking Hawaiian?

"I'm sorry, I don't understand."

"Ōlelo Hawai'i 'oe?" the woman repeated, looking at Allie expectantly. Allie shook her head and spread her hands.

"Do you speak English?" Allie asked her, wondering if the woman *only* spoke Hawaiian. Was that even possible? She didn't remember that before, but then her memory was spotty.

"A'ole no e law aka makaukau ma ho'okahi wale no olelo."

Now Allie was completely lost. Kaimana held up one finger, the international sign for "wait" and then disappeared back inside her house. She came back a few minutes later with a bag of her grandmother's coffee.

"Kona coffee?" Allie asked, pointing to the cup and then to the trees behind her.

Kaimana nodded. "Kona," she repeated, and pointed to the row of coffee trees behind her as she handed her the open ziplock bag. She smelled it and was immediately reminded of her father. He'd always smelled like fresh roasted coffee.

"Uh… *Mahalo.*" Allie knew the Hawaiian word for thank you. That and *aloha* were the extent of her Hawaiian language skills.

"A'ole pilikia," Kaimana said.

"Mmm," she murmured, inhaling.

Kaimana nodded, as if she knew this already. Allie felt hopeful then. Maybe she did understand English.

Allie held the bag, wondering what it would taste like brewed. She should've made more of an effort to know her grandmother, to know her coffee. But it had been so expensive. Kaimana watched her, smiling all the while.

Then she disappeared back inside her house and soon reappeared, carrying a teak bowl filled with hibiscus flowers and a half-strung lei. She bustled out to the porch and sank down on a wooden rocking chair, motioning for Allie to sit in the other. She began stringing the lei while Allie held the coffee, wondering what to do next.

Nearby, bright-colored birds chirped, and a warm breeze blew, rattling the delicate glass wind chimes hanging from Kaimana's porch. They made a high tinkling sound.

"Ms. Mahi'ai…"

"Kaimana," she interrupted, pointing at herself.

"Yes, uh…Kaimana, I'm not sure if you understand me, but my grandma Misu…"

"Misu," Kaimana repeated and nodded.

"Yes, Misu. She left me the coffee plantation,

but I need to sell it. Misu wanted me to get your permission before I did that and…"

Kaimana's face looked blank as she strung flowers on the lei.

Allie realized none of what she was saying was going in. She barreled on anyway.

"I need you to sign this paper, please." Allie reached in her back pocket and pulled out the folded slip as well as the ballpoint pen she'd stashed there. She pretended to write with the pen on the paper and pointed to Kaimana afterward. "You. Sign?"

Kaimana made no move to pick up the paper. Instead, she finished looping the last flower on the string and expertly tied it, her brown fingers working nimbly. She held it up for Allie to inspect and said, *"Nani?"*

Allie had no idea what she meant, so she just nodded. "Uh… *Nani.*" And nodded again.

"Ko Aloha Makamae E Ipo," Kaimana said, smiling, as she stood and draped the lei around Allie's neck. It was beautiful and soft, emanating a sweet, tropical fragrance.

"Oh, I couldn't accept this."

Kaimana shook her head and put up her hands, showing she wouldn't take it back. *"Nau wale no."*

At a loss, Allie had no choice but to take it.

"Mahalo," Allie said finally. "But about the paper. If you could just sign…"

Kaimana waved the paper away. "Dallas," she said.

"Dallas?" Allie echoed. "No, Dallas can't sign this. Dallas…" Wouldn't, even if he could.

"Dallas," Kaimana said, sounding certain he would handle it. *"A'ole pilikia. Aloha 'auinala. Kipa hou mai,"* Kaimana said, and she patted Allie on the shoulder and then went back inside and closed her door. Allie heard the lock being thrown.

"Kaimana? Ms. Mahi'ai? Are you in there?" Allie knocked, but Kaimana didn't come to the door. "Hello? Uh…aloha?" Allie knocked once more.

Again, she heard nothing.

That went well, she thought sarcastically, staring at her unsigned piece of paper and Kaimana's locked door. What now?

Allie stomped back across the plantation and found Dallas casually unloading a big toolbox from the back of his black pickup. She felt irrationally angry at him as he worked. If he wasn't so stubborn, so full of himself, maybe the two of them could've found some kind of compromise. He glanced up and tipped his straw cowboy hat in her direction, his blue eyes amused.

"Ma'am," he drawled. She ignored him. He let

out a low chuckle as she walked past. "How did that conversation with Kaimana go?"

She whirled on him, his smug grin feeling like salt in her paper cut.

"As if you don't know," Allie spat out, annoyed. Dallas had sent her over there knowing full well she'd get nowhere without a translator. "She doesn't even speak English!"

Dallas raised his eyebrows in surprise and then inexplicably burst into laughter.

Allie shifted uneasily, foot to foot. "What's so funny?" Allie felt exposed, as if she might suddenly be transported back to the cafeteria in middle school. The joke was on her; she just didn't know how.

Dallas nearly had tears in his eyes he was laughing so hard. He laid a big strong hand across his flat stomach as he howled.

"She speaks English just fine," he managed to get out.

"What are you talking about?"

"She's one hundred percent fluent, as fluent as you or I. But when she doesn't like what's going on, she'll usually refuse to speak English. Just ask the traffic cop who pulled her over for speeding last month."

Understanding dawned on Allie a beat too late. "She *tricked* me?"

"Probably just wanted to put you off for a little while," Dallas said and grinned. His blue eyes sparkled. He clearly was enjoying this. "Whatever you were asking her about, she didn't like."

Allie felt a surge of annoyance and complete embarrassment for making a fool of herself by blubbering on as if Kaimana didn't understand her, complete with full pantomime. Yet she considered the idea of a near stranger banging down her door and asking to sell the property of her once dearest friend in the world. Okay, maybe she *hadn't* been the most tactful there. She still felt like a total idiot. And Dallas got a good laugh out it. At her expense. That was the worst part. She felt her cheeks burn. He'd probably sent her there knowing full well she'd be tricked.

"You're still going to have to talk to me about selling," Allie said. "Even if I can't get her signature, I'll find a way."

"Maybe you should just get used to growing coffee. At some point, we'll have to talk about the harvest."

Allie felt a flash of anger. The last place on earth she wanted to settle down was Hawaii, the place her father died. And the last *man* on earth she ever wanted to deal with was Dallas McCormick. He reminded her of Jason, of the kind of man who thought the world owed him everything.

"I'll talk about the harvest as soon as *you* talk about selling."

Dallas's blue eyes grew cold like steel. "Not going to happen," he told her, shaking his head. She watched as he picked up the toolbox and began walking toward the big metal barn on the property. *Her* side of the property, she realized.

"Where do you think you're going?" she demanded, hands on her hips.

Dallas stopped and calmly turned. "To see if I can fix the roaster. It has to be working by harvest time. Or we need a new one."

"The barn is on *my* side of the property line. I didn't say you had *permission* to fix it."

Dallas froze, annoyance flashing across his face. Allie thought, *Good. See what it feels like, buddy, when you don't have the upper hand.*

"Allie…" Dallas's voice held a warning.

"You may not want to sell, but as long as this is *my* property, I can do what I want with it. I can knock down that barn and sell that roaster for parts, if I want to. I don't need Kaimana's permission for *that*. I could even knock down all the coffee trees on my side."

Dallas looked stricken. "You wouldn't."

"Try me."

Dallas hesitated, as if deciding whether or not to call her bluff. Allie dug her tennis shoe in the ground and dragged it across the dark lava dirt, making a line.

"*That's* your side, and *this* is mine," she declared, glaring at him. "You cross this line without my permission and…" Allie walked over to the nearest row of coffee trees on her side. She snapped one of the branches with bright orange coffee cherries on them.

"No…don't!" Dallas protested, but he was too late. She dropped the branch in the dirt and stomped on the coffee berries.

Dallas flinched as if seeing the damaged limb brought him physical pain. He frowned, his blue eyes hard and glinting. "That was one of our oldest trees," he growled.

"Good. I'll start with cutting down *that* one first."

Allie left him standing there, toolbox in hand, as she stalked off to the house, strode up the steps and slammed the door.

CHAPTER FOUR

BY THE NEXT MORNING, Allie was beginning to regret her show of temper. Not that she wasn't still furious with Dallas and didn't love seeing that smug smile wiped clean off his rugged face, but Allie usually didn't get so mad, so irrational. She'd known the minute the door slammed behind her she'd been in the wrong. It was childish, and she knew it. She usually was the calm, sensible one in the salon where she'd worked in Chicago, the one who never got ruffled about anything. But ever since Jason, she felt as if she was sitting on a powder keg, and any little thing could set her off.

Boom.

She didn't like this new Allie who flew off the handle at any small provocation. Sure, this was her grandmother's land, and she'd had plans for the sale, but did that really merit stomping on coffee cherries like a three-year-old? She should've handled it better. Maybe she ought to apologize, she thought as she gathered up a change of clothes and headed out to the outdoor bathhouse on her grandmother's property. She'd take a shower, get dressed and maybe go over and offer to talk things through. They had to come to some agreement, and Allie suspected that Dallas could probably convince Kaimana to sign those papers. She'd mentioned him by name after all. They had to work together…or neither one would get what they wanted. She felt better, more in control, calmer.

Allie had considered the whole problem as she'd tossed and turned the night before. Misu's house had no working air-conditioning, and the night had been particularly sticky. Allie had been waiting for the sun to come up, waiting for her chance to sit in a cool shower, wash off the salty layer of sweat.

Allie thought she was being quite grown-up about it as she walked into the outdoor shower. She double-checked for prehistoric-size bugs and, finding none, plopped her clothes down and went to turn on the hot water.

Nothing came out.

This can't be. She'd been looking forward to a shower for the past three hours of tossing around in the damp sheets of her bed, and now… *no water*?

She stared at the dry showerhead. "Don't do this to me," she whined.

She turned the knobs again, opening them all the way, and found…nothing. Not a single drop of water. "No!" This was seriously not happening. All she wanted was a cool shower. Her white tank top stuck to the small of her back; tendrils of hair stuck to her sweaty temple. Even her short plaid pajama bottoms felt too hot.

Allie wasn't going to take this lying down. She was going to get a shower, one way or another. She marched outside and saw the big rain-fed water tank sitting a few yards away. She decided to investigate, and as she walked, noticed a deeper line in the black lava dirt. Her toe print had been widened and deepened, probably by Dallas.

She made it to the huge water tower, and that was when she noticed the line ran straight to the middle of the base of the tank. She walked around the tank on her side of the dividing line and looked up. Half the water was on her side. As far as she could tell, it should be equally split. She crossed over the line to Dallas's side of the property, and that was when she noticed the kicker: the on-off spigots for the tank were on *his* side of the dividing line.

Well, *crap.*

God, she hated instant karma.

"I think you're on *my* property, ma'am," Dallas drawled, strolling up with one thumb hooked casually into the belt loop of his worn jeans. He wore a tight-fitting T-shirt across his muscled chest, and somehow it seemed even more sensual than if he'd been naked. Allie had to force herself to meet the man's eyes and not just gape at the ridges of his muscled pecs, plainly visible through the thin cotton fabric.

"Why did you turn my water off?" Allie demanded, hand on her hip, as she stubbornly stood her ground.

"It's *our* water, but the spigots are on *my* side, so…I can do with them what I want. Isn't that what you said?"

She really hated having that thrown back in her face. She really, really hated it.

"I…" The apology Allie had so carefully thought out that morning evaporated off her tongue. She had no desire to apologize to this man. "Turn my water back on."

A sly smile tugged at the corners of his mouth as he walked straight up to her, his tight T-shirt filling up most of her view. He only stopped when they were nearly toe-to-toe. She had to arch her neck to meet his steely blue eyes. She saw amusement there, but something else: strong-headed determination.

"Make me," he murmured, grinning again. She took in his broad shoulders, his football player–like frame. There was no way all five foot two of her was going to *make* that wall of a man do anything.

She wanted to stomp on the toe of his worn cowboy boot, or call him names, or thump on his chest with her fists, but she knew it wouldn't do any good. She felt that out-of-control temper flare again. The match was near the powder keg.

"Half of the tank is on my side. Half the water is mine," Allie argued, trying to keep her voice level and calm. *I will not lose it. I won't!*

"The spigots are on my side." Dallas grinned more widely, showing off the dimple in his cheek and his even, white smile. The fact that he looked as if he ought to be on some tourist ad for a remote stable in Colorado made her just want to punch him straight in the nose.

"Turn my water back on or I'll…"

"You'll what? Destroy some coffee?" Dallas rocked back on his heels. "If you do that, it's just money you'll *lose.* I don't plan on selling, and you need cash. I heard you quit your job to come here. You're living off savings."

"Who…"

"Through the grapevine."

"The lawyer," Allie exclaimed. "Misu's lawyer is the only one I told. He…"

"He's a good buddy of mine."

Fan-freakin'-tastic. "Is this some more of that locals-protect-locals BS?"

"You should know," Dallas said. "You used to be one."

Allie let out an exasperated sigh.

"You *still* can't make me turn that water back on."

Dallas took a step closer. His eyes flicked

down, lingering on the scooped neckline of her tank. Her anger burned hot, so hot she wasn't sure if she could keep a lid on it anymore.

"You'll turn that water back on," Allie promised. She stood her ground. His eyes met hers.

"Only if you say…please."

His blue eyes blazed with mischief, and something more. With a start, she realized he was *flirting* with her. God, the man's ego knew no bounds. He'd just cut off her shower, and he was trying to get into her pants? Seriously?

"Say it," Dallas said, his voice a rumble she almost thought she could feel in her own chest. Stubbornly, she stood her ground. "I'm waiting."

"You'll be waiting a *long* time," she ground out, spitting mad.

He dropped his head back and laughed. "Then you'll be waiting even longer for your shower."

He had her there and she knew it.

"Fine." Allie let out a frustrated breath. "Please," she muttered, annoyance in her voice.

"That's not a nice please." He took a step forward, and Allie wanted to punch him in the nose.

"You didn't say it had to be nice."

"Didn't I?"

He was so very close to her. She looked into his blue eyes and felt as if she'd fallen into the ocean. For that second, she froze, and she couldn't tell if the adrenaline zinging through her veins was fueled by anger or something else. She could smell Dallas's aftershave, and it made her head spin.

Dallas studied her mouth, and suddenly Allie's throat went dry. "Please," she whispered.

"What was that, darlin'?" He cupped a strong hand to his ear. "I can't hear you."

"Please," she managed, a bit louder.

Dallas's face hovered over hers, a smile in his eyes as he moved even closer. Allie thought for sure he'd kiss her right then, but he moved at the last minute, his lips missing hers by millimeters as he leaned into her ear.

"I'll think about it," he whispered, and she could feel his warm breath on her earlobe. It made her shiver. And not with murderous rage.

"Damn you, Dallas McCormick," she ground out, and stomped on one of his booted feet. Her flimsy flip-flop did no good against the thick leather, and Dallas just threw his head back and laughed. She could hear the laughter following her almost all the way back to her the house. Her face burned in humiliation: he'd played her. She was thoroughly tired of being played by men. It wouldn't happen again, she swore.

IF DALLAS MEANT to declare war, then, fine, two could play that game. Allie would just have to re-double her efforts to win over Kaimana, get that paper signed and sell her half. She'd love to see the look on Dallas McCormick's face when she told him she'd sold *her* half to resort developers. See how he'd fare with just half his crop and no roasting barn.

The only problem was that, whenever Allie went to Kaimana's house, she found the door locked, the blinds drawn.

Well, Allie wasn't going to give up *that* easily. She made her plans even as she rinsed off in the kitchen sink with jugs of water bought from the local grocery store. She didn't think she'd find herself wishing for an outdoor shower, but anything would be better than this.

One thing was for sure: she'd make Dallas pay.

She knew of only one person who could help her: Kai Brady. After finishing her hasty sponge bath, she got dressed and drove her rental into town.

She walked slowly down the main street of Kailua-Kona, with its brightly colored storefronts facing out to the ocean. Lines of green palm trees swayed against the blue sky nearby, and the sidewalk looked pristine, bathed in bright Hawaiian sunshine. Hula Coffee sat sandwiched between a salon and a little sushi restaurant. Painted a bright baby blue with white trim, the shop boasted an old-fashioned wooden sign carved into the shape of a Hula dancer, a Hawaiian woman wearing a white-flowered lei and green grass skirt, a halo of white flowers in her jet-black, waist-length hair. The small coffee shop was bustling even at two in the afternoon, the window-seat benches filled with people of all stripes. A handsome guy in his midtwenties, wearing board shorts and a tank top, opened the door, holding it for her.

"After you," he said, taking in her sundress, his eyes lingering on her legs. She ignored him. She didn't need complications right now. She saw Kai talking to his sister, Jesse, at the register and waved.

"Allie!" He motioned her over. "Come in. Say hi to…"

He hadn't even got out Jesse's name before the tanned, petite brunette had launched herself over the counter and clobbered Allie in a huge hug. "*Why* are you never on Facebook?" she scolded. "Seriously—we *need* to catch up! It's been a *thousand* years!"

Allie had forgotten about Jesse's bubbling enthusiasm for everything. She and Kai had the same mom and different dads, but they both had their Irish mother's warm, hazel-colored eyes. She was two years younger than Allie and Kai, and what Allie remembered was a fierce little girl who wanted to climb every tree they did.

"This is a great place," Allie said, meaning it as she looked around at the warm koa-wood tables and the easy conversation happening across the various nooks in the small but surprisingly open shop. Pastries of every kind called invitingly from behind a glass counter, and the air smelled like coffee and vanilla.

"Thanks," Kai said, standing a little straighter, clearly taking pride in his establishment. "I never imagined having a life other than surfing, but my finance guy said it's good to diversify."

"That's only because surfing is probably going to kill you," Jesse scolded. "*This* guy liked to surf the big waves. Like seventy feet!"

"Seventy…?" Allie's mouth dropped open in shock. Kai had always been fearless, even as a toddler, but somehow she couldn't quite imagine his muscled body handling such serious surf.

"That was on a slow day," Kai said, half teasing, half not. He pointed to the espresso machine. "Care for a cappuccino? On the house."

"Well, I…" Allie hesitated for a split second, but before she could even properly answer, Jesse had bounced over to get started.

"You don't want him making one. He doesn't know how," Jesse explained.

"I do so!"

"You're only here a couple days a week," Jesse teased, as they bickered warmly like the siblings she remembered. "During the *slow* times. Ask him where he is in the morning, during rush time?"

"Hey! I surf mornings!" Kai protested. "Got

to keep giving those young kids a run for their money on the circuit. I just come in here to supervise, make sure you're not sleeping on the job."

Jesse snapped a dishrag at him, and Kai just laughed. In a few moments, she handed Allie a lush cappuccino.

"This is the second time this week someone put coffee in my hands." Allie inhaled the rich aroma and then took a sip. It was the richest, most delicious thing she'd ever tasted. Nothing bitter about it, just dense, lush goodness.

"This is amazing," Allie said, dumbstruck that she actually *liked* coffee without a sugary shot of vanilla or caramel.

Kai grinned, ear to ear. "Made from one hundred percent Kona Estate coffee."

"My grandmother's coffee?"

Kai nodded.

"Wow, this stuff is *really* good." Allie took another sip, relishing it.

"The best Kona *on* Hawai'i," Jesse said.

"Your grandmother's coffee *made* this place," Kai seconded.

Allie felt a shudder of guilt as she glanced around at all the happy patrons in Kai's shop. They all seemed to like the coffee so much, and she could understand why. It was delicious, like none she'd ever tasted. But she had no intention of growing coffee, at least, not with her share.

What would happen to Kai's shop, to these patrons drinking her coffee, if they sold the land? Developed it for condos?

Not your problem, Allie thought. *Your problem is Dallas McCormick and that smug smile he wears on his face.*

"You said someone else gave you coffee?" Kai asked. "Where did you get it? *Please* don't tell me it was *you-know-what* down the street. *Please* don't!"

"Kai won't even say their name, it's that personal," Jesse said.

"Don't get me started on *why*," he said. "Big corporate lattes! Wouldn't know good coffee if it bit them in the…"

"Oh, no, don't worry," Allie said. "I haven't been to any competitors. Your aunt gave me coffee grounds, actually."

Kai immediately relaxed. "You saw Auntie K? She's always had a soft spot for you. Did she make you a lei?"

"Uh, yes, actually. Gorgeous." Allie cleared her throat. "I wanted to talk to you about her, actually. Grandma Misu wanted me to talk to her about the estate if I was going to sell, so…"

"She did?"

"Yeah, and I didn't have much luck. She, uh… she…pretended not to know English."

Kai and Jesse exchanged a meaningful glance.

"*That* wasn't very nice. Let me go talk to her," Kai pronounced, like a big brother ready to go to bat for a little sister.

"No, that's okay. I mean, I know she probably didn't want to talk to me about selling Grandma Misu's land, so I get it. But now she won't answer the door, and…"

"That's none of her business whether you sell or not," Kai muttered. "That's *your* choice, not hers. You should be able to sell if that's what you want to do."

Jesse didn't say a word. Allie could tell she didn't approve of selling, but she was grateful Kai didn't judge her. "I just feel kind of stupid. I fell for it. I really thought she didn't know English."

"Aw, she does that to everyone," Kai said. "Hell, the postal carrier didn't know for *years*, and I don't think the tax assessor *still* does."

They all laughed, and Allie felt an easy kinship between them that she hadn't felt in…years. She liked Jesse and Kai a lot. They felt like long-lost family.

"Hey, want to come to dinner tomorrow? We could help you talk to Aunt Kaimana. Maybe get this all sorted out."

"Oh, I don't want to put you out."

"You won't," Kai assured her. "I'm barbecuing, and we're having a few friends over anyway, at Aunt Kaimana's house. One more is no big deal!"

For the first time since Chicago, Allie actually *did* feel like getting out. She ignored the little voice of warning at the back of her head. She was on a mission: sell the land and get out.

But, what would one little barbecue hurt? Besides, if she could convince Kaimana to sign her paper at the party, all the better.

"Sure," she said. "I'd love to."

CHAPTER FIVE

A FEW PEOPLE turned into more like a hundred. By the looks of Kai's crowded backyard, he'd invited every local on the island for his little barbecue. Allie stood awkwardly near a banana tree, clutching a frosty mai tai, wondering whether or not she should leave. It had been so long since she'd actually been at a party that wasn't a bridal shower, she wasn't sure she remembered how to mingle. Kai was busy manning the grill, and Jesse had her hands full with mixing drinks, and she'd not even seen a trace of Kaimana. She glanced down at her white striped maxi dress and high-heeled wedge sandals and suddenly felt overdressed. Everyone else wore colorful board shorts, tank tops and flip-flops. Allie was the only woman not in an above-the-knee sundress. But she had her reasons. Her legs were bright lobster red after she'd forgotten to apply sunscreen before she'd fallen asleep lying on her stomach on her grandmother's reclining lawn chair in the backyard.

Her shoulders still radiated heat. They were so burned that even the thought of putting a strap or sleeve on them made her want to cry. The dress was the only sleeveless one she had, so she'd gone with it. Luckily, her front side was only marginally burned. In a day or so, she'd have a new golden tan. But right now, all she felt was agony.

Allie sipped at the sweet drink and glanced around, looking in vain for a familiar face. Just as she was considering knocking back her drink and bolting, she felt something pounce on her skirt. She looked down to see a fluffy brown Labrador puppy with steel-gray eyes.

"Poi! Down, boy, down!" An Asian woman about her age ambled up, deeply tan with her hair up in an elaborate do, a large white flower in her hair. She wore a black tube top and khaki shorts. "I am so sorry," she said, grabbing the dog by the collar. "He's not people trained yet."

"No problem." Allie grinned and knelt down, scratching the pup behind his ears. The dog reminded her of the lab she'd had growing up. "He's friendly, aren't you, Poi?"

"I'm Minnie," she said. "You must be Allie."

"How did you…"

"You're the new girl," Minnie said and grinned. "I know everybody here but you, so I just figured. Plus, the sunburn gave you away."

Allie shifted uncomfortably. She realized she was the only one in the yard who didn't have an all-year tan from years living here. It would take her quite a long time to work up to that, she thought. Her shoulders hadn't seen sunlight for eight months, and even an hour of sun had burned her to a crisp.

"You need some aloe? I may have some in my car," Minnie offered.

"I bathed in it before I came here. Don't worry. I've got plenty." Allie fidgeted. Her right shoulder blade in particular throbbed.

"Mind if I say, your eyebrows are…amazing. Where do you get them done?" Minnie studied Allie's forehead. Minnie still held the puppy's collar, trying to keep him from lunging again.

"I did them, actually. I used to do eyebrow sculpting in Chicago."

"I *have* to introduce you to Teri, then," Minnie said. "She owns the best salon in town." Minnie glanced around and then waved to a platinum blonde in her midforties who was wearing a bright coral-colored blouse and white Bermuda shorts. Minnie waved her over and Teri came, carrying a nearly empty mai tai glass.

"Teri! This is Allie. You know, Alani Osaka— Misu's granddaughter."

"Oh, honey! So glad to meet you!" Before Allie knew it, she was enveloped in a big hug.

"Misu was my favorite customer. She always gave the best advice." It seemed as if Teri didn't want to let her go. Allie didn't mind, though.

Instead of an awkward outsider, she was starting to feel like a prodigal daughter returned. In Chicago, she'd always lived in big, populous neighborhoods and gone to overcrowded schools, walked busy city streets, where it was easy to blend in. She wasn't used to being noticed or singled out. Small island life was a different kind of existence, she was quickly finding out.

"Teri, you won't believe this. She does eyebrows!"

"You do?" Teri asked, taking the last sip of her mai tai. "Threading or waxing?"

"Both," Allie said. "And facials, too."

"I *just* lost my eyebrow girl, and I haven't found a good replacement yet." Teri studied Allie's face. "You did your own eyebrows?"

Allie nodded.

"That's good enough for me! They look great. You might be too busy with Misu's place, but if you want a job…" She raised her glass as if a paycheck were inside.

Allie's first impulse was to jump at the offer, but then the small voice in her head told her she ought not to get too comfortable. She wasn't putting down roots. Here or anywhere else, she vowed.

"Oh, I'd love to, but I'm not sure how long I'm staying, actually."

"You're not staying?" Minnie asked, surprised.

Teri and she exchanged a quick glance. "You're just going to let Dallas run Misu's place?"

"Or sell," Allie said. "One Realtor told me it was good land for condos, maybe." The mixed feelings that passed across Minnie's and Teri's faces told her they liked that idea about as much as Dallas did when he first heard it. "But I haven't decided yet," she finished quickly. Both women looked relieved.

"No need to rush something like that, honey," Teri agreed. "Take your time. And hey, stop by the salon anyway. You want to just work something totally temporary until I can find a permanent replacement, that would be great. The tourists wait for no one! Just think about it, okay?"

"Sure, I'll think about it," Allie said, realizing it would be the perfect way to make a little extra cash while she waited to get her ducks in a row to sell. But only if Teri didn't expect her to stay long-term. She was still planning to sell and get out—quickly.

"By the way, how *are* things going with my boyfriend, Dallas?" Minnie asked, her eyes bright.

Allie felt a ripple of shock. "*Your* boyfriend? Dallas… Uh, I didn't know…"

"Don't listen to her," Teri quibbled, giving Minnie a shove. "That's how she talks about Dallas, but they aren't…"

"Hey, a girl can *dream*, can't she? Besides, my

boyfriend is the best kind imaginable: hot and completely imaginary. If I ever had a real conversation with him that wasn't a passing hello, it would ruin the whole fantasy. So how is it living next to one of the hottest guys on the island?"

"He's got an ego to match," Allie grumbled, feeling a flash of annoyance at the mere mention of the man's name.

"Ha! Lady after my own heart." Teri grinned her approval. "Thank God you didn't fall for that Texas charm. Dallas is bad news." Teri rattled the ice cubes around her mai tai glass.

"Why bad news?" Allie asked, interest suddenly piqued.

"He's a player with a capital *P*," Teri said. "He's not a one-woman man."

"He can play me *any day*," Minnie echoed in a dreamy, far-off voice. "Have you seen those abs? And that accent! I mean, 'Cowboy, Take Me Away,' you know what I'm saying? When he goes kayaking out of the bay, women just line up to watch and see if he'll take his shirt off. I mean, a guy who looks like that? Maybe he should have more than one woman. We *ought* to share him, for the sake of the sisterhood."

Teri laughed. "Minnie!" she exclaimed, giving her friend a shocked pat on the shoulder.

Allie had to admit he did have a nice chest. She could see why women would follow him around. Not *this* one, though.

"How do you know he's a player?" Allie asked, curious now.

"Besides the fact he takes a new tourist home every Saturday night?"

Allie gulped. Every week? Not that she ought to be surprised. She knew Dallas was proud of his body. Why wouldn't he want to show it off naked to a new woman weekly?

"An expensive proposition," she said, thinking aloud.

"Oh, Dallas can afford it. Rumor has it he's rich. Big sale of a family's ranch back in Texas," Minnie said. "He owns tons of stuff around here."

"Like what?"

Minnie shrugged. "Real estate. Stores. Whatever. I'm surprised he's not married already. He almost was last year."

"Until he cheated on his fiancée," Teri muttered, frowning as she held up her cup of mai tai in a grim toast.

"He cheated on her?" Allie asked, feeling suddenly angry for the woman. She knew what that felt like. Poi nudged her leg, and she absently bent down to give him a soft pat.

"Yeah." Teri took a sip of her cocktail, as if to wash the truth of it from her mouth. "They made a really pretty couple, too. She had this beautiful little girl from another relationship. They were a pretty little family, even moved in together, until she had to work longer hours, and Dallas took advantage."

Allie didn't like that. Not one bit. How could he do that to his girlfriend? Or to her little girl? She felt a surge of new anger. She'd been right about him from the start, the jerk. He was *just* like Jason. His nice-guy, aw-shucks demeanor was just a cover for the womanizer beneath.

"Longer hours?" Minnie scoffed, gesturing with her hands and nearly tipping the edge of her plastic cocktail cup. She saved the mai tai just in time. "She was gone for *weeks* at a time filming that real estate show. What is it? *Hawaii Living*?"

Allie knew *Hawaii Living*. That was Jennifer Thomas's show.

"Wait, *Jennifer Thomas* was his girlfriend?"

"Yeah, how did you know?" Minnie asked.

"I *invited* her over to the estate," Allie confessed, awkwardly rubbing her arms. "To look at the land."

Minnie and Teri stared at one another and then broke out laughing. "I bet Dallas loved that."

"Well, it explains why he was so mad," Allie confessed sheepishly. First, Kaimana and then Dallas and Jennifer—she felt at every turn like the new girl constantly stepping in it. She had a lot to learn about the island. *Not if you don't plan to stay*, that tiny voice in her head pointed out.

"Well, well, speak of the devil," Teri declared, as she looked at the back patio door.

Allie followed her line of sight and saw Dallas McCormick walking into the backyard. If he'd looked good without his shirt on, he looked even sexier now wearing a pressed white linen button-up and khaki shorts. His sharp blue eyes were hidden by expensive-looking sunglasses, but his thick blond hair was perfectly styled, and his broad chest just begged to be stroked. She saw him and her body instantly reacted, as if there was a magnetic pull straight to his navel. He pushed up his sunglasses, and she observed his clear blue eyes find hers in the crowd. For a full second, she froze, unable to move. He gave her a brief nod, and Allie felt a shiver run down the back of her spine. She hated that he looked so good. It made her even angrier.

Allie mentally shook herself. Was it something about her? Was she just destined to be attracted to unfaithful men?

"I'm surprised he came alone," scoffed Teri, as if it were a bad word. "The man can't do without female attention for ten minutes."

"Why shouldn't he? He's gorgeous *and* rich. What else do you want in a man?" Minnie exclaimed.

"Fidelity?" Allie offered, which made Teri burst out laughing.

"Oh, I like this one." She gave Allie's arm a playful squeeze.

"You two are insane. Or blind," Minnie chided. "I'm going to go stand at a discreet distance from my boyfriend and hover awkwardly. See you!" She made a beeline for Dallas, dragging Poi through the crowd. And she wasn't the only one, either. Pretty soon three girls were standing around him making small talk, giggling and flipping hair.

"Are you going to head over there next?" Teri asked, a disapproving look on her face as she watched Minnie jostle for position.

"Me? Never! He's arrogant and rude, and besides, I've half sworn off men anyway."

"Did I tell you that I like you already?" Teri asked, as she wrapped her arm around Allie's shoulders and squeezed. "Don't forget to come by the salon! We're right next to Hula Coffee." Teri spotted a young man, barely older than a teenager, crossing the yard. "Oh, there's Mason. I have to talk to him about the paint job he's going to do next week. Will you be all right here on your own?" Teri had a mothering quality about her. Allie thought it was kind of nice, being looked after.

"I'll be fine," she said.

"If you get lonesome, come on and find me." The sincere look in her eyes couldn't be missed.

"I only moved here five years ago. I remember how it feels to be the new girl on the island."

Allie felt surprisingly glad for the offer. "Thanks, Teri."

Allie took another big swig of her mai tai as she turned her attention back to the girls still swooning over Dallas. He didn't do much to discourage them, she thought. Maybe the rumors were right. She watched for a few more seconds and then decided it was impolite to stare. She'd hate for Dallas to get the impression she cared one way or another.

She still couldn't believe he'd cheated on his fiancée. Then again, part of her could. Unfortunately, her opinion of men had gone downhill since Jason. She pretty much thought any of them were capable of severe disappointment. *Especially the dangerously handsome ones.*

It was as if they were too sexy to have to learn the difference between right and wrong. Walking toddlers, the lot of them, using their charisma carelessly on anyone who stumbled into their path.

She took another drink and glanced around the yard. It was spacious and wide, and didn't have a fence. Kai's aunt's house boasted a sliver of an ocean view, the same as Dallas's half of the estate, and the water sparkled darkly under the light of a big full moon.

A mature mango tree grew near the house, and Allie recognized it as the one with a low V of branches, the one she and Kai would climb all the way to the near top. She realized it was probably all of fifteen feet tall, but then, when she was just five, it seemed like ten stories high. She saw Kaimana suddenly walk near the tree, paper plate heaped high with smoked sausage from the grill.

"Kaimana!" Allie called, just in time to see the older woman turn and stare. She quickly chewed the remainder of her bite and then bustled off toward the back door, as if trying to escape. Maybe she was. "Kaimana! Wait!"

But she sure could move fast for a seventy-something woman wearing a muumuu and orthopedic sandals. Kaimana had ducked inside the house before Allie had made it halfway across the backyard. When she got to the patio door, she found it locked.

That tricky old lady! She'd locked her out!

Unbelievable. First the fake language barrier and now this. Allie got the distinct impression Kai's aunt really didn't want to talk about Misu's land. Well, it didn't change the fact that she was the only one standing in the way of selling her share. Allie needed to talk to her whether she wanted to or not. Allie whirled on her foot, ready to stomp around to the front, when she nearly ran into a wall.

She looked up in time to see the broad chest she'd almost hit belonged to Dallas McCormick.

"Looking for someone?" Dallas's lip quirked up in a knowing smile, and right then, Allie thought he and Kaimana might be conspirators working together to keep her little paper unsigned.

"Uh, no. Just looking for the food."

"As it happens, I've got an extra plate." Dallas was carrying two full plates of barbecue, potato salad and something that looked like sliced mango. "I thought you might be hungry."

Allie glanced around, wondering where his throng of admirers had gone, and that was when she saw a few of them standing by the barbecue pit, eyeing her with interest. Had he really just ditched his fan club to offer her a plate of food? She looked at the potato salad with suspicion. Why was he being nice? The man who shut off her shower wasn't nice.

"Why? You trying to poison me?" Allie glared at him with suspicion.

"Ouch. Maybe I deserved that," Dallas admitted. "It's a peace offering. I promise. No poison."

She looked at the food suspiciously and then back at the ladies near the barbecue pit, who were trying not to outright stare.

"Come on, Allie," Dallas coaxed. "I'm trying to say I'm sorry."

"You shut off the water to the shower!"

"I turned it back on right away."

He *had*? That took Allie completely off guard. She'd just assumed it was off, which was why she'd been bathing with bottles of water in the kitchen sink for two days.

"You did?"

"You didn't notice?" Dallas threw back his head and laughed. "I wouldn't be such a bad guy that I would seriously not let you shower. I just wanted to make a point. Besides, as I recall, you *did* say please."

Allie's face burned with embarrassment. Why hadn't she checked? She'd…just assumed the worst. *God, what a fool!*

"You should have said something!" Allie folded her arms across her chest and glared.

Dallas just laughed more. "How? You weren't talking to me!"

Touché.

Allie's anger faded a bit. So Dallas hadn't left her stranded without water out of spite like she'd thought. She'd been the one who assumed he had.

Allie glanced again at the ring of girls watching them and whispering. She suddenly felt like the new girl at school talking to the star quarterback.

"Look, let's agree to a cease-fire, okay?" Dallas offered. "You can go back to stomping on coffee cherries tomorrow. But right now, let's just eat and pretend we're not going to kill one another."

Dallas's warm smile softened Allie a bit, but not enough.

"I'm not all that hungry," Allie said, and then her stomach growled loudly.

"You're a terrible liar." Dallas chuckled. "Either you take the plate or I feed it to Poi, and I'm not sure that pup can handle all this potato salad. Not to mention, Kai and Jesse will be pissed if I tell them you fed their food to the dog!"

"How do I know you didn't spit in it?" Allie eyed the plate with some disdain.

"Honestly. You go shut off a girl's water for fifteen minutes and she starts to think you're a criminal. *You* stepped on my coffee plant first."

"You deserved that."

"Maybe I did." Dallas shoved the plate toward Allie. "Eat, would you, woman? Kai's awesome barbecue is getting cold. That's a crime against... barbecue."

Kai gave her a wave from the grill, and Allie realized she was trapped now. Reluctantly, she took the plate. The smell of the food wafted up to meet her, hearty and good. She took a bite, and the barbecue melted in sweet goodness on her tongue. She almost forgot that Dallas was watching her every bite, his blue eyes studying her mouth. She felt a charge of tension between them, but chalked it up to the fact that she wanted to sell her share of the land, and he didn't. Tension would be part of everything until that was settled.

"So how do you and Kai know each other?" Allie asked.

"Everybody knows Kai, but he's a good friend, yes," Dallas said. "He was the very first friend I made on the island. I had this crazy idea to go surfing, though I'd never been. I headed into some pretty atrocious waves, and nearly bit it that first day. I don't know what I was thinking. Cowboys don't surf! I wrecked my board, and Kai saved my life. Don't tell him, though, because it'll just go to his head."

Allie laughed a little. Dallas grinned.

Then an awkward silence fell. Allie waited for Dallas to leave. His peace offering delivered, he was under no obligation to stay. Yet, he lingered.

"Thanks for the food, but you can mingle if you want to," Allie said, hoping he'd take the hint and go. She felt a little disoriented, a little dizzy with him standing so close. She could smell his aftershave, something crisp and outdoorsy, and it made her want to bury her nose in his shirt collar. It just underlined the fact that she had terrible taste in men. Jason was no fluke, which was a depressing thought.

"You trying to get rid of me?" Dallas put up some mock outrage.

"No," Allie lied.

"You are. What? Do I smell?" Teasing laughter lit up his blue eyes.

"No." Another lie. He did smell, very good in fact. His demeanor was night and day from a few days ago. Allie couldn't figure it out at all. Why was he being so nice?

"Then, how about we try some small talk? How are you enjoying your stay so far?"

"Fine," Allie mumbled, thinking so far it had been anything but. She wiggled against the elastic lining of her sleeveless dress as it rubbed mercilessly on the burn on her back. The food smelled wonderful, and she needed a distraction, so she dug in. It was delicious, and as she ate, she realized she was famished. She softened a little toward Dallas.

"There are some seats over there," he said.

"I'm fine standing," Allie quickly assured him. She preferred it actually. The burn on her legs went all the way from her calves to the backs of her thighs. She eyed the wicker chair on the patio as if it was made of barbed wire.

"You sure you won't be more comfortable sitting?"

"No," Allie said, turning a little to show him the back of her shoulders. "I won't."

"Oh! Ouch!" Dallas literally recoiled from her bright red shoulders. "*Wow*, that looks like it hurts. Is that…everywhere?"

Allie nodded. "My own damn fault. I forgot the sunscreen."

"Hey, need a ride to the drugstore? They've got a whole shelf full of aloe."

Allie chewed thoughtfully and swallowed. "Oh, I've got some, thanks. I'll be fine."

Seriously—why was he being so nice? His fan club was getting restless, eyeing the two of them together. Allie could see a few girls plotting a way in. She had trouble focusing on them, however, when Dallas's broad, muscular chest was so close to her cheek. All she had to do was lean into him, and she could rest her head there. The urge to do so was actually surprisingly strong. She wondered what it would feel like wrapped up in his arms, his big strong hands leading her in some slow dance, enveloped in his scent.

He's no good. A liar. Proposed to one woman and slept with another. Keep it together, Allie.

This made her think suddenly of Jason. How long had he been seeing that other girl? Since he proposed to her? Before? The idea made her feel light-headed and sick. Suddenly, she lost her appetite.

"You know, I'm actually full," Allie said, putting her plate down on the edge of a nearby table already cluttered with discarded beer bottles. "I think I'd better head back."

Dallas's face fell, and for a second, Allie

thought he might be genuinely disappointed to be losing her company. Then he said, "I know it might not be the best time, but at some point, you and I need to sit down. Talk about the next harvest. The coffee has to be brought in probably by next month, and it's a big job..."

And then it all clicked together for Allie. He wasn't being nice to her because he *liked* her; he was being nice because he wanted something. He wanted her help for the harvest. On property she didn't even want to keep!

It was as if he just skipped right over the entire conversation they'd had where she'd told him to sell and he'd said no, as if his word had been the end of the matter.

Allie felt the muscles around her rib cage harden against him. Teri was right. He was bad news, only out for himself.

"That's what you wanted to talk to me about?"

"We *have* to discuss it. Half the coffee is on your side of the dividing line. And so is the barn. We have to figure out a way to do this together."

"Maybe I'll skip the harvest this year." The idea of even trying to deal with it made her head spin. She saw her father in her mind's eye again, working hard to harvest the berries. Something about that memory made coffee harvesting seem like an impossible task. That was why she'd wanted to sell the land and get out—fast. She had no intention of learning how to grow coffee. That would mean staying in one place too long. *Mom had it right*, she thought. *Just keep moving. Bad things can't happen to you when you keep moving.*

"You can't just let good coffee rot."

"Why not?" Allie knew she was being diffi-cult, but she couldn't help it. She didn't like being brown-nosed, bribed with a plate of barbecue and then blindsided just when she'd started to relax and enjoy his company.

"Because…" Dallas's face grew red with frus-tration as he tried to find the right words. "Just *because*."

"Because *you* said so? Why not just say that?" Allie's voice rose, and she realized that Dallas's fan club had taken an even more obvious, and gleeful, interest, now that their conversation had veered a hard right from friendly to downright hostile.

"Conversation looks like it's getting a bit too serious here. Anyone need a mai tai?" Jesse of-fered up a full red Solo cup as she appeared by Allie's shoulder.

"No, thanks, Jesse. I was just leaving." As soon as Allie moved away from Dallas, a swarm of his admirers surrounded him, closing the gap.

CHAPTER SIX

THAT NIGHT, ALLIE dreamed of the accident. She sat in the backseat, her father driving their compact Toyota down winding coastal highway Route 19 in a torrential storm. Palm trees near the road flapped wildly in the wind. The rush of water from the sheets of rain blurred her view from the back window. Allie clutched her favorite stuffed animal, a blue rabbit named Max, hugging it more tightly with every flash of lightning and rumble of thunder in the sky. She'd forgotten why they were out: a trip to the grocery store? Some kind of errand. It was just a month after her eighth birthday. The storm had come without warning. What she remembered was her dad hitting the brakes suddenly as a dog darted into the road. She dropped Max on the floorboards of the car, and he skidded half under her and the front seat.

"Daddy!" she'd whined, reaching down as far as she could, but the seat belt dug into her shoulder as her hands reached out, too far away to touch her rabbit's left foot.

"Not right now, Allie," he'd said. "I've got to focus on the road."

"Daddy! Max!"

"*Allie!* I said *not now.*" Her dad had used his sternest voice. The roads on the Big Island were known to flood in heavy rains. Visibility was near zero. The windshield wipers whipped back and forth furiously, not quite fast enough to keep the rain off the glass.

She met his eyes in the rearview mirror. When he glanced back to the road, she undid her seat belt and slipped down to the floor, grabbing Max's foot. He was caught on something beneath the seat. She tugged but he wouldn't budge.

"Allie! Your seat belt! What are you *doing*?"

"I'm getting Max."

"Get in your seat right *now*!"

"*No!*" She'd been defiant. She was going to disobey him, and she'd made the decision to do it. She wanted Max. She didn't care if it was dangerous, or if it made her father angry. He was always telling her to keep her seat belt on, but she constantly disobeyed him. It was how she tested her limits, and she did it over and over again.

"Get in your seat!" he bellowed.

Then Allie jutted out her chin, her stubborn face.

"Move! Dammit, Allie, this is no game!" Her father's face was red with anger, with fear, and it all came roaring out as he yelled. Scared and with her feelings hurt, Allie started to cry as she scrambled back in her seat, wailing for Max. Allie snatched her seat belt across her body, sniffling.

"Allie! Quiet!"

But Allie couldn't stop crying. Might as well try to reason with the water pouring out of an open faucet. Allie saw her father struggle to reach the bunny behind his seat and then heard the click of the seat belt coming undone as he gave himself more freedom to reach.

Her father felt along the floorboards, his attention half on the road, and half on the floor. He grabbed the bunny and yanked, freeing it.

"There," he said, handing her the bunny, his eyes off the road.

That was when Allie heard the odd squeal of brakes of a hydroplaning car and was blinded by the bright white lights shining through the windshield. At first she thought it was lightning, but then she realized it was the headlights of an oncoming car.

Everything exploded in a crash of glass and metal as the car flipped end over end and landed with a bone-splintering crash. Then came the sound of rushing water, her pink tennis shoes soaked from the blast of dark water pouring in through the mangled door of the car.

Allie woke up panting, cold sweat dribbling

down her back and tears streaming down her face. Her cheeks were wet; she'd been crying in her sleep. Furiously, she wiped at her face and instinctively reached over to grab Jason, to tell him she'd had the dream. She clutched at empty sheets.

The heartache of realizing he was gone hit her so hard, she felt as if the wind was knocked out of her. A sob escaped her throat. He might have been awful in the end, but he had comforted her half a dozen times whenever the dream sneaked its way back into her life. She hadn't had it in at least a year, she realized.

Now that she was back in Hawaii, was it any wonder the dream had followed her back home?

The early light of dawn peeked through her window shades and Allie sat up sniffling and wiping her eyes. It was barely after five, but Allie wouldn't be able to go back to sleep. Despite being here several days, her body still felt as if it was on Chicago time. She slipped from bed and stooped by her suitcase to dig for clothes. She glanced up at the two white double doors of her grandmother's closet and knew one of these days she'd have to dig into her grandmother's things. Decide what to keep and what to give away. Of course, every time she opened her grandmother's closet she was overcome with memories so thick she felt as if she couldn't breathe. The dress her grandmother had once worn to play with her on the porch, or the straw hat she always had on at the beach. She found every time she started to go through her things, she'd be stymied by emotion and memories. She always shut the closet door in a hurry and vowed to attack it the next day.

She pulled on a simple tank top and jean cut-offs; all the while her sunburn itched like crazy. She glanced at the oval mirror above her grandmother's dresser and saw her skin was already beginning to peel.

"Great," she mused aloud, scratching at the back of her shoulder.

She grabbed some aloe and decided to head out to the porch with it. *No sense in missing a beautiful sunrise in paradise if I'm up this early.*

Allie saw the clouds grow pink from the rising sun as she slathered on aloe. From her seat, she couldn't quite see the water. Dallas was right: she had no ocean view. Curious about the seaside view from his side of the plantation, Allie decided to take a walk. She carried the small bottle of aloe with her as she went, walking down the little path between the coffee trees, the sweet smell of their tropical flowers in the air. *Maybe I can go knock on Kaimana's door,* she thought. Catch the woman unawares. It sounded like a good plan.

The sound of rustling in the orchard on her left caused her to stop and be still. The low-lying leaves of a coffee tree shuddered. Whatever it was, it sure was bigger than a bird. Bigger than a squirrel even.

Allie felt her heart launch into her throat. She wasn't used to wild critters on the streets of Chicago. Was it a skunk? Or, oh, Lord, something worse. Did they have mountain lions on the Big Island? Wild dogs? Allie didn't know.

The leaves rustled more decidedly, and in another instant, a furry black torpedo launched itself out of the brush.

Allie gave a little screech of surprise and jumped backward before she realized it was just a wild pig. Then she remembered: wild pigs ran loose everywhere on the Big Island. They'd been brought over by settlers and had no natural predators.

This little pig clearly had been stuffing itself on Dallas's coffee plants, since its snout was bright red from coffee cherry juice. As her heartbeat returned to normal, she waved her arms at the beast.

"Shoo, you," Allie said, advancing on the pig that didn't seem the least bit fazed, clearly used to seeing people around the farm. She stomped her feet again, trying to rouse it out of the bushes, but it just snorted, as if laughing at her, and ducked back into the thick row of shrubs. As she walked out of the row of trees, she saw Dallas's house. She remembered the dwelling from when she was little, a place always in need of new paint, but Dallas had made improvements on the house where old plantations workers used to live. It had a shine of new blue paint trimmed in white, and he'd added a new huge lanai, complete with ceiling fans and a pair of old rocking chairs on the Hawaiian porch deck. Dallas's cowboy boots sat near the front door. A big black Chevy pickup truck, relatively new by the gleam of the paint, sat under the carport.

As she passed by his house, she heard a peal of woman's laughter from the open windows, which made Allie think Dallas had company. Had Dallas gone to a bar after she'd left the party and picked up some tourist? Or, had he just picked up one of the many local admirers in Kaimana's backyard?

She found herself struck by the sudden urge to find out. It wasn't like Allie to spy, but something drew her to Dallas's house and to the sound of that laughter. She crept quietly up to his porch, furnished by sturdy bamboo chairs, probably bought locally at one of the nearby markets. She ducked down, peering in through one open window. She saw a sitting room, neatly laid out with a simple couch and a small round red rug on the floorboards in the middle.

She didn't see anyone moving about inside, so she went to the next window and found herself glancing in a bright kitchen with new appliances and a newly refinished wooden floor. She saw

Dallas first, shirtless, back to her, as he poured a cup of steaming coffee. The sight of his defined back muscles made her freeze in place as she watched his shoulders work. He had on jeans, but that was all, as he stood on bare feet on the wooden kitchen floor. *Did he not own enough shirts?* Allie thought but then, as she saw his trim waist tucked into his jeans, decided it would almost be a crime to make him wear one. He was singing along to a country song, which was loud in the kitchen, his voice low, but perfectly pitched. He'd missed his calling as a country star.

Allie glanced around and saw a woman standing in the kitchen. She didn't recognize her from the party. She was pretty despite looking unkempt—her blond hair a tangled mess and dark mascara rings under her eyes. She was distinctly overdressed for five in the morning with her strappy stilettos and some black low-cut halter sundress. The girl was pretty and most certainly a tourist: having bright red sunburn lines, new by the looks of them. As Allie watched, Dallas offered her a mug of coffee and she took it, a grateful look on her face. *One of his tourists*, Allie thought, suddenly feeling embarrassed for witnessing what was clearly the aftermath of one of his legendary one-night stands.

Allie found herself getting irrationally mad about the idea, but it wasn't as if she was in control of her emotions these days. Lately, she felt as if her whole life was dotted with land mines filled with rage. *Better that than crying uncontrollably, like you used to do.* The first week after the breakup, she'd burst into tears in the cereal aisle just looking at Jason's favorite brand. She'd take anger over that.

Allie decided she'd spied enough on Dallas and retreated from the window, but just as she was about to escape, she accidentally kicked one bamboo rocking chair, sending it clanking against the side of the house.

"What was that?" she heard Dallas ask from inside.

Panicked, she ducked off the porch, pulse thudding. She headed for the dirt path back through the coffee trees. Her heart beat madly as she tried to calm her breathing. She heard the screen door slap open and the creak of Dallas's feet walking on his wooden porch. *Just keep moving*, she thought. And then a sudden urge to scratch her sunburned and peeling back grabbed her. She slowed down to try to rub her own back, the worst of it between her shoulder blades, just out of reach.

"Allie?" Dallas sounded surprised, and Allie froze and spun around midscratch, thinking she probably looked like a crazy woman doing a little itch dance in Dallas's backyard.

"Uh…hey." She attempted reaching the small of her back. "I was just trying to see the sunrise over the ocean."

"You're technically trespassing." Dallas folded his arms across his fit chest. "You're on *my* half of the dividing line."

"Right. I'll just… I'll just be going." Allie tried to stop stretching for the impossible itch, but she couldn't.

"You need some help?" Dallas quirked his eyebrow, an amused look playing near the corners of his mouth.

"N-n-no, just fine, thanks." But Dallas was already moving closer to her. She had to fight the urge to flee. "I'm fine… I…"

"You're not fine." Dallas reached her in big, easy strides. Allie froze to the spot, as Dallas put his hand on her back. "Let me help you."

"I…" She was going to turn him down flat, but then he was there, his broad, naked chest staring her in the face, and she couldn't do anything but stare.

"Turn around," he commanded.

Her mouth had gone dry, and she'd lost the ability to understand the English language. She blamed it on the ridges of muscle in her face. His chest was amazing. Blinding, even, in its perfectly tanned smoothness. "What?" Her mind felt like mush.

"Turn around," he prodded again.

Something in the tone of his voice told her she shouldn't argue. She did as she was told. He put his fingers against her back.

"Is it here?" he asked, giving her a gentle scratch, hitting just left of the powerful itch that only made it worse.

"No, right. Go right." She squirmed as he moved slowly right, and then, like an explosion of perfection, he hit the spot she couldn't, washing her in relief.

"Oh," she moaned in pleasure. "Oh, God. That's it." He put both his hands to work, and she nearly melted with joy. "Oh, don't stop. Please."

"I wouldn't dream of it," Dallas drawled, teasing, as he increased the frequency of his scratching. She was going to faint, it felt so good. He spread his hands out, moving deliberately all around her back, hitting itches she never thought she had before she'd even felt them. Her sunburn peeled away, but she didn't care. It just felt too damn good. He had just the right amount of pressure, not too soft, and not too hard. The man was good with his hands.

Allie moaned again.

"You always this vocal when you're having a scratch?" Dallas's voice was playful, teasing, even flirty. It made Allie want to scratch a very different kind of itch.

"Dallas?" The hesitant voice of the disheveled woman in Dallas's kitchen floated to them from the porch. It felt like a bucket of cold water on her head. Allie jumped away from Dallas, not wanting to make his one-night stand jealous. Her face burned beet red as if she'd been caught making out with the man.

"Oh...you have company." Allie managed to make her voice sound both surprised and disapproving at the same time. She felt she struck the perfect balance.

Dallas, however, didn't miss a beat. If he was embarrassed to be caught with a one-night stand at five in the morning, he didn't show it. "Allie, this is Rebecca. Rebecca, Allie."

The women exchanged a brief nod. Allie would have said, "Nice to meet you," except it wasn't, and right then, she just didn't have it in her to lie.

"Dallas, I think I'm ready to go back to my hotel," Rebecca said.

"Sure thing," Dallas said smoothly, leaving her with the sensation of his hands on her back.

ALLIE DIDN'T LIKE the feelings Dallas churned up in her, or the fact that the man couldn't seem to keep a shirt on. Everywhere she looked, there was Dallas, unbearably hot and sexy, and despicably inviting. Apparently he'd not gotten the memo that said she'd sworn off men.

There was only one answer to this problem: get Kaimana to sign that damn paper and get the hell off this island before she ended up as one more notch in Dallas's bedpost.

She'd gotten into the habit of calling Kaimana twice a day and dropping by her house at least once. It had become an early-morning ritual. Allie knocked, and Kaimana either stubbornly refused to answer, or she blared ukulele music until Allie got the message and left. Once, Allie had waited two hours on her back porch, figuring she had to come out sometime, the word *welcome* on the mat like a sarcastic sneer. The woman tricked her once more, by sneaking out the front door and ducking into a friend's car, who'd been idling at the end of the drive.

While she stalked Kaimana, she tried to keep herself busy. She indulged in all the little things she'd loved so much as a kid in Hawaii: she found her favorite sticky mango candy, and the sweet pink guava juice she used to have with breakfast every morning. Then, of course, the delectable chocolate-covered macadamia nuts, a treat she'd long forgotten. The local supermarket overflowed with amazing produce: fresh pineapples, giant bunches of yellow bananas, even slices of raw sugar cane, straight from the fields. Every meal she made at Misu's felt like a trip down memory lane: she cooked rice balls in her grandmother's kitchen and tried her hand at her famous teriyaki chicken.

Now she sat on Grandma Misu's porch, slicing herself pieces of fresh mango she'd just picked from her own backyard and marveled at how much that same mango would cost imported to a high-end organic grocery store in Chicago. She had just missed the sunrise, and now she watched the pink-and-orange light play on the clouds above the rising mountain of the volcano in the distance. Honestly, everywhere she looked was a perfect postcard picture, ready to be stamped and mailed home.

Birds chirped happily, and the air was filled with the smell of some tropical flower. She tried to hang on to her anger, but in the warm Hawaiian sun surrounded by lush greenery everywhere, it slowly began to melt. There were worse places to be stuck, and Teri's part-time offer of work would come in handy when she needed to buy groceries.

Still, Kaimana's stubborn refusal to even speak to her grated.

"I really am sorry, Miss Osaka," her grandmother's lawyer had said on the phone earlier in the week. "There's really nothing I can do about Miss Kaimana's unwillingness to talk to you. Have you considered a peace offering? Or, perhaps, you can infer she *doesn't* want you to sell the land?"

"But what am I supposed to do with it?"

"Grow coffee?" the lawyer had suggested.

But what did a woman who'd spent the better part of her life on the mainland know about growing coffee? Nothing. Even calls back home to a friend who was a lawyer yielded the same results: if she didn't get the paper signed, she wouldn't be able to sell the land.

So she redoubled her efforts to get to Kaimana. This morning, she'd bring a peace offering: flowers and a bottle of wine. *Honey draws more bees than vinegar*, she thought.

As she stood, ready to make the trek over to Kaimana's, she saw Dallas—shirtless, of course, the devil—wearing just swim trunks and flip-flops, loading up a bright orange kayak into the bed of his truck. He looked good enough to eat, which sent warning bells straight through her brain.

She watched Dallas's taillights blink red as he hit the brake at the end of the drive, and then disappear as he turned on to the main highway. She walked to Kaimana's house and knocked on the door. She held up the wine and flowers in the peephole. She heard the shuffle of Kaimana's slippers against the wooden floor, so she knew the crafty old woman was home.

"I'm calling a truce," she declared to the closed door. "I've brought a peace offering." Allie waited a few minutes, but no bolt was thrown, no door opened.

"I'm leaving it here," she said, and put the bottle of wine and the flowers down on the brown welcome mat. She trotted down the steps of the porch, when she heard the bolt click behind her and the door sweep open.

Allie froze, shocked, and turned to see Kaimana smiling at her.

"Aloha," the old woman with the gray-streaked black hair said.

"Good morning," Allie said, deliberately. "I'm sorry if we got off on the wrong foot. I really didn't mean to offend. I just wanted to…"

"I'd prefer gin," Kaimana said, interrupting her. "I do love a good gin and tonic."

Now Allie was starting to get angry, what with her looking a gift horse in the mouth, but Kaimana just smiled more broadly to show she was kidding.

"Oh, loosen up, kiddo," she said. "I'm just teasing. Wine is great. Pele likes gin, too."

"Pele?" Allie asked, confused as she met Kaimana's gaze. Kaimana just shrugged one shoulder. Clearly, she'd heard this all before.

"Pele!" Kaimana pointed to the big mountain behind them.

Volcano goddess, Allie remembered. Though it was an active volcano, its smoke wasn't visible to Allie, at least not from this vantage point.

"Oh." Allie really had no idea what to say to that. "Do you believe…? I mean…"

Kaimana just stared. Her dark skin looked weathered with age spots and lines, honestly earned with a life in the sun. After a long, pregnant pause, she broke out into a loud laugh. "Oh, I'm just teasing you. I'm a Methodist."

Kaimana laughed and Allie did, too. Kaimana sank into a rocking chair on the porch and picked up a half-strung lei. She motioned to the chair next to her and Allie sat down in it.

"I know what you want," Kaimana said, finally. "I know, and I'm here to tell you, I won't talk about Misu's land."

Allie felt panic rise in throat. "But…you *have* to talk to me about it… You…"

"I wasn't finished." Kaimana held up the needle she was using to string a lei. "I was *going* to say I won't talk about Misu's land until *after* the Kona Coffee Festival. She told me she thought *this* crop would win top prize."

"Oh, well, I…" Allie hadn't even banked on harvesting the crop at all, much less entering it into a festival competition.

"You *are* going to enter?"

"Well, I hadn't thought…" Allie's mind whirled.

How was she supposed to get the crop ready for a festival?

"It meant a lot to your grandmother." Kaimana studied her for a beat longer than was comfortable. "Last year, she made it all the way to second place, but it was first place she wanted. Tell you what, girl. If you *win* that festival, if you land first place, I'll sign that document of yours and you can sell to whomever you like."

"I can?"

"Sure." Kaimana put down the lei she was working on and stood on creaking knees. She straightened her back, putting both hands on it, and groaned as she swept the silver-black hair from her tanned face. "Oh, age is not pretty," she muttered as she stretched. Her back creaked and popped under the strain.

She glanced at the still slightly pink hue to Allie's arms. "You should spend more time at the beach. Brown you right up." Kaimana said, nodding at her forearms. Tanning, however, was the least of Allie's worries at the moment. She was still thinking about how she was going to win a coffee competition when she barely even knew how to work a coffee machine, much less roast raw coffee.

"When is the festival?"

"November."

NOVEMBER WAS MORE than six months away! Allie felt panicky. She couldn't wait that long. She had no money! She'd liquidated her savings to get her plane ticket, and she'd been living pretty much on credit cards since she got here. *You could always sell the engagement ring,* she thought. And maybe she would. If things got bad…she would. She suddenly felt dizzy. She kicked a loose berry she found on the ground and sighed. As she looked up, out at the bright blue water in the distance, it occurred to her she needed a break. She'd spent a week on a beautiful island… *And I haven't even been to the beach.*

Kaimana said I needed to go, so fine, I'll go. I need a break from the endless loop of worry in my head.

CHAPTER SEVEN

ALLIE STARED AT the coffee trees resentfully as she marched back inside her grandmother's house and then ransacked her suitcase for her tried-and-true one-piece—the no-nonsense suit she usually wore. It was like her: conservative, sturdy and reliable, and those racer-back straps would never come off in the surf.

Behind it, she saw the daring bright yellow string bikini Jason had bought her for their would-be honeymoon. In retrospect, she was surprised that Mr. Whips and Chains hadn't gotten her a leather one dotted with silver spikes. She'd forgotten she'd tossed it in her bag, not thinking that it would be like one more grenade she'd taken the pin out of, ready to explode her calm.

She glared at the new bikini and was tempted to throw it into the trash. But something stopped her. Now she remembered why she'd kept it. It had been a one-hundred-and-eighty-dollar bikini. Some fancy designer that she'd never in a million years seriously consider buying. Most things in her closet came from the sales rack at a discount store. In a pinch, she could sell it on eBay. That was why she'd kept it.

Now, as she stared at the overpriced bikini, she decided she'd try it on, at least. After wiggling into the barely-there fabric, she stood in front of the full-length mirror, assessing. Her sunburn still beamed brightly up at her like a traffic light, but she could see the beginnings of a new tan. The good news was she'd been hitting the gym like a maniac over the six weeks before her aborted wedding because she'd thought she needed to squeeze into a strapless wedding gown. Now, she could see, all that work had paid off. She wouldn't have even considered wearing a bikini two years ago, but today...well, maybe she would.

Next, she tried to tackle the yellow flowered sarong that came with the suit. As far as she could tell, it was like one huge scarf. The more she tried to tie it around herself, the more she started to look like a maypole. *How do these things even work?*

Outside, she heard tires on the gravel driveway and wondered if Dallas was back already. She worked the cotton fabric of her cover-up into some kind of makeshift wrap skirt and thought, *This'll have to do.*

As she finished the knot in the sarong, she heard a car horn honk.

If that's Dallas, I'm going to tell him where he can put that horn.

Angrily, she slipped into flip-flops and trudged out the door, only to see that it wasn't Dallas's black pickup sitting in the drive. It was a big white delivery truck. A man hopped out, no older than twenty-five, his dark hair covered with a baseball cap. He held a clipboard.

His eyes went straight to her bare middle, and his eyebrows lifted ever so slightly. "I'm looking for Dallas McCormick?"

"Sorry, he's gone."

The man didn't even register her answer; he was too busy staring at her chest.

"Uh, hello?" Allie waved her hand to draw his attention away from her swimsuit.

"Oh, uh…sorry." He flushed a little when he realized he'd been caught ogling and raised his eyes to meet hers. "He's gone? You're sure? I know he called for a delivery…" He glanced at his clipboard. "Oh, no," he said, realization dawning as he read the invoice. "It's my fault. I'm supposed to be here later this afternoon! The shipment came on an earlier ferry, but I didn't realize. My boss is going to kill me."

Allie took pity on the young driver.

"I can help. What is it?"

"It's a new coffee roaster," he said as he rolled up the back of the truck to show her a massive stainless steel contraption, designed to heat coffee beans. Allie focused on the giant piece of equipment and felt like kicking it. Dallas had ordered something for *her* side of the property without even telling her.

"Can I see the invoice?" Allie asked sweetly.

The deliveryman scurried to her, eagerly handing her the clipboard. She glanced at the invoice, stopping cold when she saw the amount for the order.

"Twenty-five *thousand* dollars?" Allie's throat closed up suddenly. *Twenty-five thousand dollars?* Dallas had spent this much on some farm equipment?

The driver looked uncertain. "Mr. McCormick ordered the top of the line, and this is it. You won't be disappointed, it's…"

Allie couldn't believe it. Dallas had made a purchase this large for the entire farm without even talking to her first. She wondered how he'd paid for it. She ripped through the back page of the invoice and saw a credit card number. She nearly lost it when she saw the name on the account. It was Misu Osaka.

He'd used her dead grandmother's credit card? What the hell?

Allie felt a cold shiver run down her spine. Dallas had inherited half her grandmother's estate, but was he trying to get even more? Why would he charge twenty-five thousand dollars to her grandmother? How did he even do it?

"I'm afraid you're going to have to take this roaster back," Allie said, feeling her old anger return. Dallas couldn't be trusted. Hell, *no man* could be trusted.

The driver shifted uncertainly from one foot to the other. "It's more than a hundred dollars if I have to come back. Are you sure…"

"I'm sure."

"Maybe I should call this contact number here." The deliveryman pulled out his phone from his back pocket.

Allie bit down her anger and changed tactics. She needed to stop biting people's heads off. "What's your name again…?" She smiled sweetly.

"Dave."

"Dave." Allie took a step closer to him, and her sarong, which wasn't all that tightly secured in the first place, threatened to fall down one hip. She caught it, but not before the bright yellow string of her bottoms became visible. She hadn't planned it, but it worked anyway as a proper distraction.

Dave the driver perked up instantly, his eyes dropping to her exposed skin.

"I'm really sorry to do this to you. I don't want to get you in trouble, but Dallas didn't run this by me and he really should have. It's a big purchase. And we're co-owners now."

"Oh, I see," Dave agreed, trying to pull his attention back to her face.

"So I'm afraid I can't accept the delivery. You'll have to send it back. I don't want to get you into trouble, but it's really Dallas's fault." Allie smiled at the driver to show there were no hard feelings.

"No problem," he said cheerily, tucking his phone away. "I'll take this back and have the manager call and get this all sorted out." He closed the back door of the truck with a decisive snap. "By the way," he said, as he cleared his throat nervously. "Would you...would you want to get dinner sometime?"

"Oh, I wish I could but I'm—" Allie stopped midsentence. She'd been about to say *engaged.* But she wasn't. Not anymore. She looked down at her bare ring finger, which still bore the slightest hint of a tan line where Jason's two-carat diamond ring once sat. "I...can't. Sorry."

Dave's face fell, but then he rallied. "Hey, can't blame a guy for trying."

Allie sent him a weak smile, feeling a twinge of guilt as he hopped back into the truck and turned the ignition. He wasn't her type, so she probably wouldn't have said yes anyway. But she knew she needed to get out of the habit of thinking she was taken.

No sooner than the white delivery truck drove out of sight, Dallas's black pickup turned in, kicking up dark dust behind its oversize wheels. He headed straight to her front porch, so she didn't have time to duck inside her house for a cover-up.

"Was that the roaster?" he asked gruffly as he took in her outfit. He frowned as he looked at the curve of her bare hip and the plunging neckline of the bikini top. He wore wet board shorts and a sleeveless T-shirt, his bulging tanned biceps on display.

"Yes," she said, tapping one flip-flop on the gravel driveway.

"Where is it?" He glanced around as if expecting it to appear out of thin air.

"I sent it back." Allie lifted her chin in defiance. Dallas's face registered shock and then anger. He pushed up his mirror sunglasses into his tousled blond hair.

"You *what*?"

"I sent it back." She crossed her arms and frowned.

"Oh, no. No more crap about your side of the line! I thought we discussed this!"

"I own *half* this farm, Dallas. You can't make large purchases without talking to me first. The lawyer said…"

"We *need* that roaster for the harvest."

"You should've told me about the purchase, Dallas."

Dallas let out a frustrated breath of air. "I *tried*. You didn't want to talk about the harvest!"

She ignored the little flick of guilt she felt. He had tried to talk about the harvest, she knew, and she'd shut him down.

"Well, now I do, but first you're going to tell me why you used Grandma Misu's credit card." Allie was beginning to think the worst: that Dallas might have just been playing Grandma Misu. She'd been an old woman, and Dallas was a charming guy. He wasn't a relation, and yet he ended up with half her estate? Maybe the reasons weren't good.

"I didn't use her card!" Dallas threw his arms wide in exasperation.

"Her name and number were on the invoice." Allie crossed her arms again and glared. Jason had always given the orders in their relationship. She wasn't about to get pushed around by Dallas.

Dallas heaved a sigh. "It might have been her name, but it was *my* credit card number," he said, rubbing his forehead. "It was my account, I just let her use it. She made purchases for the farm, and when I called, that must've been the number that they had on file."

"What do you mean it was your credit card?" Allie didn't understand.

"Three years ago, your grandmother was nearly broke," he said. "I stepped in. I helped her out with a loan, paid for the new roasting barn and put her on one of my credit cards so she could still get things for the estate."

"You…did?" Allie had never heard of this. Not that she was close with her grandmother, but her mother and Grandma Misu talked all the time. Her mother would have mentioned financial troubles. Allie felt guilt like a sharp piece of shrapnel in her chest. It had never occurred to her Grandma Misu was having problems. Could it be that all these years Allie had thought her grandmother was choosing not to help them, but the truth was she couldn't?

Allie's anger drained away. Dallas had saved the estate. At least, he said he had. She'd check it out, but why would he lie about something like that? The lawyer would know. There'd be financial records. It'd be easy to prove.

"Wow, I didn't know." Allie glanced up at Dallas's face and saw the frustration fade away a little. His blue eyes studied her.

"Misu was a proud woman. It's not something she'd broadcast," he said, glancing back over the coffee tree line. "Up until the day she died, she swore she'd pay me back with interest."

Understanding finally dawned. "So she did. With half the estate," Allie said, feeling again like a complete moron. Why'd she have to go and assume Dallas was a con man? He'd done Misu a solid favor, and she'd paid him back, plain and simple. Allie sank into a porch chair. "I'm really sorry. I had no idea."

Dallas watched her for a beat, his blue eyes wary. "It's okay. I'll need to call the delivery company. See if they can turn that delivery around. We still have time to work out all the kinks before the competition."

"The Kona Coffee Festival?"

"You know it?" Dallas asked, looking bright and hopeful.

"Uh…yeah, I've heard of it." She elected not to tell him about Kaimana's condition to sign the paper she needed.

"Well, if we're going to have any chance of winning, we need that new roaster," Dallas said.

Allie groaned and let her head fall into her hands. Could this get any worse? "Okay, okay! I get it."

He glanced down at her string-bikini top. "I can't really blame the fella for listening to a pretty woman in a bikini." She'd forgotten she was on the porch half-naked. She tugged up her sarong, suddenly feeling exposed.

He walked off her porch as he dialed the number, heading down the path to his house as he chatted.

Allie watched him go, feeling glum. *What else am I going to muck up?*

Her phone rang then, and she jumped a little, startled to see an unfamiliar local number flash across her screen. She thought about letting it go to voice mail, but picked it up instead, wondering if it might be Kaimana, ready to sign the papers.

"Allie?" came a voice that was definitely not Kaimana's. "Hi, it's Teri. At the Tiki Teri salon. We met at Kai's barbecue?"

"Of course I remember. Hi, Teri."

"I hope you don't mind. I got your number from Kai. It's kind of an emergency. Can you come down to the salon this afternoon?" Teri did sound a little unsettled, and Allie could hear commotion in the background, which sounded like shouting of some sort.

"Oh, sure," Allie said, sitting up a little straighter in her seat. "When?"

"How about now?"

Allie hung up and felt a weight pressing down on her shoulders. She might as well help out at the salon since she was stuck here for a while. She had no idea how she was going to manage to pay for anything past next week and now it looked as if she'd have to find a way to survive until the coffee competition in November.

CHAPTER EIGHT

FIFTEEN MINUTES LATER, Allie was standing outside Tiki Teri's wearing a sundress she'd hastily thrown on over her swimsuit. She paused at the window. It was nothing like Michel's, where she'd worked as a makeup artist and brow tech in Chicago. Michel's was a full-service spa downtown, offering hot rock massages, fluffy white robes and the sound of running water in every room. Tiki Teri's was brightly lit, with antique aluminum and shiny aquamarine patent leather salon chairs, a black-and-white-tiled floor and multicolored plastic flip-flop-shaped lights strung up by the wall-to-wall mirrors. Bob Marley music played softly in the background, but the atmosphere was anything but calm.

Teri, her platinum-blond, chin-length hair perfectly styled, wore Bermuda shorts and a bright coral top. She was trying to console a client who was red-faced and crying.

"Teri, this is a disaster!" the brunette shouted, as she hid her face in her hands.

Teri saw Allie and nearly melted with relief.

"Allie! Oh, thank God." Teri waved her over. "Ella, this is the girl I was telling you about. If anyone can fix you, she can!" The crying client lifted her head ever so slightly, and that was when Allie saw the problem.

"I *tried* to wax my own eyebrows, but…well… see?" Ella pointed to her forehead. She was missing most of her right eyebrow from the far side in. Allie tried not to gasp. She put on her best poker face.

"Anyhow, I know you hadn't made up your mind about the job, but any way you could help her now?" Teri asked. Allie was surprised Teri had reached out, given that she'd only met her once. That kind of thing never happened in Chicago, but maybe islanders were different. *Or maybe she's just trying to be nice.* Ella gave her a pleading look.

"I can help," Allie said, feeling confident. She'd seen worse.

"You can?" Ella dabbed at the tears on her cheeks. "I've got a date with Todd tonight and I just…I just can't go like this!"

"Todd is like a living legend around here," Teri said. "Flies helicopters into the volcano."

"Gives *tours*. It's nothing quite so dangerous as all that." Ella laughed a little. "And it's just our second date." Ella grabbed her phone and proudly showed Allie a picture of Todd. He had jet-black hair and bright blue eyes and a killer smile. He was sitting in the cockpit of a massive black helicopter, giving a thumbs-up sign.

"Really?" Teri sounded skeptical. "Because people *die* doing that."

"He's the best pilot on the island," Ella declared. "But he won't want to be seen with me like this!" Ella's bottom lip quivered, and tears threatened to spill.

"Whoa, now, it'll be okay." Allie held her hands up as if Ella was a skittish horse. "Come on over here," she added, easing Ella into one of the salon chairs. "Let's get a better look at you."

A LITTLE WHILE LATER, Allie had worked a miracle with an eyebrow pencil. Ella's eyebrows arched perfectly. Allie had gone ahead and done the woman's makeup, too.

"You weren't kidding about your skills, honey," Teri said, nodding her head in admiration. "I'm going to have to call you the brow whisperer."

Ella's brow looked surprisingly natural, her makeup flawless. She looked ready for her date.

"I *love* you," Ella gushed, admiring her reflection. "How much do I owe…?"

"Uh…" Allie glanced uncertainly at Teri.

"Oh, screw it. Here's what I have! Keep it." Ella pressed eighty dollars into Allie's hand.

Allie had her hand open with the cash in it as she offered it to Teri.

"Keep it," Teri said, closing her hand over the bills. "You earned it."

"But…" Allie didn't quite feel right as she watched Ella bounce out of the salon. She thought she should refuse it, but part of her knew she was looking at a week's worth of groceries. And since it didn't look as if she was selling the land any-time soon, she'd need all the cash she could get. She took it and folded it into her pocket.

"You're a lifesaver, honey. So glad you could come by. Given any thought to that job? How about you set your own hours? Part-time, what-ever works for you."

Allie felt the cash in her pocket. She needed it, especially if she wanted to eat sometime past next week. "Sure," Allie said, thinking that she could see herself happily spending time at Tiki Teri's. She eyed a bowl of mango candy—her favorite—on the counter near the door.

"Take as many as you want," Teri called to her. "You've earned them, honey."

Allie scooped up a grateful handful and un-wrapped one for eating and left the rest in her pocket for later.

She left the salon feeling happy about her good deed of the day. She walked into Hula Coffee next door, wanting to say hi to Kai and Jesse, and also craving a little iced mocha something as a reward.

She found Jesse sans Kai working like a well-oiled machine, ringing up orders and making them. When Jesse saw Allie, she bustled out from behind the counter to give her a big hug.

"Hi, Allie!" She grinned, her freckles on her nose just adding to her warm cheer. "What brings you into town?"

Allie told her about Tiki Teri's and the eyebrow job, and she beamed. "You're going to be working right next door? That's great," Jesse said. "Leaving Dallas, then, to do all the heavy lifting on the estate?"

"Uh…yeah, I guess so." Allie glanced around at the full house of customers enjoying her grandmother's coffee. Did she really want to tell them she planned to sell her share as soon as Kaimana signed that paper?

"He's a good man, you know," Jesse told Allie.

"Who?"

"Dallas."

"That's not what I heard," Allie said, thinking about what Teri had said about his not being a one-woman man. She didn't even know why she said it just then. Hadn't Dallas saved her grandmother's farm? But did that really matter if he was a cheater and a womanizer? Then again, who cared if he was? Allie had no intention of dating him.

Jesse let out a disgruntled sigh. "Don't you dare be swayed by island gossip," she scolded as she gave Allie back her change for the iced coffee. "Most of it isn't true, and the other part is completely fabricated."

This made Allie laugh.

"Seriously, though, Dallas… I mean, Hula Coffee would not be here without him." Jesse handed Allie her iced latte. She took a big sip. "Kai and I, we wanted to start this shop, you know? Always have wanted to, but try telling a bank officer that a surfer and former whale-watching guide are good business investments."

"They wouldn't loan you money?"

"We were considered high risk. We had no collateral, since that was before Kai got his big endorsement deal, before the surfing really took off. He wasn't making much then." Jesse wiped down the counter. "Dallas loaned us the money, and we're not the only ones."

"I know," Allie said, thinking about her grandmother. "How was he able to…"

"Give away free money?" Jesse shrugged. "He did inherit some from the sale of his family ranch, but by the way he gives it away, I can't imagine he's sitting on all that much anymore."

"Why does he do it? Do you share profits?" Allie was still looking for the angle.

"We're paying him back, but he won't take interest. He's just a part of the community. He cares," Jesse said. "Locals look after one another. And all that stuff about him being a player… I just don't think it's true, honestly."

Allie suddenly had a sneaking suspicious Jesse *really* cared for Dallas. Maybe more than she let on. "Do you…and Dallas…?"

Jesse barked a loud laugh. "Us? God, no!" she exclaimed, as if Allie had just asked Jesse if she had a crush on her own brother. "There are *many* reasons for that."

"Oh." Now Allie just felt puzzled. "Do you…"

"I like girls, Allie," Jesse said, matter-of-factly.

And then it all made sense to Allie. No, she definitely wouldn't be into Dallas. He was the furthest thing from a girl there was.

"Oh," Allie blurted, and then laughed. "And here I thought…"

"That I was secretly in love with Dallas McCormick." Jesse shook her head. "Not my type. Too many Y chromosomes."

Allie laughed, strangely feeling relieved. "So why all the rumors about Dallas?" Allie just felt like where there was so much smoke, there had to be a fire. "That he cheated on his fiancée? Left her and her little girl?"

"I don't believe it," Jesse said flatly.

"What happened, then?"

She hesitated. "I don't know. He won't tell me, and I don't want to pry. It's none of my business."

"But the tourists…" Allie knew she should stop digging up dirt about Dallas, but part of her just couldn't help it.

"He only started that after Jennifer," Jesse said. "If you want my opinion, he's just rebounding—hard. He doesn't know how to stop. But make no mistake—he's one of the good ones."

Allie left the coffee shop feeling strangely unsettled. Maybe she'd been wrong about Dallas. Maybe she'd jumped to too many conclusions about him like she had about pretty much everyone on this island. Even Grandma Misu, assuming she'd spent all these years withholding support, when she couldn't give any. Maybe rushing to judgment was her fatal flaw.

Except for Jason. He sure got past all your defenses.

She didn't want to think about Jason. She didn't want to think about Dallas, either, although his stark blue eyes seemed to hover in her mind no matter how hard she tried to think about something else. No doubt he was handsome, beyond handsome. And if she were honest, he'd been nothing but nice since she'd stepped foot back on her grandmother's property. She'd been the rude one. Like accusing him of stealing from her grandmother—case in point.

The bright, warm Hawaiian sun beamed down on her, and the cool trade winds blew off the ocean, ruffling her dark hair as she strode back down the main street. She got into her car and decided, on a whim, to follow the signs to Magic Sands Beach.

Why not spend some time on the beach? She still had on her bikini beneath her sundress. She might even take a swim. The bright white sandy beach was dotted with big black lava rocks. She remembered those from her childhood, and they could be found on most beaches, a not-so-distant reminder that these beaches were still new and growing, with Kīlauea, the active volcano not too far away, pouring hot lava into the ocean.

The wind blew stronger here, and the surf was a little rougher than she expected: boogie-boarding kids were having a grand time catching waves that pulled them to shore. Some boys even got dumped upside down, laughing as they popped back up out of the crystal-blue water, shaking their blond heads and sending salt water in all directions. She walked by the big red sign that said in bold, intimidating letters: No Lifeguard. Swim at Your Own Risk. Danger: Strong Currents, but figured that if the kids could do it, so could she. She kicked off her flip-flops and pulled off her sundress. A college kid walked by, his eyes lingering a little longer than they should on her yellow bikini. She had to admit, it felt good. Down the beach she saw a couple lounging on folding chairs beneath a big, colorful umbrella.

She stretched her arms up in the toasty sunshine, taking a moment to be thankful for the warmth when everyone else she knew was probably wearing three layers of wool in Chicago, despite the fact it was April. Chicagoans wouldn't get to shed their layers until late May. She exhaled, glad not to be in the miserable cold. She wondered if Jason and his new bondage girlfriend were freezing somewhere, being battered by late-season snow. She hoped so. That old familiar anger flared up in her chest again, burning like too much hot sauce down her throat.

Out in the distance, she saw an orange kayak bobbing in the ocean. She remembered Dallas carried a similar one in his pickup, and wondered for a fleeting second if that were him. The figure was too far away to see, and Allie dismissed the thought.

She dropped her sunglasses on top of her clothes, tucked her phone and keys into the pocket of her dress and headed to the water. The Pacific Ocean felt surprising cold on her toes. As she waded in, though, her body got used to the water, and it felt good against her skin. She glanced at her tanned arms, thinking, *I'm already looking as if I belong here*. She sucked in a breath as the cool water hit her bare midriff, as she waded in chest deep. The rocky and sandy bottom felt odd against the soles of her feet, and as she looked down, she saw tiny silver pencil-like fish darting around her. Allie fanned out her hand in the water and a small blue fish skipped over her palm.

Sunlight glinted on the water's surface, making it sparkle. Truly beautiful, she thought.

About twenty feet away, waves crashed on a shallow coral reef near the shore, throwing up white sea foam as wave after wave pummeled the small shallows. Sharp lava rocks jutted up from the water, and the wave rose precariously high. *Stay away from there*, she thought as she moved in the opposite direction, taking a deep plunge into the ocean and swimming, freestyle, across the waves. She swam for a few minutes, and then a big wave dipped her, and she popped her head up, surprised to see she'd not made it very far from the reef. In fact, she seemed to be *closer* to it.

She swam harder, but the current worked against her, moving her to the rocky inlet, where waves crashed dangerously into the rock and coral. Allie pushed her arms into the water, kicking her feet furiously, but it was as if she was swimming in place. She wasn't used to swimming this long, and her muscles ached. Tingling panic tickled the back of her neck as she found herself floating toward the big surf-size waves that had suddenly blown in from the ocean. The wind picked up, sending bigger waves in her direction, and she felt as if she was swimming against a tidal wave, steadily losing ground. Her legs burned; her muscles ached. A five-foot wave splashed over her head, dunking her beneath the water. The next wave was worse: it came so hard and fast, it sent her barreling head over heels.

The next wave hit her so hard, she didn't know which way was up; her world was a mess of sea foam and air bubbles. She only barely managed a breath before the next one hit, bouncing her into a submerged lava rock, scraping her leg. She hardly registered the pain as she doggedly swam to the surface, spitting out salty ocean brine and gasping for air. Trapped between the rocky shallows and the growing waves, she saw no escape.

"Help!" she gurgled to the sky, wondering who could even reach her. The kids on the boogie boards? No one would even be able to hear her over the roar of the ocean. She fought furiously, but got pummeled by wave after wave, some sending her under, one knocking her back hard into a rock, nearly blasting the breath out of her. No matter how hard she fought, the waves kept coming.

A big wave smashed her backward, pushing her below the surface, and kept her there. She frantically tried to swim, but the current held her down, pushed her sideways and slapped her head into another rock. She saw stars, her vision clouded until she couldn't see which way was up anymore.

This is it, she thought. *I'm going to drown.*

Her lungs were on fire. Salt water burned her eyes. Everything felt futile. Fighting the current. Swimming and getting nowhere.

Was this what her dad had felt like in his last moments?

She remembered the water pouring into the car. She'd been frantic but had moved on instinct. The car had been flipped over, and she was hanging upside down, but it had been easy enough to wiggle out of her seat belt. Her father had always told her she was his little escape artist, always getting out of locked bathrooms or jungle gyms or car seats. She had just done what came naturally. She'd gone for the open broken window, half swimming out, since the car had been filling up fast with the fresh stream water. They'd crashed into a small pond, fed by a beautiful waterfall. She'd made it to shore, as the water wasn't that deep. She'd dropped Max on the way, and had gone back for her stuffed animal, bobbing in the murky water, near the car door. She'd grabbed him and clung to him.

She'd gone back for her stuffed animal. But she'd left her dad there. She'd thought he'd be out any minute, thought he'd come barreling out, angry with her about taking off her seat belt, for causing this whole thing.

She'd waited there, not doing anything, for her dad to get out of the car. But he hadn't. He'd never gotten out.

Now her lungs burned, and there'd be no stopping them from trying to take air from the water. She was out of time. Allie made one last futile kick to the surface. That was all she had left in her, one last kick. That was when two strong hands gripped her by the arms and yanked her upward. She burst through the surface of the water, hacking, sucking in air, dizzy and light-headed.

"Are you *trying* to kill yourself?" Dallas's angry blue eyes met hers, his wet blond hair plastered to his forehead. With one arm he clutched the orange kayak she'd seen. The other held on to her shoulder.

"I…" she muttered, still dazed, her head pounding mercilessly as the stars drifted back into her vision. She felt as though, any second, she would slip back beneath the waves.

"Whoa. Hang on. I got you." Dallas managed somehow to get her mostly into the kayak. It was a two-person boat, and he pulled himself up into the other seat.

Dallas angled the kayak so he paddled expertly across the current, not against it, putting distance between them and the dangerous reef. His tanned muscles worked quickly and efficiently, and soon they were in water shallow enough to stand. Allie slid over the side of the boat and tried walking, but her knees buckled.

"Oh," she cried, flailing her arms. Dallas grabbed her securely, putting his arm around her waist.

"Lean on me," he ordered as he maneuvered them both to the beach. Dully, she realized the kids she'd seen playing were standing and staring. Dallas dragged his kayak up onto the warm sand. Then he scooped weak-kneed Allie up in his muscled arms easily and carried her over to the beach near her crumpled dress. He set her gently in the sand.

"You okay?" Dallas asked, blinking, his piercing blue eyes missing nothing as he assessed her forehead and the cut on her leg.

Allie's head throbbed, and she pressed her hand only to feel a small trickle of blood there.

"I think so," Allie said. The dizziness had gone. She blinked, still not believing she was on land again. "I hit my head."

Dallas immediately turned his attention to her forehead, where he gently probed her hairline. "Doesn't look like a serious cut." He took his

T-shirt and pressed it gently to her forehead, dabbing a little. Just a little blood stained his sleeve.

"Your shirt," she murmured, mustering up what little protest she could manage.

"Forget it."

"My phone...my..." Allie reached for her folded sundress. She grabbed it, thankful to feel the bulge of her phone and keys in her pocket.

Dallas eyed her injured leg. "That cut looks bad, but probably won't need stitches. We should get it cleaned up and bandaged, though. You sure your head feels all right?"

The intensity of his stare took her off guard. His eyes were so starkly blue, like cornflowers, she thought. Or the blue sky above their heads. She could see why he broke so many hearts in town. *I must've hit my head harder than I thought if I'm mooning over Dallas McCormick.*

"I've got a first-aid kit in my truck. You okay to walk there?"

"I think I can." Allie pulled herself up on her feet, but her legs felt like strung-out Play-Doh. She didn't know how long she'd been fighting that surf, but her muscles were spent.

"You look like a newborn colt, for goodness' sake." Dallas shook his head in disapproval. "That won't do on my watch." He swept her off her feet—literally. Still holding on to her sundress, she had nothing to do but lean into his chest. He didn't even break a sweat as he easily carried her across the sand to the parking lot. She wrapped her arms tightly around his neck, very much aware that he wore no shirt, and she was clad only in a flimsy bikini. His tanned chest muscles were hard and powerful against her as he walked, transporting her as if she weighed nothing. She felt keenly aware of a warm sensation spreading in her belly, and had half a mind to blame it on her near concussion.

He gently sat her on the tailgate of his truck. Resting there, she realized the flash of bright orange kayak in the water before she went for a swim must've been him. He whipped out a first-aid kit and tended to her wounds expertly, as if rescuing swimmers was something he did in his free time.

"You're good at that." She watched him clean and dress her wound, covering it with padding and tape.

He shrugged. "I've had my share of scrapes, darlin'." The Texas drawl rolled off his tongue, sticky and sweet like honey. "You want to tell me what you were doing trying to swim Tragic Slams?"

"Tragic… Wha—?" The bump on her head must've been worse than she thought. She had no idea what he was talking about.

"Tragic Slams." Dallas focused on her head,

padding the small cut with some antibiotic oint-
ment. "It's what people call Magic Sands Beach
around here. You know how many people drown
out there every year? Not to mention the hundreds of tourists who break bones on that reef."
He gently placed a small Band-Aid on her forehead, and then went about inspecting the rest of
her for cuts.

"I didn't know."

"But you *saw* the sign, though." Dallas waved
his arm at the big warning sign she'd passed on
her way in.

"Yeah, but the kids were swimming… I just
thought…"

Dallas's stormy face, coupled with the fact that
she felt stupid for nearly drowning *and* that she
just couldn't get anything right, well, it was all
too much. A sob escaped her throat, and she burst
into tears.

Dallas momentarily froze. Then he grabbed
a towel from his truck, holding it up to her face.
"Hey…it's okay. You're fine. It's all okay."

The kindness in his voice only made her feel
like crying harder, so she did. She buried her face
in the brightly colored striped towel and wished
the ground would swallow her whole. Not only
had she made a fool of herself once, but now she
was crying about it. She'd never be able to look
Dallas in the eye again, she was pretty sure. He'd

saved her life, and she repaid his good deed by turning into a quivering mess. She wondered if she'd ever be able to *stop* crying.

Then Dallas did something even more surprising. He wrapped his arms around her in a big hug, pulling her and the towel against his chest. His arms, so big and strong and warm, enveloped her in a protective ring she almost wanted to fight, but in the end, it felt too good to leave.

"Get it out," he said softly, as he rubbed the small of her back. "Just get it all out."

"I—I—I'm such an idiot," she told his chest.

"Nah," he said, giving her another squeeze. "Just new to the neighborhood, that's all."

She sobbed some more, and he held her even tighter.

"I'm such a mess." She swiped at her eyes angrily with the towel, wondering where all the tears had come from. She thought she'd cried all she could possibly cry in the past two months.

"Hey, no shame in crying," he said. "I cry all the time."

The thought of Dallas, a big, muscle-bound, six-foot-tall cowboy crying made Allie bark a laugh. "You? Cry? When?" Sniffling, she wiped at her wet eyes.

"I got thrown from my horse once, on the family ranch back in Texas, *and* the mare stepped on me and broke my rib. I cried like a baby. And then, of course, there are all the paper cuts I've ever had. Those suckers hurt." Dallas grinned big. "That's why I'll never put in for a desk job. You want to pinch me right now? I'll probably cry."

Allie couldn't help but laugh, and instantly she felt better.

"Thank you," she said, grateful that he hadn't made her feel worse, or gloated, or berated her for her mistake. Grateful, too, that he'd saved her life. She pulled away from him, sniffling a little. "Thanks for…everything."

"Not a problem, ma'am," he drawled, pretending to tip a hat he didn't have on. "Misu would haunt me forever if I'd let you drown. And the way that woman liked ukulele music, I know she'd keep me up with it for the rest of my days."

Allie groaned. She remembered her grandmother's fondness for the ukulele, and the fact she had it on a loop, playing constantly through her house when she was little. "Bruddah IZ playing, day and night!"

Dallas hummed the Hawaiian singer's famous rendition of "Over the Rainbow/Wonderful World" on a ukulele, and Allie instantly recognized it.

Dallas wiped a tear from Allie's cheek, and she froze at the contact, her eyes meeting his. They were stark blue, and had grown serious as he gently caressed her cheek. In that second, everything changed. He was going to kiss her—she knew it. But the most surprising part was that she wanted him to do it.

And then, suddenly and without warning, the truck beneath her shook hard.

"Wha…?" Allie grabbed the sides of the truck, fearful that the emergency brake had come loose, and she was rolling away. But as Dallas grabbed the tailgate for balance, she realized it wasn't the truck moving at all. It was the earth beneath the tires.

The tremors lasted a full fifteen seconds. Nearby, a big light pole swayed. Some walkers nearby cried out in alarm, and one nearly lost his balance in the sand. Somewhere not too far away, a car alarm went off, and Allie heard the screeching of brakes.

The earth stopped moving, and the two of them glanced around, watching as people dusted themselves off. A car honked at the intersection behind them, and several took off through a green light.

"*What* was that?" Allie cried. "The volcano?"

"No, not the volcano."

"What then…?"

Dallas frowned. "Earthquake."

"They happen here?"

"Not usually." Dallas looked grim.

Dallas looked out at the crashing waves of the ocean, assessing the rough waves. He ran to get his kayak and expertly lifted it on one shoulder, jogging up the beach and putting it into the bed of his truck. "We're going to have to move." Dallas grabbed her by the waist and pulled her down from the truck tailgate. A siren blared then, loud and long. Several passersby stopped walking and listened. The kids on the beach froze, boogie boards in hand, as they stood up in the surf.

Allie covered her ears against the wail. "What's that?"

"Tsunami alert," Dallas explained.

"Tsunami? As in giant-tidal-wave-flood-of-destruction tsunami?"

"The same. Earthquake off the coast, I think, means that the big wave is coming. And we don't have much time to get out of here."

Dread seized her stomach. She thought of all the news stories she'd heard about them, about how they killed without prejudice. Numbly, Allie watched with growing dread as people began to pack up and leave the beach. The kids ran to the parking lot, and the couple with the oversize beach umbrella quickly began to gather their things.

"We're going to have to head to high ground." Dallas guided her to the passenger side of his pickup and helped her in.

"My car?"

"It's a rental—leave it," he said. "Mine's faster."

"Are we going to make it?"

"We're going to try," Dallas said and slammed his door. "But first, we've got to check on Jesse and Kai. They're on the way."

CHAPTER NINE

DALLAS DROVE WITH single-minded determination, hitting the small strip shopping center near the beach, screeching to a halt across two parking spaces. He went right to Hula Coffee and strode through the doors. Jesse was standing on a chair telling everyone to get out, get to their cars and get to higher ground. The tourists looked slightly alarmed as they turned and left the shop.

"Where's Kai?" Dallas asked.

"Surfing. He's not answering his phone, either. Do you think... Would he hear the sirens?" Concern wrinkled her brow.

"He knows the surf and beach better than anyone," Dallas said. "He'd know what to do when he heard the sirens. Come on, we have to go now."

Dallas helped her down off the chair. "We don't have much time—if any. Where's Kaimana?"

"She's visiting my mom. They're far from the beaches, out of the zone," Jesse said. "But... Kai..."

"Will kill me if I let anything happen to you, so come *on*." Dallas grabbed Jesse's arm and led her to his pickup. He was surprised when he got there to see Allie standing near Teri and two other stylists from the salon.

"They don't have cars today," Allie said. "They biked."

Dallas nodded to them all. "Okay, in the back. Jesse and Allie, ride in the front. Let's go, people. We don't have any time."

Dallas had a brief thought of Kayla. Her school was on higher ground, so hopefully she'd be fine, but… He glanced at his truck. It was full anyway, of people and his kayak—something he'd need if the flooding got bad. *Jennifer has to take care of Kayla now*, he thought, even though the fact left a sour taste in the back of his mouth. He would've driven through a tsunami to save that little girl. Now he had to force himself not to care.

But he couldn't.

He grabbed his cell phone from his pocket and put it on speaker. He had the day care on speed dial.

"Hello?" A rushed-sounding woman answered the phone.

"I'm calling about Kayla Thomas," Dallas said, as he watched Jesse swing into the passenger seat next to Allie. "Is she there or has the—"

"The children just left on a bus to higher ground, sir. I've got to go, as well. Be safe. *Mahalo*."

He felt a rush of relief. She was going to be safe.

He glanced at Allie's pale face as she squashed into the middle seat, Jesse next to her. He needed to get them to higher ground. *Now.*

Dallas hopped into the cab of his truck and turned the ignition just when a low roaring sound reached them from the beach as the tide began to drift outward, *far* outward.

"Oh, my God," Jesse breathed, as she looked through the window and saw a mile of exposed coral, fish flopping on wet sand.

Dallas hit the gas and maneuvered the truck deftly through small back alleys, hitting the highway ahead of another car. One car tried to pull out in front of him, running a red light, and Dallas swerved to miss him. Allie gripped the dashboard, her face as white as a sheet. Her leg rubbed against his, warm and firm.

The blood rush from the near kiss they'd almost shared still thrummed steadily in his veins, and his lap felt decidedly uncomfortable. He had nearly kissed her! It was as if his body had gone on autopilot, and he'd just been drawn in like a fly to a bug zapper. That never happened to him. Dallas was used to being in control. The way he felt about Allie was not something he could predict: one minute she was driving him up the wall with frustration, and the next her body was driving his crazy with desire. He knew he wanted her and that he shouldn't want her, but the explosion of need that had nearly sent him straight in for a kiss couldn't be denied.

Now, as he shifted uncomfortably in the driver's seat, he tried to push those thoughts from his mind. He had more pressing problems, like getting them all to safety. What was it about that girl that just brought trouble? No sooner had he pulled her from one disaster than another struck.

While tsunamis were relatively rare on the islands, he knew that the ones that did come hit hard and had killed more people than any other natural disaster combined on Hawaii, including twice taking out much of Hilo.

A white car in front of him slowed down for no apparent reason, and Dallas hit his steering wheel. "Come on," he muttered, glancing in the rearview and his blind spot. Seeing an opening, he glided around the slow car.

Jesse's phone binged, announcing an incoming message. "Kai has his phone. Said he's getting to his car. He's headed up to higher ground."

"Good," Dallas said, eyes intent on the road as he tried to move as quickly as possible without causing a wreck. His fingers turned white as he clutched the steering wheel. They eased upward as they climbed the mountain. Behind them, a freight train of water was about to arrive; they could hear the distant sound of its roar. Teri and her stylists gripped the truck bed as the vehicle zoomed past other cars. Everyone kept their eyes on the ocean.

Dallas glanced in the rearview, amazed to see where once was sparkling blue now was a muddy sandbank as far as the eye could see.

"This is going to be bad," he murmured. Then he hit a traffic jam; miles of bright red taillights blinked at him from the road. "No, no, *no*." He hit the horn, but it was no use. Nobody was going anywhere.

"Is there an accident up there?" Jesse asked, eyes wide.

"There's about to be one right here," Dallas half growled as he surveyed the mess in front of him. He pulled the truck over to the side of the road, maneuvering down the shoulder until he got to a small driveway turnoff.

"This isn't a road," Jesse pointed out.

"It is now," Dallas said as he pushed his truck into four-wheel drive and took the ranger's trail up through the national park. They didn't have time to wait. That water was coming, and it was coming fast. The road was uneven, and Allie flew into him after a particularly hard bump.

"Sorry," she breathed, her voice light as she tried to rearrange herself back in her seat. He wanted to tell her how much he didn't mind the contact.

"Can we get to the estate from here? That's

far from the ocean," Allie said, grasping the seat bench below her knees for support.

"Not far enough," Dallas said. "We're just below evacuation levels."

"Where are we going?"

"This will take us to the evacuation center at Kealakehe High School," Jesse said. "That's where Kai and I told each other we'd meet last time we had a warning."

"Okay," Dallas said, turning the car from the private driveway and down a small street that led to a cul-de-sac. In minutes, he'd maneuvered his way back up through the neighborhood roads, and to the three-story white concrete high school, where palm trees swayed near the school sign and lush green grass surrounded the building. The parking lot was already filling up with cars as Dallas turned in. He parked and helped out Teri and her stylists from the bed of the truck.

Jesse and Allie walked to the main building of the high school, where teachers were already showing individuals into the gym. Inside, Allie saw the bleachers thick with people. The buzz of conversation among families and friends was loud in the enclosed space.

Dallas glanced to the corner, where dozens of small children sat cross-legged listening to a book being read by a teacher. He looked for Kayla's familiar blond curls and found them. She sat snugly between two other kids in the second row, her face angelic as always, green eyes intent on the teacher with the book.

Thank God, he thought as he felt relief pour over him. He wanted to run over and hug her, but as soon as he took a step in her direction, he saw Jennifer rushing to her. Jennifer swept the girl into her arms and hugged her hard, tears of relief in her eyes. He couldn't go over now. Not with Jennifer there.

Kayla would be safe with her mother, but somehow, that knowledge didn't do anything to soothe the ache in his heart.

But he didn't have time to dwell on it as friends found them in the crowd.

"Thank God, you're okay!" This was Minnie, who collided into Allie and gave her a huge hug. "I thought your car was in the shop today?" Minnie asked Teri as she threw her arms around Teri, too.

"Dallas drove us," Teri explained. "He saved us."

"You'd do the same for me," Dallas said, knowing she wasn't his biggest fan. He didn't blame her for believing the rumors Jennifer spread. Still, he had to laugh to see Teri shift uncomfortably on her feet.

"*Told* you that you were wrong about him," Minnie whispered fiercely in Teri's ear as she gave her friend a hard elbow in the side. "That'll teach you to bad-mouth my boyfriend," she whispered when Dallas couldn't hear. Allie had to laugh.

"We heard on the radio, the first wave just hit, and it's knocked out half the resorts on the beach," Minnie exclaimed, pointing to her smartphone, where she was getting a live feed from a local news radio station.

"Whoa," Teri said. "I never thought it would happen on this side of the island."

"Everyone is saying this is something nobody predicted," Minnie said. "The first wave was insane, but it's not over."

"What do you mean?" Allie asked, blinking.

"The wave train. Every tsunami has one. Could be as many as six or seven or even more. Could be hours before this is all over." Minnie pointed to her white earbud in her left ear to show the source of her information.

"The sun will be setting soon," Dallas added. "So probably no one is going back to their homes tonight. It will be too dangerous in the dark."

Allie glanced around the filling gym, looking at the families around her huddling together with a look of empathy on her face. "None of these kids will get to go home tonight?" she asked, as she watched a mother hold a fussy baby in her arms.

"You mean even if they *have* a home to go back

to," Teri said, looking grim. The gym looked as if it was reaching capacity, and a few more people tried to squeeze in. The volunteers at the door held up the last family—a daughter and her dad—not letting them inside.

"Dallas," Allie said, grabbing his arm. "Are they going to turn them away?"

Dallas shook his head. "Not if I can help it," he said. He found Jesse in the crowd. "Call me as soon as Kai gets here, okay? If there's not room for him and Aunt Kaimana, you three come to the tree house, understood?"

Jesse nodded. Dallas made a move to go, and Jesse grabbed his arm. "Thank you, Dallas."

He shrugged off the gratitude. "Anything for you and Kai, you know that. Call me if you need anything."

Dallas left her with her circle of friends and took Allie by the hand. He saved one last look for Kayla, who was now sitting in her mother's lap. "We're going so they can let that dad and his daughter in."

"Where?" she asked, looking bewildered.

"I have a place."

ABOUT FIFTEEN MINUTES LATER, Dallas steered the truck off the main road and into a trail lined with thick green foliage.

"This looks as if we're going into the jungle,"

Allie remarked, as big, flat banana leaves hit her side-view mirror.

"That's because we are." Dallas flipped the truck into four-wheel drive as his oversize tires bounced across the unpaved, one-lane road. Leaves and branches smacked the side of his truck. He knew vehicles didn't go down this path that often, which was why he'd picked it. Dallas glanced at Allie, who wore her flowered sundress over her yellow bikini top. He noticed her bare knee poking out of the skirt's hem and remembered the smooth feel of her skin when he'd carried her to safety. He still couldn't believe he'd nearly kissed her. He'd never felt as panicked as he had when he'd seen her struggling in that surf.

He'd first seen her just as she was wading into the water. He'd only happened to be there, kayaking his usual route. He'd watched her firm, toned legs stride into the surf from a distance, and he'd been so busy admiring her assets, it hadn't registered that she was headed to Break-Neck Point. Damned if that girl hadn't gone straight for the most treacherous part of the cove, as if she had some kind of homing device for danger.

He'd felt a sharp stab of fear. He knew that beach was every bit as dangerous as the signs said, if not more.

Dallas had sprung into action just in time. Allie had been taking longer and longer to come up for air. He knew it would only be a matter of time before she'd become another statistic.

Even remembering the sight of her flailing there in the water made him sick to his stomach. He glanced over at her, alive and well in his truck, and felt thankful. He was surprised by how strongly he wanted to take care of her and, tsunami or no tsunami, he planned to keep her safe.

He steered the truck into the jungle, large branches flapping against the windshield as he went. Just when it looked as though what little was left of a road would give out, he turned and parked under a huge koa tree. He hopped out of the cab and breathed in the fresh, humid air. Here, surrounded by rain forest, far away from the sight of the ocean, it was easy to forget they were still on an island.

Allie blinked as she glanced around the cleared spot. "Are we camping?" she asked him, confused.

"Sort of," he said, helping her out of her side. He pointed up to the small, two-story cabin, built about ten feet above the ground, on a wooden deck anchored in the branches of the trees.

"Welcome to the tree house." He grinned and grabbed a bag from the back of his pickup. She stood, holding the door frame of the vehicle, glancing up, speechless.

"Need help?" Dallas offered his arm, but Allie shook her head.

"I can make it," she said, walking over to the narrow staircase gingerly on her bandaged leg. Independent and stubborn, Dallas thought.

"There's a composting toilet down here and solar panels on the roof for electricity. And, of course, a working shower outside."

Allie scoffed. "*Another* outside shower."

"In the back, down the back staircase, you'll find a small heated pond, fed by the local stream. Underground lava tunnels keep it balmy, like a hot tub. But the best part of the tree house is that we're safe from flooding. Nothing will touch us here."

In the cabin, Allie glanced around the tiny kitchen of just bare essentials: a stove top and a refrigerator and sink. A small table with tool stools made up the dining room, and a ladder led up to a loft, where the foot of a queen-size bed was visible.

"Love nest, huh?" Allie asked, pointing upward.

Dallas just quirked up one eyebrow but said nothing. He hadn't had a woman here since Jennifer. Just thinking of his ex made his stomach roil. He didn't need reminding of her betrayal.

"No—a weekend getaway. *And* a place I rent to tourists. In fact, a honeymooning couple stayed here just last week. They left two days ago. If we're lucky, they left some things behind."

Dallas poked his head in the minifridge. "Bingo! There's some water, cola…"

"Have anything stronger?" Allie asked, slumping down on a stool.

"Tequila?" He held up a half-full bottle of Don Julio Blanco.

"Tequila," Allie agreed, nodding furiously. Her fingers shook a little before she balled her hand into a stubborn fist. She'd been through a lot. Dallas felt the sudden urge to pull her into her arms and tell her everything was going to be okay. Or kiss her until she started shaking in a whole new way.

No, I promised Kai I'd stay away from her, Dallas thought. And he didn't make promises lightly. He squashed the temptation to break his promise and poured them both a small shot of tequila.

"The couple who rented this place didn't leave us any limes. Just salt."

"Salt it is," she assured him, and sprinkled some on her hand. She licked the salt off, and took the glass and downed it in one swig. Dallas, impressed, followed suit.

"That's better," she said, putting her empty cup on the wooden table.

Out in the distance, they heard the tsunami alarm sound again. They both paused to listen.

"The water can't reach us up here," Dallas assured her.

"What about the estate?" she asked.

"I don't know. Hopefully, it'll be out of reach. It just depends on how the water hits and where."

"Oh," Allie said, and Dallas couldn't figure out if she was relieved or glad to hear the estate had a chance to miss the waves.

"What about the town? I mean…"

"We won't know until tomorrow." Dallas stared at the bottom of his empty cup, rolling around the last drop of tequila left there. "But everyone at the high school should be fine."

"And Kai?"

"They said he was on his way, so hopefully, he made it." Dallas glanced at his phone. He only got one bar up here, so he hoped Jesse could call if she needed to. "There were a lot of kids near the coast, and I hope they all made it," Dallas said, his thoughts flying to Kayla again. He was glad she was safe with Jennifer, but somehow seeing them together had just reminded him of all he'd lost.

Dallas poured himself another glass of tequila. Allie instantly offered up her glass, as well. "I think we've also got some snacks. Look! They left a whole bag of chips and some salsa. Guess they didn't eat much while they were here."

Allie dug into the chips and took another swig of tequila. She chuckled, amused, and he could almost see her relaxing a little, the warmth of the tequila taking effect. He started to like this new Allie, her hair drying wavy and wild from the surf, her newly tanned shoulders emerging from her pink sunburn. "How did you find this place?" Allie gestured with her cup of tequila.

"I built it, actually," he said. It had taken him nearly a year to construct the tree house, and he'd shaped and honed every piece by hand. "It's made of one hundred percent koa wood." He tapped his foot against the smooth and richly colored wooden floorboards.

"You built this? Seriously?" Allie glanced around the small but sturdy house in awe. "I'm impressed."

"You should be," Dallas deadpanned, which made Allie laugh again. "At first, I was going to live here, but the commute was too far to the plantation. So when I was done, I just started renting it to visitors, and you'd be surprised how many come."

Another distant siren blast reached them.

Allie sobered. "Do you think it's bad down there?"

"One way to find out." Dallas dug around in a cabinet near the sink and found a radio. He clicked it on and turned it to an AM station. They were met with hefty static, until he found one weak station bleeding through the interference.

"Once again, if you're just joining us, an earthquake struck just off the coast of Kona, registering as a 5.1 on the Richter scale, nearly unprecedented for that area. The first tsunami came ashore just minutes ago, wiping out many of the tourist spots and hotels along the coast, which are now underwater. Hundreds, maybe even thousands, of people are still unaccounted for at this time. Residents had less than fifteen minutes to get to higher ground before the first wave struck, and many did not make it…"

Allie grew pale. "If we hadn't left when we did…"

"No use in getting yourself turned around with what-ifs. We made it. And so did Teri and Jesse and the others."

"But if you hadn't been there… I would've…" Allie drifted off. Her brown eyes, big and luminous, studied him. "You saved me. *Twice.*"

"Anybody would've done it."

"No, they wouldn't. Thank you, Dallas." Allie put her hand over his on the table. He felt electric sparks from where she touched him, sparks that pinged all the way up his spinal cord and straight to his brain.

"I'm lucky you were even *there.*" A small line appeared in Allie's forehead as she thought this through. "And after I turned away the coffee roaster, after I accused you of…"

"Stealing from your grandmother?"

"Right—that." Allie's face turned a deep shade of pink. "I'm sorry. After what you've done for her and Kai and Jesse…"

Dallas rubbed his neck, feeling uncomfortable. "They told you about that, did they?"

"Jesse won't let anybody insult you in her presence," Allie said. "She defends you like her brother."

"They are good people. All they needed was seed money. They've worked hard to make that coffee shop a success. Twelve-hour days nearly every day."

"Still, a lot of people wouldn't have been so generous." Allie's eyes warmed to him, and he felt something shift there. He felt suddenly on the spot.

"It was no big deal. When my dad died, he left me some family land. I had no intention of taking up the family business of ranching. It was a hard living and almost impossible to do with the big cattle companies around. Besides, I never felt as though that was home. I sold it and left and came here." Dallas frowned as he looked at his hands. "I never really felt like it was my money anyway."

"Why not?" Allie leaned forward, curiosity in her voice.

"I had a stepbrother," Dallas said. "He was my father's wife's son, but he lived with us. My mom passed when I was little, and Dad remarried when I was about ten. She already had Cal from a previous marriage. Cal grew to be like a son to my father, but there was always the issue of him not being blood. My father, he was traditional, and even though Cal was a hundred times the rancher I was, my dad didn't leave him any of the ranch."

"What did Cal do?"

"He was upset. I tried to split it with him, but he was too angry. Too hurt. He wouldn't have any of it. He took off without another word. I waited a little while, but then I sold the place and moved here."

Allie covered Dallas's hand with hers. "It's not your fault. Your father made that choice."

Dallas shrugged. "But I had to live with it."

"You're a good man." The way she looked at him made Dallas wonder if she was flirting. She parted her lips, showing her straight white teeth and a mouth he suddenly wanted to taste. *Get it together*, he told himself sternly. No time to get distracted by a pair of pretty eyes.

She offered her empty glass up for another refill.

"Are you sure that's a good idea?" he asked. "Your head feel okay?"

"Just one more."

Dallas poured her a small shot and one for himself.

"As long as we're playing truth or dare, why didn't you come to Misu's funeral? I know it bothered you that you didn't. I could tell that day…I said something."

Allie, cup at her lips, nearly spit out her tequila as she spun out in a coughing fit.

"I'm sorry. People tell me all the time I'm too direct. It's a character flaw." Dallas gave her a hard pat on the back when the coughing kept going. "You okay?"

"I'm fine." Allie wheezed and wiped her watery eyes. "I tried to come to Grandma Misu's funeral. I should've been there."

Dallas waited for more, watching her closely.

"I wanted to come. I tried to come…I…" Allie rubbed her eyes furiously and frowned.

"Hey, it's none of my business. I shouldn't have said anything before."

"No, you were right. I should've been there." Allie stared morosely downward, not meeting Dallas's gaze.

"So why weren't you?"

"The day she died, I found out my fiancé had been cheating. I thought he was the love of my life, and it turns out it was all a lie. I spent a month in bed. I lost my job. Everything. I…I was just in no shape to think about anything else. But that was selfish of me. I should've gotten it together for Grandma Misu. I realize that now." Tears glistened in Allie's eyes, threatening to spill. "If I was in any shape to fly... I mean, I would have. And then there was... I mean, well... It was just too hard."

Dallas suspected Allie wasn't telling hin everything, but he wasn't going to push for more details. He recognized the clear shape of heartbreak in her newly scabbed scars. He carried some of his own.

"I'm sorry," he said. "I didn't know about the... fiancé."

"Not something I want to broadcast." Allie shrugged. "Come pity the girl who was dumped by a secret sex freak!"

"Sex freak?" Dallas arched a curious eyebrow.

Allie covered her mouth and laughed. "I've said too much."

The corner of Dallas's mouth quirked up in a teasing smile. "You've got to tell me now. You can't just let that tidbit hang there. What was he into? Wearing diapers?"

"Diapers!" Allie shrieked, laughter bubbling up her throat as she grabbed her bare knees in surprise. "Who does that...?"

"They had a whole reality show about it, or so I heard." Dallas grinned, enjoying her shock.

"So?" He nudged her with his elbow. "Fess up. It can't be as bad as diapers."

Allie let out a long sigh. "I caught Jason—my ex—cheating. Well, his mistress sent him a love letter. And a whip. And a dog collar."

Dallas was shocked into silence as a million images rolled through his mind, none of them good. He couldn't help it then; he burst out laughing. It was the last thing he expected her to say.

Allie laughed, too.

"That *is* a sex freak," Dallas agreed. He grew serious, as the ramifications of someone into S and M dawned on him. Anger bubbled up in him as he thought of Allie's fiancé and what he might have done to her. "He didn't hit…you, did he?"

"Me? No! God, no." Allie put her hand across her chest as if the thought made her want to choke. "I don't like that. I don't think sex should be painful." Allie grew thoughtful a moment. "But maybe that just makes me boring."

"Maybe it just makes you *normal*." Dallas hit the table with the palm of his hand for emphasis. Clearly, her ex had done a number on Allie's head, and a flare of protectiveness made him want to go find Jason and have a sternly worded conversation, featuring his right fist. "I'm glad you didn't marry that prick. He doesn't deserve you. He had a wonderful girl right there, ready to marry him, and he goes and blows it. He's a fool for letting you go."

"Aw, that's nice of you to say."

"It's not nice, it's just the truth. Easy to give compliments when you just tell the truth." Dallas put his hand gently on Allie's shoulder and gave it a squeeze.

Allie paused, her warm brown eyes studying him for a moment, as a loaded silence fell between them. The warm buzz from the tequila seeped into his brain, and he suddenly felt the urge to pull Allie into his arms and get right back to that moment that was interrupted on the beach. He eyed her bare knee and the thigh above, itching to touch her soft skin.

Kai said she was off-limits, a warning thought popped in his head. *You promised him.*

The thought of Kai made him want to reel himself in. He'd been more than clear about him not getting involved with Allie.

"Teri warned me to stay away from you," Allie said abruptly, as if she read his mind somehow.

"Teri? What does Teri say?" *And did Kai mention me, too?* he wondered, but didn't ask.

Dallas snapped back to attention as he tried not to be distracted once again by Allie's pretty heart-shaped face, where her dark brown eyes studied him intently. There was no safe place to look: her eyes pulled him in, her slim thighs taunted him and her full, pouty bottom lip begged to be kissed.

"She and Minnie said you were a notorious heartbreaker on the island. Is that true?"

Dallas shrugged, running an uncomfortable hand through his thick blond hair. "My reputation is greatly exaggerated."

"Is that so? Is rescuing girls from near-death experiences your seduction technique?"

Dallas shook his head sternly. "No, it's not."

"Uh-huh." Allie's eyes sparkled. She might be flirting with him. How was he going to resist her if she came on to him? It was one thing not to make the first move, but if she did... Kai still wouldn't understand, he thought.

"I bet that's not all Teri told you." Dallas was pretty sure Teri didn't stop at him being a womanizer. She'd been Jennifer's friend for longer than his. If anyone was going to take Jennifer's side, it was her.

Allie shifted in her seat, obviously not wanting to reveal what she knew.

"Go on," Dallas said. "We may call it the Big Island, but it's anything but. I've heard the worst things people have said about me. You don't have to spare my feelings."

"She said you cheated on your fiancée."

"Uh-huh. And...anything else?"

"That I should stay away from you. That you

can't survive without a new woman's attention every ten minutes." Allie physically flinched, bracing herself for fallout, but Dallas just laughed out loud.

"That's Teri. Calling 'em like she sees 'em. Well, neither one of those things is true."

Allie blinked fast. "Why did she say them, then?"

"She's friends with my ex, Jennifer, whom you met. And Jennifer can be very persuasive." Dallas finished the last dregs of his tequila. He felt a buzz in his brain, and the sudden urge to tell Allie everything, to confess all the terrible things she'd done, the irony of the fact that she had let everyone on the island believe he was the one who cheated and lied when she'd been the one who'd betrayed him in the worst possible way. He wished cheating had even *been* the worst of it.

He wanted to tell Allie, but once again he hesitated. For Kayla's sake.

"Why would Jennifer lie?"

"Jennifer had her reasons," Dallas said. "She always does."

Allie gazed at him, steady and true. She looked as if she wanted to ask more, but restrained herself. Thank God she did. If she'd even pressed a little, he would've unburdened himself completely and told her everything. Instead, she just reached out and squeezed his hand. The comforting touch sent sparks straight up his arm. The tequila was in full force, as he felt the warmth of alcohol spread across his body.

Dallas said nothing, just moved in closer. Allie froze, sensing the change in mood. She waited, lips slightly parted. He was struck suddenly by how perfect she seemed right then, face smooth and unlined, her jet-black hair thick and silky down her shoulder. The magnetic pull he felt between them couldn't just be one-sided. He refused to believe that.

"You're really beautiful," he said before he could stop himself. He knew it sounded like some cheesy pickup line, but the fact was it was the truth. Right then, at that moment, she was the most beautiful women he'd ever seen. He'd been half-smitten that day she'd stepped out of her rental car. But now, after saving her in the surf, he felt *responsible*. He cared what happened to her, not just today, but tomorrow, and a long time after that.

"Come on." Allie wiggled on her stool, made uncomfortable by the attention. "You don't have to feed me lines just because we're stuck here."

"What lines?" Dallas stood and moved around the table so he was standing right in front of her. Allie craned her neck up to meet his eyes. "I told you, I only tell the truth."

He moved in closer, and she tilted her chin up

to meet his. She didn't inch away but sat very still. Something in her face told him that if he made a move, she wouldn't reject him. The tequila had long since dulled any of the warning bells about Kai being mad. His lips brushed hers ever so gently. She didn't push him away or cry out. Instead, she wrapped her hand around the fabric of his shirt and pulled him closer. She spread her knees, and instantly he was between them, her arms around his neck, nothing separating them but thin fabric. She tasted like tequila and something even more delicious, and though he tried, he couldn't get enough of her mouth. Her tongue met his in a little dance, and he felt as if, despite all the many women he'd kissed before in his life, she might as well have been the only one who mattered.

He lost all ability to think as she worked her hands down his back, clutching on to him as if she might fall. The rush of desire that came flooding through his senses took him by surprise. He wasn't used to wanting a woman this badly. Allie moved her hands up to the back of Dallas's neck, tangling them in his thick, dirty-blond hair. He kissed her hungrily, and she groaned into his mouth, running her fingers along his chest, and his body responded in a visceral way. She ran her hands under his shirt, caressing his bare chest, making him run hot with desire. His own hands took on a will of their own. Instinctively, his palm cupped her breast and he felt her nipple rise to attention beneath the soft swimsuit top. She moaned and arched her back, eager for more.

And then the radio interrupted everything with a loud burst of alarm.

Both of them jumped in surprise, the seal of their kiss suddenly broken. Allie pulled away, her breath ragged. "What was that?" She glared at the radio.

"Emergency broadcast system," Dallas said, turning to the radio and reaching for the volume. Allie stopped him with a hand on his wrist.

"Wait. Let's listen."

"Kailua Pier has been inundated with debris, and the Kona Village resort among several others, have been all but leveled. Several homes along Kealakekua Bay have been all but washed away. Sewer spills have been reported, as have power outages across the island. At least 107 people are still missing at this hour, and experts say we may still experience aftershocks from the 5.1 scale earthquake experienced earlier today. Residents are advised to stay at higher elevations until at least tomorrow, and maybe longer, for their own safety."

"Tomorrow?" Allie echoed. "So…we're going to have to stay here *overnight*?" Clearly, it hadn't even occurred to her until that moment that she might have to share a bed with him.

She glanced up at the only bed in the place: a queen-size frame sitting on the loft above their heads. There wasn't even a couch for someone else to sleep on, and no room on the floor, either. It was a tiny little tree house, designed for bare living. It only just occurred to him that with the tequila, and her gorgeous body in such close quarters, it would be a miracle if they *didn't* end up naked. The thought actually calmed him a little. There'd be hell to pay tomorrow, and Kai might never speak to him again, but tonight, at least, they'd both have some fun. Wasn't that the lesson he'd learned from Jennifer? Take the fun while you can before life kicks you in the teeth and steals everything you hold dear?

Or you could be the gentleman your mama raised and sleep in the pickup truck. His conscience, the killjoy. At that moment, he knew he'd have to do the right thing. If he got involved with Allie, he'd have to be willing to go the distance. He couldn't just treat her like a tourist. Kai wouldn't let him, and he knew it. If he slept with her, it would be more than just a one-night stand.

"There's only one bed," Allie said, stating the obvious. Just then, he noticed Allie's complexion had turned a bit ashen.

"Are you all right?" he asked her.

"I need some air," she said tightly, grabbed her smartphone and then bolted.

CHAPTER TEN

OUTSIDE THE SMALL CABIN, Allie crossed her arms across her chest, trying to get her breathing under control as she walked out, past the pickup and down the small dirt path leading to the road. What was wrong with her? Her body hummed with desire, a white-hot intensity that she hadn't felt since Jason, a power so strong it almost scared her. She touched her lips, almost feeling the residue of his overwhelming kiss. She'd been seconds away from ripping off his shirt, from tugging at the front of his swim trunks. And then all she'd felt was searing panic at the thought of falling into bed with Dallas McCormick.

The man who brought tourists to his house every weekend? She thought of the girl wearing the rumpled-looking dress and stilettos sitting in his kitchen that one morning drinking coffee. Did she want to become like her? One more number for him?

She had vowed not to let anyone close enough to hurt her again. But the fact was, she'd needed Dallas today. If he hadn't been there, she would've died. Her hands shook as she realized the truth of what scared her the most: she *couldn't* do it alone.

It had never occurred to her she could be so vulnerable, that she'd need someone's help so badly. That she might not have a choice. She'd always clung to the idea that she could go it alone, that she didn't need anyone, not even Jason. That anytime anyone disappointed her, she had an escape plan: go solo. But what if she couldn't?

She hugged herself tightly as she walked down the trail, flush on either side with thick green foliage. Even here, tropical flowers sprouted, vibrant pinks and yellows. Brightly colored birds darted through the canopy of trees above her head. Shaded from the hot sun, the air felt humid but cool.

The tequila still hummed in her veins, a nice, tingling buzz. She resisted giving in to it, trying to keep her thoughts orderly, sober. Could she admit to herself that she needed someone in her life? And, more than that, could she even consider that person might be Dallas McCormick?

He drove her insane. Yet he'd been there when she'd needed him most. It was more than she could say for any other man in her life. But was that enough?

Maybe it could just be a little fun. A little sex.

Yet she knew herself better than that. She couldn't just have a little fun. A little fun always ended up with her getting in way over her head. She was always reluctant to trust people, but once she did, it was hard for her not to trust them completely and absolutely.

Like Jason.

She glanced at the phone in her hand and saw she had very little battery left and hardly any signal bars. Distantly, she heard another wail from the tsunami siren. She wondered again about Kai, hoping he'd made it to the high school. She thought about all the people there, waiting on loved ones, worried about their homes and businesses. *No more moping*, she told herself. *No more pity party.*

She reached the paved road, and thought, *I could just leave.* If she didn't want to be with Dallas, she could just walk down the highway, head to the estate and take her chances. Maybe the floodwaters hadn't reached that high. Allie considered it.

She thought of the panic she'd felt when the waves swallowed her up. She had been alone then. So very alone. And she'd almost died alone.

She didn't want to die alone.

Her phone rang in her hand, her mother's number flashing across the screen.

"Allie! Honey, are you all right?" her mother exclaimed, worry giving her voice a ragged edge.

"I woke up and saw the news and… Are you at an evacuation center?"

"I'm okay, Mom. I'm fine. I…I'm with Dallas. He's the man I told you about. He actually saved me…" Allie almost mentioned the near drowning, but then thought better of it. Her mom had enough to worry about. "From the tsunami. We were on the beach when the earthquake happened. He drove me to higher ground."

"Thank goodness," her mother exclaimed, literally exhaling into the phone. "Henry and I were so worried!" Henry was her mother's husband. She'd remarried about five years ago, after Allie was out of the house. Henry was a good man, a mild-mannered accountant who doted on her. Allie could see how much happier her mother was. She'd thought she'd found someone like Henry in Jason, but she'd been so wrong. "Are you okay?" her mother asked, and this time she didn't mean physically.

"I'm okay."

"You're sure?"

"Yeah." She wasn't the least bit sure.

"Jason's mother called me. Again. She can't stop apologizing. She said she doesn't want to bother you, but she's so sorry…"

Allie felt her stomach clench. Jason's mother and sisters were all so sweet. She hoped they were giving him hell, but still…the idea that they wouldn't be her family anymore just hurt. She wished she'd never gotten to know them. It was painful to lose them. That was what made trusting people so hard, she thought. It wasn't the betrayal; it was after they'd disappeared, when they weren't there anymore.

"I can't talk about her, Mom. I don't want to…"

"I'm sorry, Allie. I just…I just wanted you to know. I'm sorry about Jason."

Nothing Jason's family could do or say changed the facts of what Jason had done. Allie knew that.

"I know. I'm fine, Mom. Got to go. Phone's dying!"

She clicked off, swallowing a lump in her throat. As she fought for her composure, she realized the sky above her had darkened, signaling that daylight was going fast. As the sunlight faded, Allie felt goose bumps rise up on her arms. Did it get *cold* up here? A shiver ran down her spine, telling her she was far from the tropical climate of the beach. They were high up on the mountain. Farther up, she'd heard that snow sometimes fell at the peak. Leaving would be foolish, she thought.

Allie turned and headed back into the forest toward the cabin. By the time she rounded the final bend, the sky had turned dusky, and she smelled a campfire. She saw Dallas had made a small blaze in the fire pit in a clearing near his truck. The pit had a metal grill attached, where he'd set a pan filled with baked beans. He also had some sausage on a stick, which he carefully rotated in the fire. Allie's stomach growled as the maple smell of sweet barbecue sauce hit her nose.

"Found some more things our honeymooners left. Hungry?" he asked her as she cautiously approached. He didn't mention the kiss or her sudden escape. For that, she was grateful.

"Starved," she said, rubbing her hands together.

"Have a seat," he said, nodding toward the other folding chair across the fire from him. She felt relieved to be sitting outside, away from the single queen-size bed in the tree house. She happily sat down, watching Dallas expertly maneuver the oversize sausage link over the flames. Observing the skin grow crisp in the heat, he added, "Just about…done."

Expertly, he pulled the sausage away from the fire, heading toward the open tailgate of his pickup truck, where Allie saw he'd spread out plates, the tequila, some bottled water and their cups from inside. He gently slid the sausage off the metal roasting fork and sliced it easily with a carving knife he'd brought from the kitchen, dividing the meat between two plates. He grabbed a tea towel and wrapped it around the handle of the pan, gently lifting it from the metal grate. He served up some beans and more tortilla chips and handed her the blue plastic plate. She immediately began to scarf down the food; the spicy sausage tasted especially good. Dallas watched her out of the corner of his eye as he served himself dinner. A small smile played at the corner of his lips.

"You *were* hungry," he said.

Allie nodded between gulps. "Yeah, thanks. I was. This is a feast. Why did the couple leave all this?"

Dallas shrugged. "Who knows why tourists do what they do?"

Dallas ate slowly and thoughtfully. "I wasn't sure if you were coming back," he said as he sat in his chair. The firelight threw shadows on his tanned skin. "But I figured I'd cook enough for two just in case."

"Yeah…I almost didn't," Allie admitted.

"I'm glad you did. It gets cold up here."

Allie shivered a bit, and Dallas walked over and put his fleece jacket around her shoulders. "Scoot up to the fire. It'll warm you."

"Thanks," she said, watching his every move, remembering what his strong arms had felt like when they'd carried her to the beach. The way his lips had felt on hers. Soft, inviting.

She shook herself. What was wrong with her? Getting involved with Dallas was a bad idea. A very bad idea.

The air temperature dropped rapidly. Another

chill shook her as she finished up her plate. She put her hands up to the fire and felt the warmth from the flames spread across her palms.

"If you really want to warm up, you could try a swim in the heated pond." Dallas nodded backward toward the tree house. "It really is warm, 24/7."

"Not boiling with lava, I hope." Allie hugged herself as she put down the plate on the ground near her.

"Nothing like that. It's the perfect temperature. Here, let me show you." Dallas put his empty plate down and walked back by the tree house. Allie followed, watching as he made his way between two lush trees. Several large stones made a path through. "Here, it gets tricky." Dallas offered his hand and helped her over a small boulder. His fingers felt big and dry and strong as they led her. Allie could hear the sound of water, and when Dallas swept several thick branches to one side, she found herself staring at a beautiful pond, fed by a trickle of a waterfall down a wall of black lava rock. Even in the silvery moonlight, the scene looked like something from a glossy tourist brochure, the bright white moon above their heads reflected in the clear pool. Dallas kept hold of her hand as they made their way on the slippery black rocks to water.

"Go ahead, dip a toe in." Allie could see Dallas's bright white smile in the dusk. She kicked off a flip-flop and dipped her right foot in.

"Wow," she exclaimed in surprise. "This is like a hot tub!" She kicked off her other shoe and waded in up to her shins. "This feels...so good."

"I told you."

"I'm going in." Allie let go of Dallas's hand so she could lift her sundress up and over her head. Without another care, she tossed it over her shoulder, with Dallas struggling to catch it.

She hesitated when the water reached the cut on her leg. She winced slightly as the bandage got wet, but the stinging soon subsided.

Allie's yellow string bikini glowed in the moonlight as she waded out across the warm, slick rocks beneath her feet, and stopped when the water reached nearly chest height. She dipped her head under, feeling a rush of fresh warm water envelop her. She could feel Dallas's eyes on her as she went, and she hoped he liked what he saw. She turned, pushing water with her hands.

"You coming in?"

Dallas hesitated on shore, still holding Allie's sundress. He seemed to be having some kind of inner conflict. *Probably because the second he kissed you, you ran off.*

"Come on. You scared of getting wet?" Allie splashed water in his direction, not really intending to hit him. A few drops landed on his otherwise dry shirt. He looked down, and a big grin spread on his face.

"Oh, you've done it now," he said, his blue eyes sparkling with mischief. He dropped Allie's dress on the rocks and pulled out his cell phone from his back pocket, gently laying it far from the water. He lifted up his shirt, and his bare chest looked as impressive as she remembered, even more so in the silvery moonlight, the clear ridges of his abs leading like a ladder down into his drawstring swim trunks. She found herself wondering what he looked like with no clothes on at all. He ran a hand through his sandy-blond hair and walked around the pond, grinning. Then he gave a rebel yell and launched himself into the middle, sending up a wall of water that splashed Allie in the face.

She giggled and sprayed him back, and soon they were in a full-on water fight, Allie showing Dallas no mercy.

"Ah!" Allie shrieked as Dallas sent a wall of water her way. She kicked at him, sending wave after wave toward him, the last one hitting Dallas straight in the face. He shook off the water, spray flying every direction.

"Oh, you'll pay for that," he promised, and stood, hands up like claws, as he circled her.

"Oh, no!" Allie shrieked a laugh and scurried away from him, sending up sprays of water in a defense. Dallas shook them off, intent on getting to her, and the more she fought, the more determined he got. The pond was only so big, and it was only a matter of time before Dallas managed to wrap his arms around her waist, pulling her to him.

"Gotcha!" he declared, even as she squirmed and giggled.

"No!" she cried.

"Give up, Splash Lady of the Lake! I've got you surrounded." Dallas tightened his grip on Allie's waist and lifted her up out of the water as if she weighed nothing.

"I surrender! I surrender!" The last laugh escaped Allie's throat in a rush of air. "Put me down!"

"You asked for it." Dallas heaved her up in the air, and she went splashing back down in the pond. She came up laughing and pushing wet hair from her eyes.

"No fair! I surrendered!"

"Oh? Should we try that again?" Dallas lunged for her once more, and she retreated, only to find herself trapped against the waterfall and Dallas. Allie pressed her back into the hard rock wall behind her.

"Now I have you." Dallas grinned, putting up two monster-size hands above her head. Allie craned her neck to see the playful streak in his stark blue eyes. But now, suddenly, she realized it was no game. He was so close to her, she could feel his breath on her cheek. His bare chest was so near now, she could touch it. She saw beads of water dripping near his taut pink nipple, and without even thinking about the consequences, she put her finger there, following the line of water down his smooth chest. The muscles were just as firm and seductive as she'd imagined they'd be. She looked up, meeting his gaze, and realized the moment had gotten serious fast.

In an instant, his mouth was on hers, and the raw desire exploded in a symphony of sensations. His tongue moved into her mouth, and she opened for him, eager to taste him, eager to feel every part of him. Every logical thought, every hesitation disappeared in that moment as they fed on each other hungrily, their kiss taking on a life of its own. Dallas's hands roamed down her body, finding the small of her back as he deftly maneuvered her to him. Pressed against him, she could feel the tautness of his stomach and the thickness in his shorts rising to meet her. Dallas hungrily asked for more, and she gave it to him. He eventually broke free first, only to trail kisses down her neck, down the curve of her cleavage, stopping at the tied string of her bikini. She let out a thick groan, her body responding to him forcefully, her belly growing warm beneath the water as she could feel blood rushing there.

Allie had nearly died that afternoon, and now all she wanted to do was live. She didn't want to think about how vulnerable she'd been, how lost. Right now, all she wanted to do was celebrate life in the most primal way possible.

Dallas tugged on her bikini top with his teeth, instantly undoing the tie in the front, and suddenly her top fell away, her breasts exposed. She hardly had time to care before Dallas began worshipping each one, flicking each brown nipple with his tongue, gently caressing her heavy breasts in his hands. If she'd liked his tongue in her mouth, she liked it even more here, as he gently sucked each nipple, teasing her, tantalizing her. She had no time to worry about being half-naked in front of a stranger. There, in the moonlight, all she wanted was more. She arched her back, moaning, feeling the throbbing want between her legs. It was too late to stop now. There was no way she wanted to.

Then Dallas returned to her mouth, kissing her fiercely as he pulled her to him. Instinctively, she clutched his neck and wrapped her legs around his waist, knowing he wanted her as much as she wanted him. She pressed her bare breasts against his chest, feeling the hard warmth and safety of his arms around her as he carried her away from the wall. He deepened the kiss even as he moved her closer to the rocky shore.

She found her anticipation growing as Dallas kissed her hard again, stirred at the naughtiness of it. He pulled her to him, and she could feel his arousal, hard and strong and unyielding, against her belly. Dallas pressed his hands into her waist, pulling her to him, when his phone rang.

He ignored it, but Allie already saw the face of the phone near her.

"It's Jesse," she said, disappointment ripping through her as she realized there was no way they could not answer. She might be in trouble. Or Kai. As much as she wanted to throw the phone in the water, she knew she couldn't.

Dallas groaned, reluctantly pulling away from her as he reached for his phone. Allie crossed her arms across her bare chest, suddenly very aware she was nearly naked. "I'm not finished with you yet," he swore in his thick drawl as he answered the call. Almost instantly, his expression grew somber. "Calm down, Jesse. One thing at a time. What about Kai?" Dallas listened patiently, his eyes growing more serious. "When was the last time you heard from him?" Allie felt a sudden chill as she waited for news. Dallas listened for a bit. "Uh-huh. Okay. Let's not jump to any conclusions, all right? No need to worry until we have something to worry about. I'll see what I can do, Jesse. You sit tight."

Dallas ended the call and frowned. "Is everything all right?" Allie asked, already knowing by the expression on Dallas's face that it wasn't.

"Kai never made it to the evacuation center," he said, sounding grim. "He's missing."

CHAPTER ELEVEN

"YOU'RE NOT GOING," Dallas declared, as he cleared out his pickup bed of everything but the kayak and paddle, and rounded the driver's-side door. "It's dark and it's dangerous, and the wave train might not be done. There could be more aftershocks out there."

"It's been hours, the tsunami was close in and my phone says they think the worst is over." She held it up to show him. "*And*, there's no way you're going without me. Kai is my friend, too." Stubbornly, Allie climbed up into the passenger side of the truck and slammed the door. Her wet bikini top was already bleeding through her sundress, but she didn't care. She wasn't going to be left behind. All she wanted was for him to even try to test her on this. He'd find out just how much she meant business. "You'll have to carry me out and duct tape me to the tree house, because I *won't* stay willingly." Allie crossed her arms across her chest and glared at Dallas.

"Don't tempt me, woman," he said and sighed as he eyed the fixed set of her chin. "Okay, fine, but this is a search-and-rescue mission. We're in and we're out as quickly as possible. From everything I can tell from the news, we're going to be facing catastrophic damage, downed power lines, demolished buildings with leaky gas lines, you name it."

Allie nodded. "I got it. I can do this."

"Okay, then, let's go." Dallas slammed his door.

"Go…where?"

Dallas turned the ignition and eased on the gas. "Jesse said Kai left the beach but stopped to help evacuate Rainbow Daycare south of Kona. He went to check on his cousin's daughter. Kai never got to the high school, and now his phone is going straight to voice mail."

"That's just like Kai," Allie said. "Stopping to help. Do you know where Rainbow Daycare is?"

"Sure do," Dallas said, voice low. "Jennifer's daughter, Kayla, goes there. I used to drop her off every day."

Allie felt a sudden constriction of her throat, as irrational jealousy gripped her. She imagined the gorgeous real estate agent and Dallas playing family, him doting on an adorable little girl… and then Dallas leaving them. It felt as if she'd been splashed with a cold bucket of water. Dallas had abandoned them, and he could leave her, too. He'd said he hadn't cheated on her, and she believed him, but he couldn't deny that he'd left. That much was true.

Maybe he wasn't the kind of man who stayed. Maybe the interruption at the pond was fate trying to help her not make the mistake of her life.

Allie watched Dallas's profile carefully as he tried not to look worried.

Allie slipped her hand in her pocket, finding the forgotten pieces of Teri's mango candy there. Absently, she pulled two out, offering Dallas one.

"Do you think Kayla was there? When the tsunami hit?"

"No. I…saw her at the evacuation center. She made it out." Dallas gripped the steering wheel so hard his knuckles turned white.

"Good." Allie felt genuine relief as she unwrapped a piece of mango candy and ate one. She was glad the kids got out. The idea of a wall of water demolishing a place filled with little kids… she shuddered at the thought.

"Still, I should've gone to check on her," Dallas said, voice sounding ragged.

Allie recognized the guilt in his voice. She knew what it meant to feel as if you hadn't done everything to save someone you love.

"We didn't have twenty minutes, Dallas," Allie said, hoping her reasoning would get through. "All the news reports said we missed the water by maybe *minutes*. We were lucky to get out, and to get Teri and her stylists and Jesse out in time. If we'd stayed even five minutes longer, none of us would've made it."

Allie saw the hard, glassy look in Dallas's eyes and realized her words might not matter. How many times over the years had she been told it wasn't her fault that her father had died? When had she ever believed it?

"Besides, you said yourself, she was fine," Allie said.

"I know." Dallas ran a hand through his thick blond hair, and it jutted out in all directions. Allie wanted to ease his worry, but wasn't sure how. "But I lived with her for nearly three years. I was there when she had her first day of preschool. And, then… Well, I know she's not my responsibility anymore, but…"

"You still care about her," Allie finished. Allie wondered just how deeply his feelings for them still ran.

The streetlights beside them were out, and the houses along the ridge were dark. Another power outage, added to the many. Dallas studied the road intently, the bright beams of the truck lighting the way.

"I nearly adopted her. If we had gotten married, I would've been her stepfather. Her own dad hadn't been involved at all."

"What happened with you and Jennifer?" Allie

had to know. He said he hadn't cheated, but she couldn't make the puzzle pieces fit.

Dallas let out a long sigh. "Jennifer is pretty damaged," he admitted. "I guess I'm a sucker for damsels in distress."

Allie barked out a laugh as she thought about just how much of a damsel *she'd* been lately. "No kidding."

Dallas sent her a rueful smile. "Jennifer's damage is all on the inside. Her father left when she was little. She got pregnant with Kayla right out of high school. She was one of these girls who wanted attention from everyone—it didn't matter who. She'd go with any guy in front of her. I thought I could change her, could get her to understand that all she needed was me, but it took me a long time to realize you can't fix someone else, no matter how much you love them."

Allie agreed this was true. It was one of the reasons why she knew it wouldn't work with Jason.

"We were together two years before I caught her cheating the first time, with one of her rich real estate clients. Against my better judgment, I took her back. For Kayla's sake. We were a family, and I felt I owed it to her to work it out. We went to counseling. We really tried. But then I found out she hadn't quit stepping out on me. In fact, she'd made it her regular hobby. The last time, I found her in our bed with the reality TV producer she still works with."

"Oh, Dallas." Allie felt instant empathy, putting herself back in the afternoon she'd opened that package meant for Jason.

Dallas's eyes narrowed as he watched the road. "I wish pride was the only thing she took from me."

"What do you mean?"

Dallas swallowed. "She…" Dallas paused, holding back. Allie could tell this was something he didn't want to share, that this was the hardest part of the betrayal.

"You don't have to tell me."

"It's… Well, it doesn't matter. After that, I couldn't stay anymore, and I had to say goodbye to Kayla. I asked Jennifer if I could still adopt her, but Jennifer was livid, angry at me for walking out."

"How could she expect you to stay?" Allie couldn't believe the woman's gall.

Dallas's shoulders sank in weary indifference. "She gives everyone in her life an excellent reason to leave, and yet she's always surprised when they do."

"It's terribly sad, but you can't blame yourself," Allie said, realizing how empty the words might sound to him, knowing how they'd sounded when her friends told her the same thing. When someone cheated, there was always an undercurrent of "Why didn't you make him happy enough to stay?" No one said it out loud, but Allie felt it dozens of times, in the questions people asked. *Did he ever tell you he was unhappy? Did you know he was pulling away?*

"I know the feeling. I do. But those were choices Jennifer made, and what happened now—if something happened to Kayla that we don't know yet—you can't take responsibility for it." Allie felt more certain of this than she had of anything in the past year. She only hoped Dallas believed it.

She reached over and put her hand over his on the gearshift of his truck. He glanced down at their hands. When he looked back to the road, he hit his brakes. Water completely covered the road up ahead. Allie craned her neck, peering into the darkness. A poolside lounge chair floated by them, and she realized debris littered the water: splinters of wood, pieces of glass and a random single flip-flop crowded together. Watching the neon purple flip-flop bobbing in the water, her stomach shrank. She wondered what had happened to the person wearing it.

"Are all the roads like this?" she asked.

"I hope not." Dallas put the truck in Reverse and then whipped it around, backtracking to a small residential road that he took south. "I'm going to try to get us closer." All the homes were dark and quiet as they glided past. These houses, just beyond the reach of the tidal wave, had been spared. Dallas slowed the truck as they reached the main road. He stopped, and they both stared out the windshield in complete shock. Here, some of the water had receded, but even in the narrow beam of the headlights, they could see the path of destruction. An entire gas station and convenience store had been completely wiped out; random piles of brick, smashed wooden planks and pieces of road signs littered the ground. Water lapped at some of the debris, and, inexplicably, a huge round sea turtle lay half-stranded between an overturned dumpster and someone's old spare tire, a large flipper smacking against the muck.

"I don't believe it," Allie breathed, the complete destruction impossible to process. Just that morning, she'd driven down this road, alive with stores and people. Now not even the small palm trees remained; they'd been completely uprooted by the force of the tidal waves, as had any small building in their path. Distantly, she saw that the tall concrete resorts still stood, dark outlines against the night sky. She wondered how flooded they were, and whether tourists were stranded in the top floors, looking down at the ocean below. Nearby, Allie heard a loud snapping sound. A spark lit up the street about fifty yards down. A broken streetlight hung half in the water, and the power line above it, severed, still sparked with live electricity.

Dallas looked at the mess, trying to get his bearings. "Rainbow Daycare is just a little north of here. Should be about a block that way." Dallas pointed. He studied the sparking light pole and then got out and turned his back to it, walking round to the bed of the truck and removing his two-seater kayak.

"You're going out in that?" Allie looked at the sparking streetlight, thinking that might not be the worst of the danger.

"I have to. I have to see if the building is still there. If there are any survivors. If Kai is there."

"I'm going with you," Allie said, lifting her chin stubbornly once more.

"Fine," he replied, resigned. "I'll paddle. You take this." He gave her a handheld spotlight. She flicked it on to test it and then climbed into the front of the kayak. Dallas eased it into the floodwaters, through the debris. Allie shone the spotlight on to the water, amazed at the sheer bottleneck of wood splinters, as if a giant had come and squashed everything and then used a huge hose to wash it away.

On the edges of the road, she saw parts of buildings, some still half-standing. A three-story condo had half of it washed away; the other half still stood, with a gaping hole down the side.

"Water did this," Allie said, almost in disbelief. Allie shone the flashlight to the right and saw what looked like an arm out of the water. "Dallas! There." Dallas pulled the oars through the water, pushing the boat in that direction. But, when they got there, the body, a man wearing bright blue Bermuda shorts, was floating facedown. He still wore a plastic wristband, a luau ticket from the night before. Dallas got close enough to take a pulse.

"Long gone," he said.

Allie didn't know him, but finding this man, a tourist by the look of the sunburn on his neck, chilled her. She felt a heavy sadness as they moved away from the body, a stranger they didn't know, but still. He had a family somewhere. People who cared about him. Maybe even a daughter or a son. Worry built up in her chest for Kai. Now, suddenly, the tragic reality of the situation sank in: people were dead.

And then she thought of her father, drowned, just like that man floating facedown in the floodwaters. She should've felt a rush of gratitude about surviving. But instead, all she felt was how unfair the world was. *Why am I the one who always survives? Why am I the one who gets to crawl out of the car window?*

"Are you okay?" Dallas asked her, and she realized she'd zoned out.

"Seeing that man…it just…brings back bad memories," she said. The car crash seemed so suddenly real and vivid.

Dallas let it drop, and Allie felt relief. They moved slowly past the sparking signal light, away from the live wire snapping high above their heads.

"Hello?" Allie called into the quiet night. "Kai! Anyone out there?"

She waited, but no response came, just the snapping of the electric line and the sound of water lapping at the boat.

"Kai! Can you hear me? Kai!"

Allie saw a shadow moving to her right, and moved the light there, hoping to find a survivor. Instead, her beam landed on a dark, menacing triangle poking out of the water, gleaming and unmistakable: a shark.

"Dallas," Allie whispered urgently, her beam of light on the moving target, the dorsal fin at least twenty inches high. The massive shark moved quietly, deadly through the debris. Allie sucked in a breath and held it.

Dallas stuck his paddle in the water behind them like a rudder, and the kayak shifted away from the dark shadow, moving soundlessly away from them.

"Tiger shark," he whispered back. "Scavenging." He frowned as they watched the huge fin turn and move away from them, back out in the direction of the ocean.

Allie let out the breath she'd been holding. "How did it get here? The water… It's not that deep."

"A shark that size only needs about four feet, maybe five." Dallas resumed his paddling down the flooded street. "It came in with the wave, and it stayed for a late-night snack."

Allie shuddered as she grasped the floodlight in her hands tightly. She slowly swept the water in front of them, fearing each new shadow that appeared might be a new dorsal fin. Now that she knew what was in the water below them, the murky waves seemed even more menacing.

"Whatever you do, don't fall in," Dallas warned from behind her.

"I don't plan on it." She eyed the water that swept past the bow of the kayak before turning her attention once again to the dry shore. "Kai!" Allie called out over the floating minefield of debris in front of them. "Anyone! Can anyone hear me?"

Allie's stomach sank as they moved through the water, with no sign of human life. Buildings lay completely destroyed in oversize heaps of broken matchsticks rising up from the flood.

"There. The sign." Dallas pulled the paddle out of the water and pointed with it. Allie shone the light in that direction, and miraculously, the tall metal sign for Rainbow Daycare stood, mostly intact, its huge steel pole securely in the waves. Beyond that, the building lay half-standing, its front door and half of the first floor washed away, gaping and skeletal, the water flowing inside. The second floor still had its windows and roof attached, and sat above the water.

Allie aimed the flashlight at the door and windows, fearing what she'd find.

"Kai!" Allie shouted as her light brought up no sign of anyone, dead or otherwise. The child-care center lay dark and empty, water sitting in most of the first floor.

Dallas rowed the kayak straight up to the daycare center, carefully avoiding the fence top, just bobbing up in the water. Dallas's oar hit something hard, and as they rowed past, Allie realized it had been the top of a large slide, the upper part of the ladder just visible below the surface of the water. Allie shone her light down and saw the rest of the playground there: a jungle gym and swing set, all bolted down to the ground, the chained swings floating in the waves upside down, the seats floating along the surface of the water.

Dallas kept rowing, and when he got to the building, he pulled up alongside a broken-out window. He grabbed the empty sill with his oar, pushing the boat to the building. He peered in.

"The second floor is dry," he said. "I'm going to go look for Kai."

"Dallas—wait! It's not safe." She looked at the day-care center and thought of all the ways it could be dangerous: leaky gas lines, weak floors or collapsing roofs.

"I'll be quick," he said as he climbed out of the kayak and into the window. He gave her the oar, and she held it, keeping the boat in place near the window. "Stay here," he warned, and flipped a small LED flashlight out of his back pocket.

"Dallas…"

"Stay with the kayak. Make sure it doesn't float away."

She gripped the oar more tightly. "Okay." Allie's voice sounded small as she followed Dallas with the beam of light, watching as he disappeared into the darkened building.

DALLAS CAREFULLY MADE his way through the Rainbow Daycare center, his heart in his throat as he dreaded what he would find inside. The small playrooms upstairs had been touched by the water: chairs and tables were overturned, soaked crayons leaked color onto the wet carpets. No children here, or their caregivers, either.

The water had blown through and then receded, though it still covered much of the first floor. He made it to the main stairwell, and shone his flashlight into the salt water that covered most of the first flight of stairs.

"Kai!" he shouted down, and then waited, but heard only the sound of water gurgling across the handrails. There was no way to explore that first floor, and even if he could, he thought, anyone down there would be dead. There was just too much water.

Dallas thought about Kayla, the sweet girl who'd always begged him for shoulder rides with her dimpled smile, and felt a dull pain through the center of his chest. He missed her. *She's with her mother, where she belongs*, he told himself, but somehow it didn't make him feel any better. He turned the corner and saw a single white stuffed animal floating in the stairwell, and had a moment of panic, thinking it was Kayla's bear, Mr. Cuddles. But soon he realized his mistake. The bobbing stuffed white kitten with a bright pink collar belonged to someone else. Dallas turned back to the second floor, opening the closed janitor's closets and bathroom doors, knowing in his bones the building was empty, the search futile, but unable to stop until he'd checked every room.

"Kai! You in here?" he shouted, his voice suddenly loud in the enclosed space, bouncing off the tiled walls. No one answered him. Maybe he got out. God, he hoped so.

He heard a muffled call from outside. Allie. He'd left her outside with sharks and who knew what.

"Allie!" He rushed back to the window, panting, blood pumping and ready for a fight.

Allie, safe and in one piece, focused on the water beyond them, her eyebrow furrowed.

"Listen," she urged him. Dallas did as he was told. First, he heard nothing, and then came a distant *plink*.

Could be nearly anything. A chair leg hitting an exposed pipe, maybe. A chain caught in the water, banging against a car bumper. The sound was far away and hard to place.

"I think we should check it out," Allie said.

Dallas figured why not—he'd checked the day-care center already and found nothing. He climbed back into the boat, and they went paddling farther down the debris field. It seemed as if they'd gone a long way before they heard another *plink*. This one, a little louder.

"Hello?" Allie's voice echoed a bit in the dark night.

No one answered.

Dallas kept paddling until they heard another *plink*. They were getting closer. Finally, after a good ten minutes of rowing, the *plinks* came louder and more often.

"Hello?" Allie called. "Is that someone?"

The *plinks* came furiously, this time in response to Allie's voice.

Allie and Dallas exchanged a glance, both thinking the same thing: that nothing about the metal-on-metal sound was accidental.

After a little more distance, Dallas paused in rowing as the kayak glided through wooden debris. "Hello?" he called this time. The metal *plinks* came once more, louder.

"There!" Allie directed the light at a car, floating tires up. A man, his back to them, clung to the front fender.

Dallas sped up the paddling. They turned the corner and saw Kai, clinging desperately to the car, a bleeding cut across his forehead.

"Kai!" Allie shouted, putting down the light and leaning forward. "Kai! Are you all right?"

Kai turned, opening a bleary eye. "I've been better," he half croaked, his voice raw and hoarse. "I think my leg's broken."

Dallas glanced down and saw his friend was right: his leg seemed oddly disjointed, and he floated in a pink cloud of blood.

"We have to get you out of there."

"Don't worry about me. Is Po all right?"

"Po?"

Kai pointed to the top of the floating car. There, a little boy lay. He looked no older than three or four. He sat up, holding a small metal pipe, which he'd been clanking against the car's muffler.

"Hey, are you all right?" Allie asked the little boy, who nodded, his almond-shaped eyes wide and serious.

"That's my buddy," Kai said. "You did it, pal. Good job with the pipe." Kai grinned, but he looked pale. Dallas glanced around, looking for something that might act as a floating stretcher. A commercial refrigerator, like the kind filled with soda at the convenience store, bobbed nearby. He saw a few plastic bottles of soda and some broken shelves lined the bottom along with a little water. The tsunami had ripped off the original glass door at the hinges. Amazed at the force of the wave yet again, he grabbed the refrigerator by the closest edge, pulling it toward them.

"Allie, help me empty this," he said.

She turned and got to work, pitching bottles of Coke overboard and pieces of shelves. They were nearly done when the sound of debris smacking together made Allie turn, shining her light in the distance about a hundred feet.

"The shark's back!" she cried, voice high, her light on the tip of the tiger shark's fin. She caught it for a split second before it dipped silently below the surface. "Dallas!"

"It's not going to have you as a snack," Dallas promised Kai, whose grip tightened on the car.

Po, on top of the car, whined anxiously. "Shark!" he cried, pointing and looking scared.

"Don't worry. We'll get you, okay?" Allie said. "Just sit tight."

"Give me your hand, Kai." Dallas was already reaching out, trying to pull Kai into the open case. The first time, the case nearly tipped over, and Kai fell back in the water. They tried twice more, failing each time.

Furiously, Allie shone her light back and forth, trying to find the shark. "I can't find it, Dallas. I can't find the shark." Panic laced her words.

"Something brushed me," Kai murmured, trying to keep calm. "Something big."

Allie shone her light frantically, but all she illuminated was blue water.

Dallas knew it was now or never. The shark, drawn by the blood from Kai's leg, circled beneath the waves, trying to decide if Kai was worth a bite.

"Come on!" he cried. With one mighty heave, Dallas pulled, and Kai shouted in pain as his broken leg came out of the water. He thumped into the open refrigerator case just as Allie shouted, "There!" Her spotlight caught the fin of the shark, sweeping so close to the kayak its tail nearly slapped the boat. Dallas grabbed some rope from the storage compartment of the kayak and tied the case to the back of the boat.

"That was close. Too close," Kai said, leaning his head back on the edge of the refrigerator. "Your turn, Po."

Allie shone the light on the shark as it disappeared underwater again.

The little boy sat on the floating car, shivering, his eyes wide with fear. He'd seen the shark, and the stubborn line of his chin said the last thing he wanted to do was go near the water or in a small kayak.

"Come in, buddy. Come in here with me. It'll be okay." Kai tried to coax the boy off the car and into the refrigerator case, but the boy didn't want to budge. Suddenly, Allie reached into the pocket of her sundress and pulled out a piece of mango candy from Teri's shop.

"Hey, Po. Do you like mango candy?" The boy's eyes grew bright with excitement. "You can have *all* these pieces. Just let Kai help you."

The boy studied the sweets in Allie's hand. Then he glanced warily at the water. Eventually, he made his choice and hopped into the case with Kai. Allie handed the boy the small bunch of candy, and he swiped it eagerly, ripping open his first piece.

"Good thinking," Dallas told Allie with approval as he started to paddle them away from the car.

"How'd you find me?" Kai asked.

"I came as soon as Jesse called, telling us you weren't answering your phone."

"Lost my phone as soon as the first wave hit." Kai grimaced as he shifted his weight, trying to get comfortable. "I'd left the beach, packed up my board and was on my way when I drove by the day care to check on my cousin's daughter, Reese, and saw a bus full of kids and a frantic preschool teacher. The bus driver was arguing with her that they had to go and was threatening to leave her. I stopped, and that's when she told me Po was missing. Turns out, he'd run off across the street to the gas station. He thought he saw his mom's car."

Kai ruffled Po's hair.

"I sent the bus along, promised the teacher I'd look for Po, and she, in a panic, left," Kai said. "I found him at the gas station, wandering around, not even crying. He's one tough kid." He ruffled Po's hair. "But then I saw the water come. We ran to the day-care center, headed upstairs. The first wave shook the building and knocked the power out and tossed some furniture around, including a pretty heavy snack refrigerator. That's what broke my leg. The second and third waves were really bad, and the third washed us out of the second floor completely. That's when we ended up outside."

Po blinked at Kai, a big black mud smudge across his nose, dirt and mud the only signs he'd been in a tsunami at all. "Po can swim, let me tell you. He's a surfer in the making. He rode that third wave as if he was meant to be there." Kai ruffled the boy's jet-black hair again. The boy smiled. "I tried to stay close to the day-care center. We spent a lot of time swimming to it, but my leg made for slow going. I knew Jesse would send someone there if she didn't hear from me, and I figured it was our best shot. Plus, Po here said they keep a big thing of goldfish crackers and apple juice boxes in the top shelf upstairs in the snack room, and we were getting hungry, weren't we, Po?"

The boy nodded sharply.

"Did you see any other survivors?" Kai asked them.

"No," Dallas said softly, thinking of the man who didn't make it.

Kai whistled. "There were still cars on the street when it hit." He shook his head, solemn. Everyone in the boat grew silent as Dallas paddled, and the only sound for a while was the plastic oar dipping in and out, dripping salt water. After what seemed like forever, they got back to the sparking signal light not too far from where they'd parked.

"You doing all right, Po?" Allie asked the little one, who was busy chewing on the sticky candy. The boy nodded furiously. When they finally got to the shoreline, Dallas saw the water was farther from the truck than he remembered. The floodwaters were receding, slowly but surely. Allie helped Dallas pull the kayak up and dragged the floating refrigerator case to the shore, which took some doing. Once safe from the water, Dallas backed up his truck, bed side facing Kai, so that all they'd have to do was lift him a short ways. Dallas held one of his arms and Allie held the other, and together they lifted him to the truck bed, where they laid him down. The effort caused him quite a bit of pain, and he grunted as he slid down on the metal, his face going pale. Dallas glanced at the wound, wishing he knew enough first aid to help, but didn't as he stared at the leg, clearly bent the wrong way. The bone had broken the skin, and blood dripped down. All in all, Dallas didn't like the look of the leg, not one bit.

"We've got to get him to the hospital," Allie said. "Where's the closest one?"

"Kona Community Hospital," Dallas said as he swung himself in the driver's seat. Allie helped Po into the cab of the pickup, but he wanted to turn around and stare at Kai through the window.

Kai gave him a "hang loose" sign, and the boy mirrored it. Dallas handed Allie his phone. "Call Jesse, would you? Tell her what's happened."

Allie pulled up his contacts and dialed while Dallas drove through the roads that were far enough from the water that they were left largely undamaged.

"Jesse? It's Allie. We've got good news and bad…" Allie began.

Dallas tuned the rest out. He had to focus on driving. A few streetlights were out, making intersections treacherous. Not many people were on the roads, but enough were, and he hadn't planned to save Kai just to get in a car accident. He glanced in his rearview, watching the bobbing head of Kai against the back window, hoping his friend was all right. Kai looked way too pale and weak. He'd lost a lot of blood.

"Okay, Jesse. We'll meet you there." Allie ended the call. "She's on her way," Allie told Dallas, who just nodded.

After easing through a blinking red light and down the street, Dallas saw where most of the people were: the hospital parking lot. Cars and trucks were parked in every available space. Without an alternative, Dallas pulled close to the emergency room entrance, the spot where an ambulance had already stopped, and put on his parking lights. He went into the ER to see if he could get help, and found chaos instead: gurneys and beds lining the hallways, patients overflowing into the waiting area. He grabbed a nurse in blue scrubs and tried to explain what they had, and she hurried out the door with him and a wheelchair.

Together, all three of them got Kai out of the truck and into the hospital. She took one look at the leg and whisked him straight through the people waiting in the hallway. Dallas didn't take that as a good sign at all. He noticed Kai had turned even paler, and worried again about how much blood he'd lost floating in that water.

"I'm taking him in to see a doctor," the nurse said as she pushed him through the automatic sliding doors of the interior room of the ER. "Wait here, please."

She held up a hand, leaving Allie, Po and Dallas standing in the hallway.

"Kai!" Po called. The boy's bottom lip quivered, as if he might cry.

Well, now what? he wondered.

Allie put her arm around the boy's shoulders, gently guiding him away from the closed doors. "Come on, Po. Let's see if we can find a snack machine."

He looked at her in wonder as she calmly but decisively distracted Po from what would have no doubt been a huge, heart-twisting fit. She seemed to have a magic touch.

had been in her hospital bed when her mother had delivered the bad news. Allie had been asking to see her father for days. He'd died before he'd ever made it to the hospital, but she hadn't known it until much later.

"We should try messaging his mother again," Dallas said, looking at the sleeping boy.

Po hadn't known his phone number, but he did know his mother's first and last name. Dallas had found someone on Facebook he thought might be his mother, and had messaged her through the site, hoping she was the one.

"We don't know if that's even her account," Allie pointed out.

"Or *if* she made it," Dallas added, grimly.

Allie hugged the boy a little more tightly. "Let's not think like that," she said, watching the boy's peaceful face as he slept. "We could try calling the police again."

"Why? To be put on hold? The last time we waited for fifteen minutes! They're out dealing with life-or-death emergencies. We're not in any danger. I'd put us on hold, too." Dallas shifted in his seat.

Before they could come up with a plan, Jesse hurried through the entrance doors, her tear-streaked face frantic.

"Where is he? Oh, God! Is he okay?" The torture on her face made Allie's stomach twist into

CHAPTER TWELVE

ALLIE SAT WITH Po on her lap and Dallas next to her in the crowded waiting room. They'd tried, but failed to reach Po's parents. Dozens and dozens of worried mothers, fathers, wives and husbands pensively sat, hoping to soon hear about the loved ones being treated in the hospital, many of whom were already walking wounded themselves.

Allie glanced down at her own worn bandage, the one covering the cut she'd gotten in the surf, and thought, *I fit right in.* Allie watched sadly as a man with a bandaged arm held his wife, a woman with a splint on her leg, while they waited for news of their daughter. Allie met the glance of the worried mother and sent her an encouraging smile. She just nodded and went back to hugging her husband.

Po, the adrenaline finally wearing off, laid his head against Allie's chest and fell asleep. She cuddled him as they waited. Allie didn't like hospitals, as a rule. She'd spent a long time recovering in one after the accident that killed her father. She knots. Allie didn't have brothers or sisters and didn't know what it was like to have a sibling. She'd always wanted one.

Dallas embraced Jesse, explaining about Kai being in surgery. Dallas gave up his chair for Jesse, who collapsed into it, fretting and exhausted.

"How did you get here so fast?" Dallas asked.

"I borrowed Minnie's car to get here, but she wanted to stay behind to make sure no one took her spot at the high school," Jesse explained. "Who's this little guy?" Jesse nodded to Po, who was sleeping in Allie's arms.

"Kai saved this boy," Allie said. "He's a good man. He'll be fine."

It seemed to be the time for reunions, because Allie didn't get another word out before a woman came bustling through the emergency room doors calling for Po. The Asian woman in her twenties, wearing a halter top and shorts and wedge sandals, hurried in, worry etched on her face. The young mother searched the crowd.

"Here!" Allie called, waving. The woman rushed over.

"Po!" she cried, unable to help herself, as her face lit up in relief and happiness.

The boy awakened at the sound of his name, rubbing his sleepy eyes. "Mom?" he asked groggily, coming to slowly.

"Po!" the mother cried, picking up the three-year-old off Allie's lap and crushing him into a smothering hug. The boy brightened and hugged his mom back, his small, thin arms holding tightly to her neck. "How can I thank you? I've been worried sick. I...I just can't thank you enough!" she gushed to Dallas and Allie. Both squirmed under the praise.

"Don't thank us," Dallas corrected. "Our friend Kai saved him. He's in surgery for a broken leg."

The woman's face paled. "Oh, I hope he'll be all right."

"This is his sister," Dallas said, introducing Jesse. The mother hugged Jesse then, squeezing Po in the middle.

"I'm Jun," she said, her face brightened by her big white smile. Allie noticed how young she really was. She couldn't have been older than twenty-four at most, and she wore no wedding band. A young single mom, Allie thought. Allie wanted to know more about her, but the ER waiting room was no comfortable place to get acquainted. The way she held her boy said she loved him more than life itself.

"Thank you. Tell your brother thank you for us. He's my hero. I just can't thank you enough." The mother grew teary, emotion drenching her voice. "Po is...my everything." She hugged him once more. "You have no idea... I couldn't get to the day-care center. It was flooded, and no one knew where he was. He wasn't at the evacuation center…" She nearly choked on her words as she squeezed him more tightly. The hug was so fierce even Po began to squirm.

"Mom!" he protested.

She peppered his face with kisses. "I'm not letting you go for *days*, mister! Just get used to it." She tickled him under one arm, and he burst into giggles. Her somber, dark, almond-shaped eyes turned back to Allie. "How can I help you? Can I get you anything?"

Jesse just gently squeezed her arm. "Say a prayer for us, for Kai," Jesse said.

The woman nodded vigorously. "I will. I promise." Po yawned, and his mother cradled his head against her shoulder, his long feet dangling by her hips. "I need to get Po home. But if you need anything, you call. My apartment's not too far. And let me know when Kai wakes up. I want to come thank him myself."

She exchanged numbers with Jesse.

"Thank you." The young mother took Po out the door, Po waving over her shoulder. He held up the last piece of mango candy and grinned.

Jesse watched them leave and sighed. Allie could sense the worry in her every breath. She put her arm around her friend and hugged her.

The wait seemed to go on forever. Every time

the doors opened and a white-coated or scrub-clad doctor bustled out, every face in the room snapped to attention. For hours, they waited, and each time the doctor came out, she delivered news to someone else. Allie watched as families received the answers to their prayers and rejoiced, and some had all their hopes crushed in a single sentence. The bad news made the air feel heavier, the dread worse, as if tragic endings might be contagious.

After what seemed like a lifetime, a doctor in blue scrubs arrived for Jesse. Allie held her breath, as if that somehow sealed a pact with God: *please, let him be okay.* Allie reached out and grabbed Dallas's hand. He squeezed her fingers in reassurance.

"Hi, I'm Dr. Bradley and I operated on Kai today. He suffered a complex fracture that nicked a major artery, and he lost a lot of blood, but he's going to be okay."

A sob of relief escaped Jesse's throat, and she pressed her fists to her mouth to stop the tears. Allie felt a wave of gladness roll through her as she hugged Jesse, and Dallas wrapped his big arms around them both.

"Would you like to see him?"

KAI SHARED A room with another man who'd suffered injuries in the tsunami. The room was intended for one patient, but two beds had been pushed in, the whole hospital overcrowded. His family stood around his bed on the other side of a flimsy curtain. Jesse, Allie and Dallas waited at Kai's bedside. He was groggy and out of it, but managed to kiss his sister on the cheek.

"Don't you *ever* do that to me again," Jesse scolded, squeezing him in a hug until he begged for release. "I know you like big waves and publicity, Mr. Surfing Champ, but a *tsunami*?"

Kai chuckled. "I promise I won't do it again on purpose." He glanced at Dallas. "Is Po okay?"

"Reunited with his mom and doing fine," Dallas assured him.

Kai visibly relaxed. "Good, I'm glad." He locked eyes with Dallas. "Thanks, man. I... Thanks for..."

"No need to thank me," Dallas cut in, shaking his buddy by the shoulder. "You'll just never live it down. Usually you're the one pulling *me* from the water. Last time we went surfing..."

"You dropped into the water like a stone," Kai said. He glanced at Allie. "This guy surfs like a ninety-year-old woman."

"Hey, a *spry* ninety-year-old *with style*."

They all laughed. As the mirth died down, Allie felt a sudden fatigue sweep over her. She yawned without even meaning to, and abruptly covered her face with her hands.

"So sorry," she murmured, feeling quite tired. The midnight search-and-rescue mission had gone on awhile, and then the surgery had lasted nearly until dawn. Pink sunlight lit the hospital window.

"It's late—or early, depending," Dallas said. "We should get going, but we'll be back later to give you more of a hard time."

Kai grinned. "Thanks, man."

Jesse hugged them both. "I'm going to stay with him. Make sure my older brother doesn't get into any trouble. Once the nurses find out he's Kai Brady, they'll be *all* over him. I'm going to make sure they don't rush him into a Vicodin-induced wedding."

"Good call," Dallas agreed.

Everyone paused a second, glad Kai was alive, not wanting to even think of the next step: what his long recovery might be like. When—or if—he'd surf again. She glanced at his leg splint, which was held up by an elaborate set of wires and pulleys above his bed. Kai sighed and leaned back in his bed, looking pale and tired.

"Try to get some rest, Kai," Allie said, squeezing her friend's hand. He gave her a nod, and his head fell back on the pillow. Keeping awake and upbeat was a struggle, she could tell. Dallas led her out of the crowded hospital and to his pickup truck. As they both climbed in, her worry for Kai bubbled over.

"Do you think he's going to be okay?" she asked.

Dallas shook his head. "I don't know. I really don't. That leg…"

"You think it will heal all right? Will he be able to surf?"

"I didn't want to ask," Dallas said as he steered the truck out of the hospital parking lot. "That's something Kai will have to talk about with his doctors. I'm just glad he's alive. For a while there, I had my doubts he'd make it. If we'd found him just a beat later…"

"Don't think about it." Allie reached out to touch Dallas. "We got there. That's what matters."

Clouds crowded the sky. It looked as though it might rain. *Just what we need, more water,* Allie thought as a big fat raindrop plunked down on the windshield.

Dallas met Allie's gaze, and his stark blue eyes sent shivers through her. "Thank you."

"For what?"

"For coming with me. For helping. With Po and Kai. You were…amazing." The complete admiration in his eyes took her by surprise. He squeezed her hand.

"It was nothing." More rain fell, big drops, and Dallas flicked on the windshield wipers. Allie felt uneasy, as if the stress of the past several hours was only now reaching her. The rain didn't help. She hated driving in the rain.

"It was many things, but *nothing* ain't one of them," he drawled, bringing her palm up to his mouth and kissing it ever so gently. She felt the feather-like kiss all the way to her toes.

Why does he have this effect on me? Allie wondered. It wasn't long before her thoughts wandered back to the pond, about just *what* kind of effect he could have on her. She blushed just thinking about it.

"I'm serious, there aren't many women like you," he said.

"Like me what?"

"That think of others first, before themselves. You're a good person, Allie." She felt herself cringe at the compliment. She always had a hard time with compliments. She always thought the person giving them wanted something.

The rain poured down in sheets, and Allie felt a strong sense of déjà vu. They weren't on the same road where her father had the accident, but it *felt* like it. The dark green foliage on the side of the road, the blurring rain on the windshield. Allie felt her chest constrict. She hated driving in the rain, always had since that day, but today, for some reason, the memory felt closer than it had in years. As if it had happened yesterday.

"Allie?"

Her heart rate sped up, and suddenly she felt as if someone was standing on her chest. Why couldn't she breathe?

"Stop the car," Allie muttered.

"What?" Dallas asked in confusion. "We're almost there."

"*Please*. Stop the car!"

Dallas did as he was told, pulling over on the muddy median. Allie grabbed the handle of the door and opened it, tumbling out. She bent over her knees, trying to suck in air, the heavy raindrops pelting her body, her face, just like they had on that day. *I think I'm having a panic attack.*

"Are you sick?" Dallas asked, now worried as he walked over to put an arm around her. The kind gesture undid her. The pressure from her chest lifted, but now the floodgates opened and the tears came. They poured down her cheeks. "I don't understand." Dallas furrowed his brow, his blue eyes bewildered. "What's wrong? Talk to me."

But Allie couldn't. All she could do was bury her face in his chest and cry.

CHAPTER THIRTEEN

DALLAS CALMED ALLIE down enough to get her back into the truck. They sat, Allie wearing one of Dallas's oversize sweatshirts he'd found in his truck cab, her damp hair hanging down past her shoulders in dark clumps. Tropical rain ran down the windshield of the truck, the wipers still going, the headlights beaming out into the rain, spotlighting a huge papaya tree growing alongside the road.

"Just take me home," Allie said, swiping at her eyes with the back of her hand.

"We need to talk about this."

"I don't want to." Allie's jaw clamped down, and Dallas realized she had practice keeping people away. But he wasn't going to take no for an answer.

"We're not leaving here until you tell me why you were crying."

"We *can't* stay here." Allie's eyes grew big as she glanced to the side of the road, where the headlights of a car could be seen in the distance.

They sat in a little dirt turnaround, but Allie's face said it all: she didn't want to just sit.

"If you want to go, then you need to tell me what's wrong." Dallas wasn't above waiting here until she confessed. He took the key out of the ignition to make his point. The lights stayed on; the windshield wipers, however, abruptly stopped.

"Why do you want to know?" The question came out like a squeak. She sat hunched in the front seat of his truck, as if he had just asked her to admit to being a drug dealer, as if she'd done something unpardonable. Dallas wanted to know what it was. He'd known she'd been holding out on him, and now it was time for her to come clean. He couldn't imagine it was nearly as bad as she thought it was.

"Because I can't help you fix your problems if you don't tell me what's wrong." Dallas's tone was matter-of-fact, and that prompted a reluctant smile from Allie. "And if you don't tell me, I'll just assume it was something I did, and then you'll have to deal with that."

Allie coughed a laugh. She saw the glint of the key in his hand and reached for it. Abruptly, he pulled away, holding it out of her reach. "Give me that!"

"Not until you tell me."

"Dallas. Drive us out of here." Allie glanced anxiously out the back window of the truck. "With the rain and the flooding already from the tsunami, we could get washed away or something."

"We could," he said. "You'd better start talking, then."

"Dallas!" Now, she was mad. Good, he thought. Better mad than distraught and crying. He'd take an angry woman over a weeping one any day.

"No." He shook his head, holding the ignition key far from her. "Tell me why you were crying. *Then* I'll start the car."

"Ugh," Allie grunted, angrily crossing her arms across her chest. *"Fine."* She swiped her sopping wet hair from her forehead angrily.

Allie took a big breath as if bracing herself for a fall. "When I was eight, my dad and I were driving in the rain. I had a stuffed animal, my favorite. I dropped it on the floor and undid my seat belt. Dad was mad, and he was turning around to help me get it. He wandered over into oncoming traffic and hit a truck. We overturned and fell into a creek by the side of the road. I got out with hardly a scratch. Dad didn't. He drowned in that car. I just stood there. Not helping him. Instead, I went to get my stuffed animal. I could've helped him, but I got my toy instead. When the ambulance got there, I was the only one left to take to the hospital."

Dallas felt his heart constrict, thinking about Allie as a little girl, scared and alone by the side of the road, waiting for help. He thought of the day he'd found out his dad had died. He'd been nineteen, and the news had still hit him like a ton of bricks. He couldn't imagine what it was like for little Allie at eight.

"Were you okay?"

"No," Allie said, voice small. "I had a concussion. A bad one. They operated on me to relieve the pressure on my brain."

"Allie, I'm sorry. That's terrible."

"It *is* terrible," Allie agreed, staring dully at the raindrops falling on the windshield. "If it hadn't been for me, my dad would still be alive."

Dallas couldn't believe what he was hearing. "It's not your fault he died."

"It *is*. I caused the crash. I didn't go back for him. I sat and stared at the car. I was…I was *mad* at him for yelling at me. That was the whole problem. The thing was, I didn't *want* to help him. I was angry at him, so very mad. I sat there, my arms crossed, angry." Tears pooled in her eyes, the years of guilt and pain obvious as she furiously wiped at her face.

She *really* believed it was her fault. Dallas wanted to shake her by the shoulders, make her see reason. Instead, he reached out and grabbed her hand and held it. He looked into her dark, nearly black eyes. "It's not your fault. You were just a kid."

Allie half shrugged, not listening or not caring to *hear* the message. He got the feeling someone else might have told her that before.

"I mean it, Allie. I don't think you're hearing me. *You...were...just...a...kid.* You were hurt and scared and way too young to think you were supposed to save the day. So what if you were mad? Kids get mad, Allie. Kids have fits. *They're kids!* I don't know how many years you've been blaming yourself for it, but it has to stop now."

"Why?"

"Because it's *just* not true!" He banged the flat of his palms against the steering wheel for emphasis. "And if it's one thing I hate most in the world, it's a lie."

Allie shook her head.

"Fine, then." He threw up his hands. "So by your logic, Po is responsible for Kai's broken leg."

"What? No, of course not!" Allie sounded almost offended.

"Po wandered off. Kai had to go looking for him, and then because of that, Kai broke his leg. It's Po's fault. Let's go call the police. See if they'll arrest a three-year-old."

Allie cracked a reluctant smile. "No. Don't be ridiculous."

"Don't you see? You were just a few years older than Po. The crash? Your dad dying? It's *not* your fault." Dallas felt he had to make her understand.

The fact that she'd been holding on to this lie her whole life just wasn't right. He could see understanding dawning a little, but he knew she was reluctant to really embrace the truth. He knew what he'd been through after his dad died, and it was clear to him that Allie still hadn't processed through all her grief. In the close quarters of the truck, it was obvious. "You couldn't have gotten your dad out of the car. It would be like asking Po to carry Kai to a hospital. Impossible."

"But I should've *tried*. I didn't even *try*." Allie sniffed.

The rain continued to pound the windshield. Next to them, cars slushed by on the small, two-lane road, their headlights beaming in the storm.

"A car flipped like that… It's dangerous. You could've drowned. It could've caught on fire. Do you think your father would've wanted you to die trying to help him out?"

"No, but…" Allie clearly still did not quite want to embrace the parallels of their story. "I survived. He didn't. It was my fault the car crashed." She pushed her wet, dripping hair from her eyes with both hands.

"Okay, so even though you weren't driving, it was still your fault. Fine. You want to take some of the blame? Okay." Dallas tried a different tact. "But I think that you don't want to let go of this guilt because then you might have to face some other ugly truths that you might not like too much."

"What do you mean?" Allie tucked a damp strand of her dark hair behind one ear.

"I mean if it's not your fault, then you might want to blame your dad."

"Dad didn't do anything wrong!" Allie exclaimed.

"Yes, he did." Dallas moved, reaching out to touch her elbow. She didn't flinch. "He died, Allie. He died, and he left you, and you were just a little kid, standing on the side of the road, scared and alone. And then he left you alone all the rest of your life, because *he died*. He left you, even if he didn't mean to do it. You've got every right to be mad at him for that."

Tears streamed down Allie's face as the truth of what Dallas said hit her full force. He knew he was getting through.

"I…" Allie shook her head, more tears glistening on her cheeks. Dallas reached over and opened the glove compartment, offering her a wad of drive-through napkins. She took them, wiping her nose.

"But it was so long ago… Why am I crying?" Angrily, she swiped at her wet cheeks.

Dallas pulled her closer to him, and she came, sagging against his side, with his arm around her. She leaned her head on his shoulder, sniffling.

"I'm no psychologist, but if you want my two cents, it's probably because your fiancé betrayed you and that dredged up all kinds of memories from the first, and worst, betrayal you never really dealt with. Not to mention, you nearly died twice! I'd think that's enough trauma to bring back some traumatic memories."

Allie tensed in his embrace. "God, I think you're right." The truth of it settled on her as she seemed to try it on for size. "How did you…know all that?"

"I'm a good read of people," he said. "Plus, my own dad died when I was nineteen. I had a lot of anger for a lot of years. I was just old enough to realize what it was."

"I'm so exhausted, so tired of all this." Allie snuggled into Dallas's shoulder.

"You need some sleep. It'll all look better after you get some sleep."

"That's what my dad used to tell me," Allie said, brightening. She looked up at Dallas, and he glanced down. Her eyes were big and dark, and her thick eyelashes still glistened with tears. She watched him, very still, and suddenly Dallas remembered the pond—and everything he hadn't gotten to do to her. He'd loved the feel of her sexy body, loved how eagerly she responded to him. She was just delicious in every single way, and he craved her like some kind of drug. Her breast nudged against his rib cage, and he suddenly remembered the feel of her perfectly taut nipples in his hand. Just the thought made his body stand at attention.

All he wanted to do was kiss away her tears, her sadness.

Yet he knew this wasn't the right time. Kai was in the hospital. Could he go back on his promise to his friend when he was hurt? And then there was Allie herself, so very vulnerable, clearly dealing with some heavy stuff. He shouldn't take advantage. He hadn't even meant to let things get so far in the pond, but something about the taste of her just drove him a little crazy.

Like now, as she gazed up at him, all he could think of was tasting her lips one more time.

"Dallas…" she murmured, moving closer to him—or was he dipping down to her? Either way, their lips met halfway, and again, he felt the luscious taste of her as she opened her mouth to greet him. Allie opened herself up to him as their tongues met in an ancient, primal dance. She held nothing back in that kiss, which electrified every nerve ending in his body. Her wanton submission to him, just in that moment, made him wonder how free she'd be in his bed. Dallas pulled her close, and suddenly she was straddling him, her back to his steering wheel. He could feel her warmth between her legs, as she rocked seductively on him, grinding him slowly but mercilessly. Dallas felt so full, so close to exploding, he gripped her hips, almost begging them to stop. The pressure on him felt almost too much, was nearly enough to make him come right there. Their kiss turned even more savage, and Dallas felt as if he was awake in his own best wet dream.

He should stop this. He knew it, but part of him didn't want to stop, didn't know how. That part didn't care they were right out in public near a busy street. He just wanted to be inside her, deep inside her, feel her warm wetness. He wanted to make her shudder with pleasure again and again; he wanted to see pure ecstasy on her beautiful face.

He slid his hand up her skirt, felt her warm, taut thigh. He squeezed it, and she groaned, pushing herself into him more as the kiss turned even more furious, more desperate. He cupped her perfectly round backside, and she arched into him, pressing farther into his lap. The pressure drove him mad, nearly made him lose it right then. How could he stop this? Why would he?

Allie pulled back, slipping out of his zipped sweatshirt, revealing her low-cut sundress. He glanced at her perfect cleavage and laid a trail of kisses there as she moaned, throwing her head back.

A hard rap on his fogged window caught them

both by surprise. Allie jumped, and Dallas put a protective arm around her and pulled her close, blinking up to the rain-soaked window. He saw the flash of a deputy's badge and uniform before the bright white of a flashlight blinded him.

"Police," the man said, tapping once more on the window. Dallas recognized the voice of Kona patrol officer Lyle Lawson. Dallas turned the key in the ignition and rolled down the window.

"Hey, Lyle," Dallas said, blinking against the bright light. "You trying to blind me?"

Lyle's face lit up in recognition. "Dallas, you old dog! Didn't know that was you. Computer's down and can't run plates. How have you been, man?" All seriousness was gone; the officer grinned. He'd shared more than one round with Dallas at the local tourist bar off duty. He shone the light on Allie, who blinked and shaded her eyes.

"I see the tsunami hasn't slowed you down any. Doing what you do best, giving the all-star tour to our visitors, I see." He gave Dallas a playful punch in the shoulder. Dallas could feel Allie flinch. Dallas thought about correcting Lyle, introducing her as a local, but stopped himself. *Was* she a local? She had made it clear she didn't plan to stay. He thought about getting into the complications of the fact she was Misu's granddaughter, and just let Lyle think she was a tourist. It was simpler.

Allie squirmed in his lap, uncomfortable and embarrassed. Awkwardly, she slid back over the gearshift to the passenger seat. Cool air hit his lap and he felt sorry for it. If he could tell Lyle to go to hell and get away with it, he would. But Lyle didn't deserve it, not really.

"You be careful out here," the officer said. "I got a report of looters."

"The waves just hit!" Allie exclaimed, talking for the first time.

"I know. But that's the perfect time for some people." Lyle shook his head with resignation like a man who'd come to expect the worst from people. "Been up all night trying to sort out this mess. They just sounded the all clear. You could go check on the Kona Coffee Estate. No need for the two of you to be stuck out here in the rain." He winked at Dallas, and Dallas really wished he hadn't. Allie crossed her arms over her chest.

"Uh, yeah, I guess we'll be on our way," Dallas said, hoping Lyle would take the hint and get. He was a solid stand-up guy underneath, but he had no idea how to talk to women, or around them. Right now he was making Allie feel one inch tall. She stuffed her arms back into Dallas's sweatshirt, not looking at him.

"Oh, yeah, man, didn't mean to interrupt the

party." Lyle glanced at Allie's bare legs appreciatively, which made Dallas want to punch the man in the face. Only the idea of getting hauled in on charges of assaulting an officer kept his hands on the steering wheel.

He thought about calling Lyle out, denying his island reputation, but figured he'd only give the officer an excuse to dig himself in deeper. Lyle had seen Dallas take home one too many drunk girls to believe he'd just dropped them off at their hotel. Which he had done, every single time. He didn't sleep with girls who were too tipsy to say yes. The tourist he had slept with had had *one* mai tai.

"See you at Lu's!"

Dallas cringed. Lu's was where tourists and hard-partying locals hung out. You only went there if you wanted to get drunk fast, which was exactly what Dallas had wanted to do the year after he broke up with Jennifer. Drunken bar fights were a regular weekend occurrence there, but he didn't want Allie to think that was how he liked to spend his time.

Dallas held up a two fingers. "Bye, Lyle." He watched the officer retreat to his police car, pulled up behind them. He turned to Allie. "Sorry about that… Lyle…"

"Is an old friend. I get it." Allie hugged herself

a little and then yawned. "I guess we should go to the estate, right?"

"Are you sure?" he asked, hopeful that maybe she had something else in mind. All he wanted to do was get back to that minute before when she'd been kissing the life out of him. "The tree house isn't far. You could rest there. We've been up all night."

"Why not just stay up? Sun's out." The rain was letting up, and the storm seemed to be passing. The sky cleared again, and the sun shone through the clouds above them. She glanced through the window and then added, "We can go back to the plantation. Don't you want to see if everything's okay?"

Dallas did want to, but he wanted to resume kissing Allie more. But Lyle had ruined that for him.

"Sure, let's go." He turned the ignition in the truck and turned back onto the road. They fell into a silence as disappointment settled in. He'd never thought he'd ever be able to want someone after Jennifer. Allie was so unlike his ex-girlfriend, it was almost comical.

Still, he wondered if he was ready to get involved with someone else. He still remembered that day he'd found Jennifer in bed with the producer. She'd left the door open, almost as if she'd wanted him to find her there, as if she dared him to do something about it. Well, he had. He'd packed a bag and he'd left.

Nothing she'd said then would convince him to stay. She'd threatened to do all kinds of terrible things to him, to spread lies about him, to turn Kayla against him, too, and vowed he'd never see her again. But he'd been done with the emotional blackmail, done with her, done with a relationship he saw could never be fixed, because *she* didn't want to fix it or herself. She liked how she was, the destruction she caused for other people, and she had no intention of ever changing. He'd spent too long trying to fix her wounds. Part of him knew it wasn't entirely her fault. She'd had a crappy childhood, and most people she'd known in her life had failed her. But at some point, he thought adults needed to stop blaming other people for their troubles and decide whether they were going to set their own selves on their feet or spend their lives playing the victim. Dallas hated leaving Kayla, but in the end, he felt he couldn't help her by staying. They'd both be pawns in her mother's narcissistic game.

The hardest part of that day had been saying goodbye to Kayla. He'd come back to the house to get more of his clothes. Of course, she couldn't understand why he was leaving. She was a bright girl, with her mom's piercing green eyes and blond hair. Her dad lived somewhere in California, but that was all Dallas knew about him. He'd been out of the picture since she was born.

He'd had her promise to call him if she ever needed anything, even though he knew her mother would never let her.

"You're a fine, smart, wonderful kid," he'd told her, before he'd choked up. "I wish I could stay, but I can't."

Kayla had just blinked at him, confused. "Why not?"

"Because…sometimes adults don't always get along."

"Say you're sorry," she'd advised him, holding Mr. Cuddles close. "And Mommy, too. Mommy can say she's sorry."

His heart had broken then. She was too little to understand that there were some things you simply couldn't apologize for. It was the hardest thing he'd ever done, walking out on that little girl with the big green eyes bright with tears.

He'd thrown his suitcases in his truck. He'd driven away from the house they shared, and was grateful to Misu, who'd let him move back into his old place, the guesthouse on her property.

Dallas had thought that was the worst of it. But Jennifer wasn't done with him. That very same day, she'd gone online, used passwords she'd guessed right and transferred all but one dollar out of his accounts. It was close to fifty thousand dollars, more or less, and everything he had that wasn't tied up in investments or CDs, which he couldn't touch for at least two more years. She'd stolen from him, not just Kayla and his trust, but everything in his bank account, too.

He could have gone after her for it, could've called the police, but then what? Kayla's mom would go to jail. That was, *if* he could have proved he hadn't given her the passwords and told her to take the money. She'd argue he did.

And if he had pressed charges, everyone on the island would have heard about it. The gossip would have flown fierce and decisive, and Kayla would hade been hurt by it. She'd grow up being the daughter of the thief, or she'd grow up in a foster home if her mom went to jail. Either way, Kayla got hurt. Dallas had refused to go after Jennifer for the money, and he'd chosen not to battle the gossip, either. Anything he said to defend himself would just prove Jennifer's guilt. Dallas knew the power of gossip in a small town. He'd come from one. He wasn't going to do that to Kayla. He hurt Kayla enough by leaving, and he damn sure wasn't going to hurt that precious girl any more. If he had to be the bad guy, it was a price he was willing to pay.

He glanced over at Allie in his passenger seat, as she stared away from him out her window. He knew all about guilt, about how it could eat you up inside. He hoped she believed him that it wasn't her fault about her dad. He could see plainly that she was a woman who struggled with trusting people, too, and he could see why. The most important people in her life had failed her. He wanted to help her get past this, but wondered if he even could. He thought of Kayla, knowing he had his own burden to carry. He tried to imagine a time when he didn't feel bad about leaving, and couldn't. It might well haunt him for the rest of his life.

CHAPTER FOURTEEN

As Dallas and Allie drove back down to the Kona Coffee Estate, they saw most of the higher elevations untouched by the tsunami. Carloads of fleeing Hawaiians steadily made their way back to their homes, and Allie worried for them: Would they find their houses intact? Or return to splintered rubble? She remembered the tourist they had seen floating in the floodwaters. How many people had died? How many families would be torn apart? How many daughters would lose their fathers? With so many people likely to be suffering, Allie felt selfish holding on to her little traumas of her past.

For the first time, she thought, maybe she needed to let them go.

Somehow she'd been afraid to take a closer look at her past, afraid that if she did, she'd find only more blame. But Dallas had helped her see how wrong she'd been to keep it all bottled up for so long. She was afraid to look too hard, afraid of the anger she'd feel toward her dad.

It's not your fault. She tried that on for size, and

actually for the first time, she actually started to believe it. *It's not my fault.* She wanted to say it out loud, to make the words official somehow. Dallas was onto something. All those years her father had missed with her, all those birthdays, and holidays, and first days of school. Her heart ached when she thought of all those times she'd wished her father had been there. And he wasn't. And she'd blamed herself.

But she couldn't be mad at him, either. It wasn't her fault or his.

Sometimes, she guessed, it wasn't anybody's fault. Not really. Bad things just happened in life, and it was about what you did next. Did you let them keep you down forever? Or did you pick yourself up and try again?

Get knocked down seven times, get up eight. Wasn't that what Grandma Misu had always said? It had been her favorite Japanese proverb. Maybe it was time she listened.

She wasn't sure what she was going to do with that information, but she'd figure something out. She was grateful to Dallas for the advice, and yet, she also knew she had to be careful. Dallas wasn't someone she could get involved with. He may not have cheated on Jennifer, but everywhere she turned, she saw new evidence that he liked to play around. She didn't want to think about how quickly her body responded to him, how eager she was to throw caution completely to the wind, consequences be damned. What would've happened if that officer hadn't knocked on their window? Allie felt as if she wouldn't have been able to stop herself. She realized, a beat too late, she didn't even have a condom. Did he? Would they just jump in blindly and hope everything worked out?

Never before had she even considered doing anything so reckless.

But did she really want to be one in a parade of women through his bedroom door? Allie already knew the answer. She'd shared her fiancé with another woman and she'd hated it. She hated the idea of someone not thinking *she* was enough. She was done sharing. The next time—if there was a next time—she wanted a man who could be true, who didn't need his head turned every ten minutes by something or someone new.

Allie glanced at Dallas's rugged profile as he kept his eyes steady on the road. She couldn't hope to keep him interested, not in the long term, not when he'd had so many conquests under his belt. She'd be a fool to risk it. Her heart was barely mended, practically still in pieces. She should find that cop who'd interrupted their little make-out session and thank him for preventing her from making a mistake of a lifetime.

They drove to the Kona Coffee Estate, and Allie could feel Dallas tense as they made their way up the seemingly untouched driveway. The fence was intact, as were the first rows of thick coffee trees, their branches heavy with bright red berries ready to be picked. As they ascended the drive to Misu's house, Allie saw it stood untouched by the disaster, completely and radiantly in one piece. She'd never been so glad to see her grandmother's porch. She realized, belatedly, that all her grandmother's things were inside. *I'd have lost what was left of her if the tsunami had taken it.* Allie felt an immediate rush of gratitude. She'd have more time to sift through her grandmother's things.

And then she felt an even bigger sense of gladness: the property was still whole. She could still sell it. She had to convince Kaimana, but that came after the coffee festival. She still had a chance. The thought buoyed her, made her feel instantly lighter. *My escape plan is still in place.*

But was that what she wanted? She didn't know. She wasn't sure anymore. Did she want to be alone in a world where disaster could strike at any minute? Wasn't it better to be with people you loved than alone?

Dallas parked the truck near Misu's house and Allie ran in, just to be sure. Just to check that somehow the water hadn't made its way inside with no residue on the outside. Allie found the house just the way she'd left it: her suitcase open on the bed, her rinsed dishes from breakfast in the sink. Nothing was out of place. Nothing touched. Allie went outside to tell Dallas the good news, and found him back by the roasting barn, inspecting all the equipment for making coffee. He wore an expression of intense concentration as he went through each piece of equipment, checking it out from top to bottom.

"Everything okay?" Allie asked.

"All good," Dallas said, relief on his face. Allie and he shared a grin, and for the briefest of seconds, she wanted to launch herself into his arms, to kiss him to death. *We made it!* she wanted to shout. *We're going to be fine!*

"My house," Dallas said, as if remembering it for the first time. He rushed out of the barn, and Allie followed him. He strode down the small path between the tall coffee trees, but skidded to an abrupt stop when the trees parted. Allie nearly collided with his back.

"What…the…" But then Allie saw why he'd stopped. Here, on this side of the property, closest to the shore, the water *had* come, and it had come in force. Several rows of coffee trees had been completely leveled flat, swept off by the floodwaters. But even more shocking, half of Dallas's house had been washed away; the other half lay in a tangled, slumped mess on muddied ground.

"Oh, Dallas," Allie moaned, reaching out to

touch his elbow, but he was gone, moving away from her, his hands deep in his thick blond hair, as if he hoped to pull it out and make everything in front of him disappear. He walked to what was left of his front door and through it, sinking into thick mud up to his ankles. "Dallas—be careful!" Allie followed him up to his collapsing porch and peered into his house. Half of it: the kitchen and living room looked strangely unscathed. The back bedroom and indoor bathroom, however, had been mostly swept away. Pipes lay twisted and torn, coming up from where his bathroom had been. A toilet with no door or walls sat strangely in the middle of the muck.

He disappeared back to his bedroom and came out with a handful of clothes.

"All I could salvage right now," he said, his face registering shock. "I don't know what to even... Where to start..."

Allie gently took some of the clothes from his arms. "It'll be okay," she said. "You can stay with me until we get this fixed." The words were out of her mouth before she even realized what she was promising. Dallas staying under her roof? Was that a good idea? She glanced at his muscled forearms, wondering just how long it would be before he was kissing the life out of her, before she was back in that logic-free zone where she just wanted to take off all her clothes.

She flicked away the temptation. This was about offering Dallas *the couch*, she told herself. Nothing more.

Dallas blinked at her, as if not understanding a word she said. "You can stay at Misu's house until we get this fixed," she said once more, as if that somehow made it right. It wasn't *her* house she was inviting him into.

Dallas suddenly put his arm around her, hugging her to him silently. She rested her head against the solid muscle of his chest and wished he'd never let her go. Eventually, he released her and strode toward the house again, grabbing one of his working patio chairs away from the sagging roof. Allie set his clothes on it, and he went about the task of trying to find what he could save from his house. Allie started to help him, and then she remembered: Dallas's house wasn't the only one closer to the shore, wasn't the only home near here on low-lying land.

"Kaimana," Allie said suddenly. "Kaimana and Jesse's house!"

Dallas stopped what he was doing, and their eyes met. Instantly, they both walked quickly down the path of coffee trees toward Kaimana's old farmhouse. The water had taken out the big mango tree in her front yard and swept it off to an unknown destination. It had also clearly made it up the porch steps, which carried a mud line from where the waters had receded, but the rest of her house remained in one piece.

As they stood there assessing the damage, Kaimana herself opened the front door and shuffled out carrying a mop and a bucket. She froze when she saw them, her gray-streaked hair, long and loose past her shoulders. A white flower was tucked behind her ear, and she had on a bright blue flowered muumuu along with her signature macadamia-nut necklace.

"Are you all right?" Allie called as she walked up to the porch.

Kaimana dropped her mop and made her way down the steps. She pulled Allie into a big hug, surprising her. "Where have you been? You scared me to death! You weren't at the shelter." The sudden warmth surprised Allie.

"This is your fault, huh?" She pointed at Dallas accusingly. Dallas just held up his hands, trying to convey innocence. "You wanted to play hero or something? Going out to the floodwaters for my Kai?"

"I…"

"I'm grateful you did, you big dummy!" Kaimana pulled Dallas into a big hug, too. "You're a good boy." The big-boned woman gave Dallas's blond hair a good tousle, and he turned a little red as he disentangled himself from her.

"Is there anything we can do for you…anything

we can get?" Allie asked, as Kaimana finally released her.

"You got any gin over there? I could use a stiff G and T." This caused everyone to laugh a little. "Nah, I'll be fine. Little damage, no big deal." Kaimana shrugged. "It'll be clean in no time. And Kai is doing much better. I went by the hospital this morning. He was awake and singing your praises. You know it kills him to do that, Dallas."

"I know." Dallas grinned.

"He'll have to take you surfing and try to drown you again, just so it's even."

Dallas laughed. "Fine by me, anytime."

"How is the estate?" A worry line wrinkled Kaimana's forehead.

Dallas fell silent. "Most of the crop is fine and so is Misu's house," Allie said quickly. "But… not his house."

"It's just stuff," he said, trying hard to mask the seriousness of the loss. "It can be replaced. And Allie is letting me sleep on the couch at Misu's, so I'll be fine."

Kaimana uttered something in Hawaiian to show she approved.

Dallas glanced over his shoulder, up at the bright sky. "I need to head back and use this daylight while I can," Dallas said.

"You go on. I need to talk with Allie." Kaimana's face left no room for argument, so Dallas just shrugged.

"Sure. I'll meet you back at your place," he said and trod off down the trail leading away from Kaimana's house. When he was gone, Kaimana ushered Allie to a seat on her porch.

"Have you talked to your grandmother yet?" Kaimana asked, taking Allie by surprise.

"Talk to her? I don't understand…" *She's dead.*

"I talk to her every Tuesday afternoon," Kaimana said. "I visit the Alae Cemetery, and we have a nice long chat."

Allie instantly felt relief. Kaimana wasn't talking about seeing dead people, she was talking about speaking to a grave.

"Oh."

"You should come."

"I will," Allie promised, feeling a knot in her throat.

Kaimana clapped her hands, making Allie jump a little. "Okay, so be sure to tell her about the contest. She'll want to know you're entering. You still plan to enter the festival?"

"I forgot about it," Allie lied.

"You've got months yet. That's enough for several batches."

"Several?"

"Sure, you harvest beans every month, roast them up and then pick the richest ones for the competition. Easy." Kaimana dusted her hands as if it were a chore easily done. Allie didn't think it would be that easy. Especially not now, with the island still rocked by the aftermath of the tsunami.

"Once you win the festival, you could always sell to Dallas. Of course, that is *if* you want to sell."

Sell to Dallas. That would be a perfect plan, wouldn't it? He'd get to keep the plantation and she'd get to travel around the world.

"Right…that would be a good plan." Allie had to admit it was the perfect out. "We'll win that contest. Dallas would be an excellent buyer. You're right." Allie felt a strange sense of disappointment when she said those words. Hadn't she been relieved to find the land in one piece to sell? And now she could give Dallas the good news. *No need to worry about rebuilding your house, just move on in to Misu's and call it home.* "You're right. It's the perfect solution for everyone."

"Is it?" Kaimana asked, one eyebrow raised, her eyes playful within the wrinkled folds of her aged face. She was a wise woman who seemed to be able to see right through her.

"Well, anyway, I have to help with the cleanup right now, and then, I mean, the festival is months away."

Kaimana nodded sagely. "Of course. It's a long

time. Lots of things can happen in that amount of time. You'll need to work closely with Dallas to bring in the crop, roast up that coffee."

"Will I?" Allie felt strangely upbeat about the prospect. What was wrong with her? One second, she couldn't wait to sell, and now she seemed plagued by second thoughts.

"I know you need to go, but I have one thing for you..." Kaimana bustled back into her house. She emerged with a small wooden tiki carving, a short squat god grinning wide and wearing a tall pointed hat, twice as big as his body.

"It will bring you luck," Kaimana promised. "One of the old Hawaiian gods."

Allie studied it. The small wooden carving fit easily into the palm of Allie's hand. He had a wide-mouthed grin that looked almost like a figure eight.

"I guess I could use all the luck I can get," she said, meaning it. She put the little figure into her pocket and strode back toward the house. Her phone rang, and when she pulled it out, she saw a local number flash across the screen.

"Oh, thank goodness you're there." Teri sounded rushed and stressed. "I didn't have Dallas's number, and we need some help down here, if he could spare his pickup truck. The water receded, but there's a lot of debris. I'm not sure if the salon is going to make it."

Allie stiffened, concern rushing over her as she thought about the shopping center and the salon. "Oh, Teri…"

"We're trying to organize a big cleanup, but it's slow going. Do you think you could come and help? We're also looking for any cars that can haul trash away."

"We'll be there."

CHAPTER FIFTEEN

ALLIE AND DALLAS drove separately to the shopping center that housed Tiki Teri's hair salon and Hula Coffee. He hadn't even hesitated when Allie told him about Teri's call. Despite having his own mess of a house to deal with, he'd instantly gone to help his neighbors. Allie realized the proof of his commitment to the community in how quickly he volunteered his assistance, how he instantly put the needs of others in front of his own.

As they pulled into the shopping center, Allie saw the buildings were still standing, amazingly; but Teri was right, they'd had some pretty intensive flooding. The parking lot was covered in debris: random splintered boards, old crates, even an overturned small fishing boat. Teri and Minnie were already there working, as were several other familiar faces that Allie recognized from Kai's backyard barbecue.

Dallas and Allie didn't have to ask; they both dug into the cleanup effort. Dallas gave Allie a pair of workman's gloves and then she was off, helping Teri haul bits of broken glass and debris from the salon. They worked steadily, filling the commercial dumpsters someone had rounded up and put in the parking lot. The whir of fire truck sirens could be heard steadily throughout the day as people began the long, arduous process of cleaning up. Municipal trucks came out in force, with technicians working on downed power lines and leaking gas pipes. What Allie couldn't believe were all the people who weren't on a county or city payroll out working and helping, the line of volunteers that snaked into the shopping center eager to assist. Allie found herself working side by side with lifelong residents, and even a few tourists who'd enjoyed coffee at Hula Coffee, all happy to roll up their sleeves and help in a time of need.

She watched Dallas wordlessly hauling big pieces of wood away from the stores, his muscles bulging. He'd discarded his shirt at some point. Sweat beaded on his shoulders as he carried heavy pieces above his head. She could watch him all day, she thought. Then she remembered she'd have to tell him about Kaimana's plan at some point. She decided not to think about it. The time now was for working.

The goodwill and the team attitude floored her. Never before had she seen people come together from so many backgrounds to work together, and in such harmony, at the teeth-gritting task of picking up what the ocean had brought in.

"Now *this* is the aloha spirit," Minnie declared, stopping briefly from her task of hauling away soggy drywall to take a quick picture with her phone. She posted it instantly to several sites, and Allie knew the word would be spreading and more volunteers would show. The tsunami was a terrible tragedy, but Allie felt as if the spirit of the people here was an amazing sight to see.

Get knocked down seven times, get up eight.

Now she understood that saying more than she ever had. Allie wondered if Grandma Misu had seen this fighting spirit in her neighbors all these years in Hawaii. Allie couldn't help but admire the people. She found herself considering how it would feel to live with such neighbors. *Could I settle down here? What would it be like to live on an island where everyone looked out for everyone else?*

As she tucked a piece of broken plate glass into the dumpster, watching others do the same, Allie saw a man turn on his car radio up to the loudest volume. Ukulele music punctuated the din of work, and Allie remembered then, suddenly, a long lost memory: her father's funeral.

In true Big Island style, it had been a mix of cultures and religions: part Christian, part Buddhist, all Hawaiian. Incense had burned near the

golden Buddhist plates set near his open-faced
coffin while a pastor had said a few kind words
in the open-air service near the cemetery. It had
been standing room only, all the folding chairs
taken, as half the Kona district had come. Allie
remembered live ukulele music played throughout the ceremony, and she remembered her father, lying lifeless in the coffin, his face peaceful.

The sky above them had been crowded with
clouds, threatening rain on that humid day.

She remembered that she'd worn one of Aunt
Kaimana's white-flowered leis around her neck.
Kaimana had approached her after the ceremony.

"Waimaka o ka Lani," she'd said, speaking in
Hawaiian as raindrops fell from the sky. *"Waimaka o ka Lani."*

Allie suddenly remembered what that meant:
"The heavens cry when a loved one passes."

Allie felt something seize up in her chest when
she thought of her father's funeral. All the many
people there, just like now, helping her family
when they needed them most. She wondered why
she couldn't see it then, why she'd only thought
they were there in some way to judge her: the
little girl who'd survived. She'd been so wrong,
she realized.

"Allie!" called a little boy, and Allie looked
up to see Po running to her, his mother coming
behind. He gave her a big hug, and when Allie
set him down he grinned wide.

"Got any candy?" he asked.

"Po! That's not nice!" his mother chided behind him.

"It's okay," Allie said, smiling at the mother. "I'm sorry, I don't have any, Po." The boy temporarily looked deflated but recovered quickly. "That's okay. We went to see Kai! He gave me his chocolate pudding." The boy wore a smudge of what looked like dried pudding on his chin. "He said hospital food is gross! But, I don't think so." Po grinned even wider. "Dallas!" he shouted, as the man strode over and gave the boy a solid high five.

"How you doin', little man?" he asked.

"Good!" Po grinned. "We went to the hospital!"

His mother ruffled his hair. "We went to thank Kai, and as we drove by, Po saw you and Dallas here. He wanted to say hi. Is there anything we can do to help?" Po's mother looked around at all the people working.

"You might want to ask Teri," Allie said, nodding toward the salon owner, who was busy directing volunteers.

Po's mother scooped him up. "Come on, Po. Let's talk to Teri."

Dallas grabbed his phone from his pocket and glanced at the time. "I should probably go see Kai," he said.

"Let me come with you," Allie offered.

"Allie!" called Teri, waving her over. Allie

hesitated, not wanting to miss seeing Kai, but also feeling as if she didn't want to let Teri down.

"Looks as though you're needed," Dallas said. "You stay and help. I'll tell Kai hi for you."

"I'll be by when I can," Allie promised.

DALLAS DROVE TO the hospital, amazed at the devastation he'd missed in the dark cover of night: entire shoreline neighborhoods had been washed away, as had shops and gas stations.

He'd never seen his beloved Kona District in such shambles. His half-knocked-down house was really the *least* of it. The tsunami had taken away more than stores and homes and gas stations. It had taken people's lives and their livelihoods. Nothing about the Big Island would be the same after this, he knew. But he was also confident they could rebuild.

Judging by the way she'd rolled up her sleeves to pitch in with the relief effort, helping people she barely knew, Allie was a special woman, he could see. That's what he'd have to tell Kai when he broke the news that he did plan to date his oldest friend, local or tourist; he didn't care what category she fell in.

Dallas found Kai without visitors, save for the nurse named Maggie, according to her name tag. She was hovering near his shoulder and giggling. He probably had a lot of nurse attention.

"Mr. Brady, you are so funny," she murmured, flirting.

"*Mr.* Brady, huh?" Dallas leaned against the doorjamb, crossing his thick, muscled arms across his chest. "We on formal terms now?"

"Dallas, you old dog." Kai grinned. "Not my doing. You have to ask Jesse. She's insisting everyone call me that."

Maggie smiled shyly at Kai and then scurried out of the room. "Somehow, I don't think that's going to keep the nurses away from you," Dallas said as he watched Maggie flit down the hall. A line of other nurses whispered at the nurse's station, keeping their eyes on Kai's room.

Kai shrugged. "Hey, bro, I can't help it if the women love me."

"Uh-huh. You sure you didn't just break that leg for the attention?" Dallas cocked one eyebrow, and Kai laughed.

"That's right. More *female* attention. Just what I need." Kai exhaled a tired-sounding breath. "*Speaking* of female attention, Jesse told me you took Allie to your tree house? Are you serious with that?"

Dallas felt put on the spot. "The shelter was full."

"So you take one of my oldest friends to your *love shack*?"

"Nothing happened."

Kai just glared at him.

"Nothing *much* happened," Dallas amended, thinking about the feel of her topless in his arms. Technically, they didn't have sex. *If* he wanted to get technical, which he did right at that moment.

"Dallas McCormick!" Kai raised his voice, upset, his face flushed. "I *told* you not to mess around with Allie. She isn't one of your conquests. You promised me, Dallas. You promised me you'd stay away from her."

"I promised I wouldn't treat her casually, and that's not what it is," Dallas protested.

"Uh-huh. Right." Sarcasm laced Kai's words.

Dallas felt anger pinch his temples. He was tired of everyone assuming the worst about him, including his best friend.

"I'm not messing around," Dallas growled. "I wasn't looking for this, Kai. Lord knows I've *tried* to find fault with that woman, tried and failed. She's not only the most beautiful woman I've ever met, but she's also smart and funny and completely and totally selfless *and* one helluva stubborn pain in my ass. She drives me crazy, but I can't seem to get enough of her anyway, so that either makes me suicidal or a glutton for punishment, I don't know. But what I do know is that I'm going to spend as much time with her as possible because being with her might make me insane, but being without her is worse."

"You done?" Kai asked, as he raised an ironic eyebrow.

"No, I'm not, not where Allie is concerned." Dallas had begun to pace. He ran a harried hand through his blond hair.

"Okay, Dallas… I—" Kai glanced at the door looking worried. Well, let him worry about one of his nurses overhearing. Dallas didn't care.

"I'm not done!" Dallas thundered, really gearing up now as he stood rigid by Kai's bedside, his back to the hospital's hallway. "You know what else? She's completely and hopelessly a danger magnet. But do I care? No! I just want to make sure she's safe, and given the past week, I can already tell that's a full-time job. But I *want* that job. I'd do anything to get that job. But you and everybody else on this island keeps telling her I'm pretty much a grade-A asshole, and I'm tired of it."

Kai glanced over Dallas's shoulder. "Dallas…" Kai began, but was cut off once more.

"I may *not* deserve Allie, that's true, but I'm damn well going to try to, because she's exactly the woman I've been looking for my whole life. Not you or anybody else is going to stop me from going after her, because I can't even think about a world where I don't. Even if she is a walking natural disaster, even *if* she's got more emotional baggage than a full set of luggage, I don't care. So even though it's none of your business *who* I have sex with or *when*, I'd really like you to be okay with this. I'm not asking your permission to date her, because you're not her father, but you're the closest thing to one right now, so there. I'm asking. I want you to be okay with this."

Dallas took a deep breath and released it. Kai had been rendered speechless, which was exactly Dallas's intent. Let him say something *now*. Let him lord imaginary conquests over him or tell him he was not serious enough to date his friend; let him even *try* to pull any of that crap. Dallas was ready.

Kai cleared his throat and glanced at the door. That was when Dallas realized someone was standing behind him in the doorway of the hospital room.

He turned in time to see Allie, holding a bouquet of flowers from the gift shop downstairs, standing stock-still. It was clear by the startled look on her face that she'd heard every word.

"Do *I* get a say in this? Or do you two men get to decide who I sleep with next?"

ALLIE HAD TO ADMIT, watching Dallas turn bright red made her day. He'd been ranting when she'd walked up to the door, and she'd paused to listen, wondering what had made him so mad. When she realized it was *her*, she'd been shocked. Frankly,

stared at Dallas, his chiseled chin inches from her own.

"Will you have dinner with me tonight?"

"But...the cleanup, and..."

"You can't clean up debris when it's dark," Dallas said. "This is not a casual invite, Allie. This is an official date. Will you have dinner with me?" His blue eyes waited expectantly for her answer.

"Yes," Allie breathed, feeling a jumble of excited nerves dance in her stomach. "Yes, I will."

CHAPTER SIXTEEN

ALLIE HAD THE rest of the afternoon to worry about just what she'd gotten herself into. The dinner wasn't what she worried about. It was *after* dinner that was cause for true concern. Would she sleep with him?

It wasn't as if she could exactly kick him out and tell him to go home after dinner was over. He'd be sleeping under her roof. And that was where the trouble came in.

Well, he's already seen you nearly naked, so that's hardly a problem, that sarcastic little voice in her head said. It was true they'd done a fair amount of fooling around, but still. Technically, they hadn't rounded home base yet. For Allie, that meant something serious: a line yet crossed.

And because he *had* gotten her top off once, would he expect to again? And, more important, would she be disappointed if he didn't?

Her mind was a whirl of contradictory problems, which she understood if she voiced them out loud would make no sense. *An amazingly sexy man asks you on a date—be happy about it!* And yet, Allie couldn't quite relax. After all, she'd been too conditioned her whole life waiting for that shoe to drop.

And then there was another problem: she still had no condoms. After finishing up at Teri's near sunset, Allie pulled her rental car into the parking lot of what was once the drugstore and found the store intact, but closed, a handwritten sign on the door stating their doors would be shuttered until the power came back up. *Probably for the best*, she thought. *No condoms, no sex*. That would be her new rule.

When she arrived home, she discovered she'd beaten Dallas there and felt a little bit of relief. She'd have time to shower and get ready. She ought to be exhausted from lack of sleep, but she didn't feel tired at all. She took a change of clothes out to the shower. The hot water washed off the grime of the day. She was amazed at how many places she'd managed to get dirty. Even the crook of her elbow carried some mystery grease. Her muscles ached from the unaccustomed work, but it had been worth it. They'd done nearly half the debris clearing working together. By the end of the week, they'd have it all done. It felt good to help Teri, and it felt good to be part of a team. No, more like a family.

She'd be sore tomorrow, but right now she just felt a good, weighty tiredness in her bones, the kind of worn-out that only came from a day of useful work. The gloves had mostly saved her hands, although she could already feel a blister forming near the base of her thumb.

As she shut the shower off, a bright green gecko ran down the shower curtain. She wasn't even startled.

"You go eat that centipede—wherever he is," she told the little lizard. It paused and cocked its head to one side, as if actually listening, and then darted down and to the ground.

She put on her best clean sundress—a lavender sleeveless mini—and paired it with her favorite silver dangly earrings. She whipped up her damp hair into a messy bun on her head, a few dark strands falling down by her ears. She looked down at the newly bandaged cut on her leg, thinking again how lucky she was Dallas had saved her. Kaimana's good-luck tiki sat near the bathroom sink. On a whim, she tucked it into her dress pocket.

Allie heard Dallas's truck barrel up the drive, but she took her time applying her makeup in the small outside bathroom with the tiny mirror. By the time she finished, she was starting to feel nervous, and her body hummed with an excited energy. She blotted her lips and stared at her reflection in the mirror.

Country music wafted to the open-air bathroom, catching her attention. Dallas must've salvaged some speakers from his house, as well as some charcoal by the smell of the heating grill. Allie found Dallas near the back porch, closing the lid of the big grill. He wore linen shorts and a solid blue polo shirt, which somehow made his eyes look like the deep, cool blue of the Pacific Ocean.

He glanced up at her, giving her an appreciative once-over. "You look…gorgeous," he said, pulling her close for a hug, where his hand lingered on her lower back. "Good enough to eat," he murmured in her ear. Her thoughts went instantly to the pond, and she felt a hot flash run through her. Her mind whirled with possibilities. When he pulled away, Allie could tell Dallas was thinking along the same lines. A playful smile tugged at the corner of his lip.

No condoms, no sex, she reminded herself, and then began to worry her resolve would melt away by the end of the evening. Already, she was forgetting why jumping into bed with Dallas McCormick was a bad idea.

"After you," Allie said, motioning toward the patio door. Dallas smiled slowly.

"Oh, no. It's *always* ladies first in my book. My mama raised a gentleman." He tipped an imaginary cowboy hat in her direction, and she laughed. She liked flirting with Dallas. Maybe a little bit too much. Once inside, Dallas uncorked a bottle of red wine and filled two glasses.

"Where did you get this?" Allie asked, taking a sip and loving the smooth, expensive taste of a prime pinot noir.

"It's what I could salvage from my place. As well as two steaks thawing in my freezer and some fresh green beans." Allie saw two rib eyes marinating in a sweet and spicy steak sauce in a container on the counter. "I thought I'd treat you to a Texas barbecue," Dallas drawled.

She couldn't help but wonder how many times he'd done the same for a tourist passing through. Maybe he kept wine and steaks at the ready at his place. Just in case. She felt a twinge of jealousy and then tamped it down. He'd said his reputation was greatly exaggerated. He'd even argued with Kai about it, and yet…she'd seen a tourist at his place early in the morning with her own eyes, about to make the walk of shame home to her hotel. For some reason, she couldn't shake the image of him handing her a cup of coffee.

"So the tsunami will cut down on the tourists," she said.

"Yep. It'll be hard on some of the local businesses, but I think we'll survive. And we'll rebuild all the faster." Dallas took a sip of wine, and then grabbed the container of steaks. "Grill should be about hot enough. Let's go see."

Allie followed him outside and watched him open the dome-shaped lid of the barbecue pit, the white-hot coals blazing from within. He grabbed a barbecue fork and set the two rib eyes on the metal grill. Marinade hit the coals and sizzled, sending up a puff of steam. The steaks cooked for a while as the two sipped their wine.

"And I heard Lu's might be closed indefinitely. It was knocked out. So that will cut into some weekend fun." She tried to make her voice light, but somehow it came out pensive.

Dallas glanced up at her. "I won't miss it," he said.

"You won't?" Allie couldn't keep the surprise from her voice.

"I'm done babysitting tourists for a while."

Allie let out a snort of disbelief. "*Babysitting? Is that what you call it?*" She couldn't help but laugh. Now she had him. "Like the one I saw at your place."

"So she got under your skin, did she? So you *do* like me. Like me enough to spy on me and stalk me!"

"I wasn't stalking!"

"Uh-huh." Dallas looked as if he enjoyed teasing her and watching her squirm.

"You were having a one-night stand," Allie said, hoping to change the subject.

"They're not illegal, you know," he pointed out.

"But, no, I didn't have a one-night stand. I was making sure she had a safe place to stay. She got too drunk the night before, so drunk she couldn't remember the name of her hotel. It was either drop her off at the district jail for her to sober up or have me take her and then bring her back to her hotel in the morning. And the jail is a terribly uncomfortable place to sleep."

Allie was dumbstruck. "You didn't sleep with her?" she asked, amazed.

"Absolutely not! She was far too gone for that. It wouldn't be right."

"Would you have, if she'd been more sober?" Allie knew she ought to stop asking questions, but she couldn't. She just had to get to the bottom of it. She felt she'd never asked enough questions with Jason. If she had, maybe she would've dug up his proclivities earlier. She'd not make that mistake with another man again.

Dallas just laughed. "No. I would've just taken her home. I'm a glorified taxi service, that's about it." He flipped the steaks on the grill. The juices dripped downward into the flames and sizzled, as the mouthwatering smell of seared barbecue filled the air.

"But the police officer..." Allie was trying to piece the puzzle together.

"Who? Lyle? He just wants to live vicariously. He wishes he could talk to women, but he can't.

Anyway, I've tried to tell him that I just make sure the girls get home safely, but he thinks that's code for having crazy sex." Dallas shrugged. "I'm tired of trying to convince him otherwise."

"Oh." Allie processed this. If Dallas *didn't* really sleep with all those women, then Teri and everyone else on the island was wrong about him. Everyone except Jesse, who'd told her she didn't believe the rumors. Was it possible this was the truth? The idea that he didn't just roll into bed with anybody made her feel strangely better. Did that mean what they had was special?

"You sure do seem concerned about my sex life," Dallas said, sneaking a sly look at her. "If you're really worried about me getting enough, I know one way to make sure I get some. I might have to take you back to that pond, though…"

"I…" Allie trailed off as white-hot and decidedly naughty thoughts ran through her mind. In the moonlight, she felt her cheeks grow warm.

"But that can wait," Dallas promised. "First, dinner."

Dallas served up the steaks and green beans, and they sat together on the patio beneath the stars. Allie dug into her delicious food, her body eager for the energy she'd depleted with her hard day's work.

"This is delicious," she murmured, taking another sip of wine, the combination of steak and wine on her tongue divine.

"I'm glad you like it," Dallas said. As they finished the meal, Allie glanced up at the sky. It was so crowded with stars, she could hardly tell where the constellations were. Stars she'd never seen before, living in the big city, popped up in and around the Big and Little Dippers.

"So many stars," she exclaimed. "They look brighter here on the island than the mainland. Almost as though they're closer to us."

"I've thought that, too," Dallas mused, looking up. "There's Orion. He's my favorite."

"Where?" Allie glanced up. Dallas leaned over, his shoulder nearly touching hers.

"There," he said. "See those three stars? That's his belt."

"Oh, yes!"

"He was a famous hunter, you know. He boasted he could kill any living thing on earth, that nothing could beat him. Of course, then he was killed by the bite of a tiny scorpion."

"Ouch. That was a blow to the ego."

"It just goes to show that you should never get too cocky," Dallas said.

"Oh, a philosophy you live by, do you?" Allie teased.

"Most of the time."

Allie finished her last sip of wine and put her

glass down on the table. She stood and stretched, reaching for her plate to take it back to the kitchen. Quick as lightning, Dallas grabbed her wrist.

"Hey," he said, and she turned back to see him studying her.

"What?" she asked, half afraid she had some remnant of dinner on her face.

"You're beautiful," he said, his eyes looking dark in the moonlight as he pulled her closer, tugging her down on his lap. She collapsed there, a giggle on her lips, even as his hand caressed her cheek, and she went very still. Before she knew it, his lips were on hers. Allie felt her body respond, as if he'd flipped a switch. She pressed into him as he pulled her to his chest. She tangled her hands in his thick blond hair, and he groaned into her mouth. Allie, sitting on his lap, felt she couldn't get enough of him. He broke the seal of the kiss first, panting.

"Should we take this inside?" he asked her, and all she could do was nod, a million hormones flooding her brain at once, lighting it up like a Christmas tree. He stood, picking her up and carrying her easily back inside the house, the porch screen door flipping out and then slapping back against the door frame. He laid her down on the bed in her room and deepened the kiss, his body on top of hers, the weight of it delicious. He slid his hands up the length of her dress, running his fingers beneath to her bare skin, and she gasped, breaking free of his kiss and arching into him. He ran kisses down her neck to the low-lying cleavage of her neckline, and all rational thought fled. She tugged on his shirt, and then it was off, revealing miles of taut muscle. She slid her hands down the ridges of muscles, his smooth hardness driving her wild. Distantly, alarm bells went off. She ignored them as long as she could, but as her hands slid to his waistband, she realized what she was forgetting.

"Wait," she murmured, gasping. Her body felt as if it was on fire, but she had to call a time-out. "I…uh…don't have a…condom." Allie felt her face burn a little, embarrassed at saying it out loud. There was something about saying the word that just brought her straight back to her sixth-grade sex ed class.

"Condom!" Dallas exclaimed, as if he'd only just thought of it, and maybe he had. "I have one. I mean, I *think* I have one." He looked stricken for a moment. "Hang on one second." Dallas jumped up and ran to the bag near the kitchen. He dug through it, cursing. "I thought I saw one." He dumped out the contents of a shave kit, but nothing but razors and shaving cream and a tooth-brush fell out. "Damn."

"Dallas…" Allie began, but he cut her off.

"One more second! Don't move a muscle!" he

called, still rooting through his bag. She rolled over on the bed.

The urgency with which he was searching made her giggle a little. He *really* wanted to seal the deal. He cursed and slammed down the bag.

"Did the tsunami wash away your supply?" she asked half teasing, half not.

"I don't *have* a supply. I haven't even had sex in a nearly a year!" he admitted.

"A *year*?" Allie echoed.

"Wait! I know where one might be!" Dallas sprinted out of the house wearing only his shorts, and Allie watched him through the small slit of a window run to his pickup truck and tear open the driver's-side door. After frantic searching in the glove compartment, he came up with a thin square in triumph. He clambered through the door holding on to two linked packages with a goofy grin on his face.

"I found two," he breathed, exhaling.

"It's really been a *year*?" Allie still couldn't get over it. "So you really don't hook up with tourists."

"I've only had one hookup since I broke up with Jennifer a year ago. *One* tourist. Not *tourists*."

So he *didn't* need a new woman's attention every ten minutes. Teri had been wrong. And that made Allie secretly ecstatic. She jumped up from the bed and threw her arms around him, dragging him down on top of her.

"I've never seen a woman so excited about an old Trojan," he teased, as she kissed his neck. "Where *were* you when I was eighteen and carried one of these around in my wallet for a year?"

"Ha. Ha," she said. She glanced at the worn packaging. "You sure this isn't that same one?"

"No," he said, pretending to be indignant. "I *eventually* used that one, thank you very much. This one is probably just, you know, a year old. Do they go bad? Should I smell it and see if it's off?"

Allie giggled. Something about Dallas made everything *comfortable*. She felt as if she could talk to him about anything. "Give me that," she demanded.

"Most of the lettering is still on the package. I say, let's give it a whirl," Dallas drawled, kissing Allie's lips once more. It wasn't long before the playful kisses turned serious. He whisked Allie's dress over her head and, wearing only her lacy underwear, she undid the button on his linen shorts and slid them and his boxers down with them.

He sprang to attention, and she realized he *was* much bigger than Jason as she wrapped her hands around him. He stood before her as she sat on her knees on the bed running her hands up and down the length of him. He groaned, leaning into her touch.

"Allie," he growled, his pupils wide and hungry.

She teased him until he begged for mercy, exploring his body in the same way he'd explored hers at the pond, with her hands and her mouth.

"Allie, God…you're going to make me…" He didn't get to finish his sentence as he wound his hands tightly in her hair. "Allie…"

Just when she knew he couldn't take much more, she pulled away, reaching for the condom, ripping open the package and freeing the thin circle of latex. Expertly, she put it on him, and then she stripped, wiggling out of her underwear.

His eyes swept her body with appreciation. "You're so damn sexy," he murmured, and then he crawled on the bed, kissing her as she dragged him down on top of her. Allie spread her legs beneath him eagerly, and he dived in, filling her in ways she never imagined. She gasped at the sheer force of him as he pushed deeper inside her. Explosions of sensation rattled her as he worked, managing to hit every one of her pleasure centers. Just when she thought she couldn't take it anymore, he switched their positions, and she took over the rhythm as he gently cupped her breasts. He met her gaze as she sat on top of him, grinding against him, his eyes hot with need.

She dipped forward, and he put one of her nipples in his mouth, sending her into another universe of sensation. He let that one go and concentrated on the other one, gently, deliberately, and all she could think of was his kisses again at the pond, and the memory of that sent her body completely over the edge. The climax came before she could stop it, her body shuddering in delight as she cried out. He grabbed her hips, pushing himself deeper as she came, making her ecstasy all the more intense.

"Oh, God, Allie," he murmured, as her series of tight contractions had their effect on him. She squeezed him harder, unable to stop herself, and he groaned, his breath quickening. "You feel so damn good," he exclaimed as he intensified his thrusts, coming just after her with a low shout. Allie collapsed on top of him, sweaty and spent, listening to the sound of Dallas's frantic heartbeat in his chest.

"Wow," he murmured.

"Uh-huh." Allie still felt rocked by her own orgasm, her brain abuzz in endorphins, her body all but exhausted. Her tired muscles protested the extra work, but she ignored them. It was well worth it. She rolled off him, exhaling. Dallas wrapped his muscled arms around her and cuddled her to his chest. He happened to glance at the floor.

"What's that?" he asked, pointing to the tiki statue on the floor that had rolled out of Allie's pocket.

"Kaimana gave it to me for good luck," Allie said, reaching for it. Dallas took it from her hand and studied it, and then burst out laughing.

"Not for good luck, more like to *get* lucky," Dallas said. "That's Lono. The Hawaiian god of sex and fertility."

"No!" Allie cried, swiping the little figure from Dallas's hands and staring at it as if she could disprove it by looking. "Kaimana did it again! She fooled me. That woman…"

"Has a wicked sense of humor," Dallas agreed, laughter rumbling in his chest as he placed the little tiki on the bedside table. It stared at them, big mouth open, as if laughing, too.

"Honestly," Allie fumed. Although she couldn't be too mad. Sex with Dallas had been amazing. If that was Lono's doing, she'd be fine with it.

"Hey, I think it's working again," Dallas said, nudging her, already ready for round two.

"It would be a shame to waste that second condom," Allie said.

"Who said anything about wasting?"

CHAPTER SEVENTEEN

THE NEXT TWO weeks were filled with tsunami cleanup in the day and amazing, white-hot sex at night. Allie had never gotten so little sleep and not cared a bit. Dallas made her feel anything but bland, and after the amazing positions they tried that week, Allie realized something astounding: she wasn't the boring one in bed at all. Jason had been.

The thought made her giggle. It was true: Jason stuck to mostly two positions, and hardly ever altered his strategy. With Dallas, Allie realized that she'd been missing out on all kinds of fun. She almost wanted to call Jason and let him know that there was life beyond missionary, but she decided just to gloat from afar.

A bulldozer came to level what was left of Dallas's house. He put his arm around her as the construction crews did their work, but that night, she distracted him in bed, easily taking his mind off the worry. She didn't have time to think about what might happen in the future, or if Dallas might run off one day or find a way to disappoint her. She was too busy with all the work: helping Teri when she could, figuring out what coffee plants could be saved for the harvest. She'd also taken on another project: cleaning out her grandmother's closet. She'd been inspired to do it after calls had come out for gently used clothes for tsunami victims who'd lost everything. She'd managed to clean out all of her grandmother's closets and drop off several bags of clothes to the Red Cross. She kept some of her grandmother's jewelry, and of course, her grandmother's prized book of recipes.

Of course, after the major clean out of her grandmother's house, she realized that it was quickly becoming their house, with her things hanging in the closet next to Dallas's. For once, she ignored that little voice in her head that said, *Dallas is too good to be true. Dallas will disappoint you just like Jason.*

If she ignored the voice long enough, she was sure one of these days it would go away. Dallas, for his part, started talking about weeks and months later: what they'd do for the festival. At least she didn't have to worry about him leaving before then, she reasoned. She was safe for a couple of months.

And besides, she hadn't decided to stay. She still had the land to sell, she reasoned. She still had an escape plan.

ONE MORNING, ALLIE came awake to the sound of voices in the kitchen and the smell of bacon sizzling in the pan. She threw on a pair of yoga pants and a T-shirt and wandered out, curious about the visitor. When she got there, she saw an older man, heavyset with mostly gray hair, a mix, Allie guessed, of Hawaiian and Asian descent. He and Dallas were talking seriously, while Dallas tended to breakfast at the stove and the man drank coffee from a white mug.

"Good morning, Allie. I'd like you to meet Henry Leong. He and his workers have been helping us harvest coffee for years."

Henry removed his worn baseball cap and shook Allie's hand. "Nice to meet you," he said. "I knew your grandmother well. She was a wonderful person." A slight blush crept up the side of Henry's cheek, and Allie wondered if this man might have just had a crush on Grandma Misu. "I was very sorry to lose her." He fiddled with the brim of his hat, his wrinkled and age-spotted hands running over the edge of it. Allie patted his shoulder, glad to know that her grandmother had had a man like him to support her on the farm and maybe in her life.

"I promised her we'd win the competition this year," Henry said. "I'm hoping the tsunami didn't hurt our chances."

"We didn't lose many trees," Allie offered,

taking a seat at her grandmother's small kitchen table. Dallas poured her a cup of coffee.

"But we lost some of our best," Dallas explained as he handed her a full cup. She took it gratefully. "Henry agrees, it might be tough finding the right harvest this year."

Allie thought of Kaimana and her paper. "But we have to win the competition."

Dallas looked surprised. Henry did, as well.

"Isn't that what Grandma Misu wanted?" she amended quickly, finding some bit of lint on her shirt to focus her attention on.

"Yes, it's true." Henry nodded. "But we will have at least three rounds of harvest and roasting to get the perfect combination."

"That's a lot," Allie said, just like Kaimana had said. "Why can't we get them all at once?"

"The beans don't ripen all at the same time," Henry said. "That's why we need to pick them by hand."

Allie nodded, remembering again her dad standing on a ladder, reaching the cherries at the top of the tree. "When do we start?"

"How about today?" Dallas said as he served up a plate of bacon and eggs. "Eat up. You'll need the energy."

ALLIE HAD NEVER worked so hard in her life, and that included hauling trash from tsunami-wrecked parking lots. The basket she wore around her neck was full of red coffee cherries, her back ached, and her fingers felt raw and sweaty, blisters popping up even through the work gloves she wore. Her neck felt stiff, and sweat dripped down her back. The straw hat she wore kept the sun off her face, but her hair was a matted, damp mess beneath it.

She reached up to grab one last red cherry from one of the low-lying branches and then decided the basket had become too heavy and full, and took it over to Dallas's waiting pickup truck to add to the collection of full baskets there. Henry and his workers crowded the lines of trees, expertly and efficiently picking berries from the trees. They could pick far more than Allie could in a day. She was still learning how to best twist and pull the small coffee fruit from the vine.

"Tired yet?" Dallas asked, offering her a cool drink of water.

"Exhausted," Allie admitted, taking a deep dreg.

"Well, you'll appreciate a good cup of coffee even more now," he promised.

As the last of the day's pickers put full bushels of cherries into the back of Dallas's pickup, he drove them to the pulper at the barn, the big metal machine that took the red skin and pulp off the cherries, revealing the bean, or seed beneath. After pulping, the beans went into a fermentation tank.

"This is where the bright, clear flavor comes from," Dallas told her as he showed her the wet beans in the huge fermenting bin.

Allie felt intrigued by the whole process, each new step both exhausting and thrilling at the same time. She could also see Dallas come alive throughout the process. She could see the thrill in his eyes, the absolute joy of doing what he loved to do. The joy was infectious, and she felt she could learn to love this, too.

The new roaster was delivered during this time, and Dallas eagerly fired it up, the gleaming piece of equipment everyone's hope for a winning batch of Kona. Dallas lit the gas burner beneath the huge contraption, and he fed dried beans into the giant metal drum. They popped and cracked, and Allie watched, fascinated as the cherry pits turned into the darkened coffee beans she knew so well. The roasting barn filled with the smell of fresh coffee, and Allie felt the presence of her dad and grandmother nearby, approving of each step. Dallas made clear there was an art to roasting the perfect Kona coffee: it was all about a delicate balance of heat and time, and lots of careful stirring.

"A lot like love," he said, and gave her a meaningful glance. At the very word, Allie felt a tingle in her toes. *Love* could not be what was happening here, could it? She could not even remotely allow herself to think about the possibility of *love*. That was inviting disaster.

Dallas went about taking out the first batch and then feeding it into the grinder. Allie put the warm, freshly ground coffee into individual bags, each with its own special hula girl label. Allie couldn't help feel a special kind of pride as the crates of newly packed beans began to stack up in the barn. There was a certain kind of satisfaction from growing something and harvesting it with your own hands. She could see why both her father and grandmother had dedicated their lives to this, and why Dallas did, too.

After grueling work, the roasting and harvest was nearly done. The helpers had all gone home with enthusiastic thanks from Allie. Hula Coffee would be saved the problem of having to find a new house roast, at least in the interim.

"Moment of truth," Dallas declared, as he took a bag of beans and ground them up, ready to pour into their coffeemaker. Allie waited anxiously, eager to taste the fruits of her first coffee harvest. She watched anxiously as the coffee dripped into the clear glass pitcher, the rich black liquid slowly filling the carafe. Allie inhaled the beautiful smell of 100 percent pure Kona coffee, and realized there wasn't anything as delicious to her as that smell.

Dallas poured a small mug for himself and for Allie.

"Cheers," he said, and they clinked glasses. Allie giggled, as she took a sip of the brew. It was rich, yet not bitter. She swallowed her first taste as she watched Dallas take his time with his. He smelled the cup first, a deep inhale, and then gently took the first mouthful, as if he were sipping a fine wine.

He swallowed and then frowned.

"What's wrong?" Allie asked, immediately sensing something was off.

"It's good, but not good enough."

Allie took another sip. Her taste buds weren't as refined to the nuances of the perfect cup of coffee. It seemed good to her. "It's not?"

"No." Dallas put down the cup, frustration on his face. "It won't win the competition. It's not as bright as it should be."

"Bright? I don't understand."

Dallas tried to explain the certain zing a winning cup of Kona needed, but to Allie, it felt like trying to understand a foreign language. Then he pulled out a packet of Queen's Best.

"This farm won last year," he said. "It's won five years in a row."

Dallas set it brewing in a separate coffee machine and, when it was done, handed Allie a small cup. "Taste the difference."

Allie went about sipping the new cup and the old one. "Ours is more bitter," she said.

"Exactly," Dallas exclaimed. "And?"

"More acidic," Allie said, closing her eyes and letting the full taste of the coffee roll over her tongue.

"Right." Dallas nodded. "We need to be less of both."

"How do we do that?" Allie wondered aloud, as she stared at both half-drunk cups, still thinking a bit of magic was involved to make one taste so much better.

"We'll have to harvest another round of beans, roast them up and hope they're better," Dallas said, tossing the dregs of his own coffee cup in the sink of the kitchen. "It's all in the bean. How it grows, how it's picked and the way it responds to the roast."

Allie felt the enormity of the task ahead of them and sighed. "How many more chances do we get?"

"Two more," Dallas promised.

THE NEXT SEVERAL months passed in a blur of work. Allie had never gotten so tan, picking coffee cherries in the Hawaiian sun. Dallas divided his time between the harvests and overseeing the rebuild of his house. As each new piece went up, Allie tried not to think about what that meant: one day soon he'd move out. Of course, there'd be the Kona Coffee Festival and competition before that. And if they won, Kaimana would give her what she wanted: the ability to sell her share of the land. Why should she be upset if Dallas planned to move out, if she did, too?

What did she want, she wondered? A grand gesture? A marriage proposal on one knee? Surely, she'd seen enough disappointment in her life to know that none of those things came without a price. She felt herself brimming with uneasiness, waiting for the bubble to pop. It had to soon, didn't it?

She brewed a fresh pot of amazing Kona coffee in her kitchen, and she looked out the back window and watched Dallas stride purposefully toward the barn. Every morning, he'd gotten up before her. Living together the past few months, she'd learned he was a morning person, rising just after dawn, working hard to get that perfect batch. He'd been obsessed about roasting the best coffee. After the past two rounds, Allie could hardly tell the difference. Her palate had gotten a little better with tasting differences between coffee brews, but they were all so good, she didn't know why Dallas seemed so sure they'd lose.

She took a sip of the rich coffee and sighed,

wondering if there were worse things than losing the contest. *Would staying here be so bad?* she thought as she looked out across the bright green coffee trees, laden with red cherries. She set her coffee cup down on the counter and grabbed a new yogurt from the fridge for breakfast. Unlike Dallas, Allie needed some wake-up time and a little food before she could go charging into the day.

Besides, he'd made sure she hadn't gotten much sleep. They didn't do much of that in bed, especially not last night. She thought of his hands on her the night before and felt warm all over.

As she opened the lid of her yogurt, a bit of strawberry pink splashed onto the counter. When she moved to grab a paper towel to wipe up the mess, she knocked over the coffee bag, spilling black Kona grounds into the mess.

"Great," she muttered, as she went about wiping the spill. Guess that proved she wasn't quite awake yet. As she wiped the yogurt and coffee grounds together, she got some on her hand, and noticed that it felt like some expensive exfoliate the Chicago spa she used to work for had charged customers hundreds of dollars for.

The caffeine facial had involved high doses of caffeine and vitamin C, designed to brighten skin and erase puffiness. The facial cream had been little more than yogurt and caffeine, which made Allie wonder: Would the coffee grounds work the same way? She glanced at her reflection in the smooth glass of the kitchen window and noticed the puffiness around her eyes.

What the hell, she thought. *Might as well try it.*

She mixed up a bowl of coffee grounds and yogurt, swirling it together, and then she went in the bathroom and lathered it on half of her face. She wanted a before and after effect, and wanted to know if the mask would be as rejuvenating for her skin as she predicted it would be. After a few minutes, she washed the mask off, and instantly noticed a difference: the puffiness was all but gone, and the left side, the side that had the yogurt coffee mask, was brighter, fresher looking.

"I'll be damned," she thought, glancing at her reflection. "It worked."

She lathered up the other side of her face, and just then heard the back door open and slap shut, and Dallas's boots on the wooden floor. He walked by the open door. "Morning, darlin'," he murmured, nuzzling the back of her neck. He smelled like hard work and the open air of the coffee fields. He looked at her reflection in the mirror and nearly jumped. "Whoa, what is that?"

"An experiment," Allie said. "If we can't use coffee to win a brewing contest, we can use it for an expensive face cream."

"We can?"

Allie nodded, excited. "I can use some of that batch you decided was too dark to sell."

"You're going to used burned coffee?" Dallas shook his head. "Seriously?"

"It might even be better for the scrub. I'm going to experiment."

Dallas grinned and wrapped his arms around Allie, lifting her off her feet.

"You're my dream woman, you know that?" He kissed her gently on the lips, and Allie felt the zing right to her toes.

IT HAD BEEN months since the tsunami, but the island was only slowly returning to normal, or the *new normal*, as most Big Island locals were calling it. Life started feeling steady and predictable once more. The debris was gone, and construction was in full swing on rebuilding old homes. Tiki Teri's and Hula Coffee reopened to huge fanfare. The disaster had brought the locals closer together than ever, which was a good thing, since tourists were still slow to return. The tsunami had made major headlines across the world, and only the disaster seekers came these days, hoping to see carnage. Allie was glad the island disappointed them. Still, the bars and restaurants that survived remained only half full, the lack of tourists clearly noticeable.

The whole island held its breath for the upcoming weeklong Kona Coffee Festival, which drew in its share of tourists. This year, everyone had higher hopes than usual that it would bring in a good crowd.

"It'll turn around. It has to," Teri told Allie at the salon one afternoon. Allie had dropped by to give Teri her order of Kona coffee to fill up the coffeepot she kept at her business. Many of the locals didn't have money to spend on beauty at the moment, too concerned about rebuilding homes or feeding their families.

Tiki Teri's had new drywall and a fresh coat of paint. Teri had been able to salvage her aluminum salon chairs and most of her decorations, and the fresh paint made everything sparkle. All things considered, the place looked great, and no one would've ever guessed that a wave had barreled through it. Still, it was empty—not a single customer. The patent leather seats beamed, shiny and newly recovered, but no one sat in them.

The bell on the front door dinged, and both Allie and Teri looked up, hopeful for a customer, but they saw Jesse walk in, still wearing her Hula Coffee apron.

"Well, don't look so happy to see me," Jesse joked. "I just thought you might want to see this guy. Look who's off the couch!"

Kai limped in behind Jesse on aluminum crutches, a sheepish grin on his face. He'd been out of the hospital for some time, but had largely been a hermit. Rumors abounded that it meant the end of his surfing career, that the break had been too bad and that he'd been laid up on the couch suffering from depression. Jesse, however, said it was largely because he'd been on pain meds that gave him vertigo. She was determinedly upbeat about his prognosis, and that was how Allie would be. Allie knew how the rumor mill had hurt Dallas, and she had about decided not to believe a thing she heard on the island.

Teri clapped her hands, and Allie jumped forward to give him a hug, nearly knocking him off balance.

"Whoa," he said. "Easy, now. Don't send me back to the hospital." But he grinned, showing his bright white smile. Allie was glad to see him up again, even if it was on crutches. He looked good, and she hoped the reports of his depression were largely exaggerated.

"How's that leg?" Allie asked, eyeing the brace still on it.

"Won't know till I have more rehab." He knocked at the white Velcro brace wrapped around his knee. "Muscles are still really weak. Sorry I couldn't help with the coffee harvest this year."

"Don't be silly!" Allie exclaimed. "You had healing to do. Besides, you know Dallas loves to have something to lord over your head."

Kai chuckled a little. "That's true," he said. "How's business, Teri?"

"Awful," she moaned, playing with one of the oversize pearls of her necklace. She was impeccably dressed as usual in a linen shift dress, her bleached-blond, chin-length hair perfectly coifed. "The tourists have disappeared. I never thought I'd live to see the day I'd say I *miss* them, but there it is!"

"I hear you," Jesse said. "Since the Red Cross left, and the other volunteers, business at the coffee shop has really slowed down. It's bad. I heard some of the other shops are in worse shape. Everyone is counting the days to the festival next week, but who knows if the tourists will show?"

"Ironic, isn't it?" Teri said. "Here I thought we'd gotten over the worst of it by not being leveled by a tsunami, but then here comes the slow bleed of no customers!"

"That's why we've got a plan," Kai said. "How do you feel about a luau?"

"I love poi and roasted pig as much as the next girl, but what's that got to do with business?" Teri asked.

"Probably nothing, but I've got a reporter and a big blogger from Honolulu coming to cover how the whole community is celebrating still being here, and with any luck, we'll get some attention, and talk up the coffee festival, and we'll have tourists again."

"That's a great idea," Allie exclaimed, feeling hopeful for the first time.

"Everyone needs this," Jesse said. "It'll remind us all what's important. It's like Aunt Kaimana says, when you're at a luau you're *ohana*—family."

"Have you talked to Jennifer Thomas? Maybe she could get the film crew of *Hawaii Living* here, too," Teri offered.

Allie fell silent, even as Jesse looked worriedly at her. She wouldn't meet Jesse's gaze.

"Uh, no…we haven't, but…" Kai didn't get to finish his sentence. Teri stumbled over his words.

"I'll call her," she offered brightly, having no idea that the very thought of Jennifer coming to the luau was like a knife in Allie's stomach. Jennifer was the last person she wanted to hear about or see. She felt a flare of jealousy at the very mention of her name.

Kai shifted his weight on his crutches, uncomfortable. He was in a spot where he couldn't exactly turn down publicity. Allie knew it. Maybe Jennifer would flatly refuse, she thought.

"Want to sit down?" Teri offered.

"No, thanks, Teri," he said. "We're going to tell others about the luau. Spread the word. It's on Punalu'u Black Sand Beach Friday at seven.

It's a potluck luau, so everybody bring something. I'll provide the pig."

"It's too bad Misu isn't here. She made a wonderful mango fruit salad."

"It was so good," Jesse agreed, and the group fell silent. Allie remembered Grandma Misu's mango salad, bathed in a citrus dressing.

"I think I know where the recipe is," Allie exclaimed, recalling her grandmother's recipe book. "I can make it."

"There you go!" Kai said, nodding his approval. "That's what I'm talking about. We're going to show the world the aloha spirit and just what it means to be *ohana*."

CHAPTER EIGHTEEN

LATER THAT WEEK, Dallas sat in the roasting barn, holding a cup of steaming coffee and hoping *this* was the winning one. It was the latest batch through the new roaster, and all the estate's hopes lay here in this one cup.

He smelled the aroma: good so far. Rich, tasty, bright.

He closed his eyes as he lifted up the white mug to his lips and took a sip. The deep Kona brew hit his tongue, less bitter than the last, and yet...

"Not good enough," he muttered, and put the coffee mug down in a hurry, sloshing some on his worktable. "Just not good enough."

The coffee would be great in bags on store shelves. He'd made a damn fine brew, but Dallas knew it had to be one notch better to win the coffee competition. Kona farmers would be bringing their finest samples, and he'd have to be near perfect to compete. They'd be lucky to bring in fourth or fifth place with this year's batch. He frowned as he stared at his steaming mug of the latest round of roast. He racked his brain trying to figure out if there were any steps he'd missed from last year.

The festival was in a matter of days, and they were simply out of time. He'd run three separate harvests through, and for some reason simply couldn't quite repeat the magic of last year.

Misu, what am I doing wrong? he thought, glaring at the baskets of roasted beans.

Dallas knew growing good Kona coffee took hard work and a little bit of luck. Maybe the rain didn't fall so much this year, or maybe the sun burned too hot. Every yield came out a little different; every bean carried its own unique flavor. It could just be the luck of the crop. But he wasn't going to give up the idea of winning this thing. He had to do it, for Misu's memory, and for his own pride. He wanted to show the world that he could run Misu's farm, that he could make amazing coffee.

And I want to show Allie I can do this.

Dallas realized with a start he really did want to impress that girl, prove to her that he could run this estate and show her that putting down roots here was a good idea. Winning the competition would just show her it was possible. It seemed the best way he could think of to calm her skittish nature. He had a lot riding on winning this year, a lot more than he'd ever had the past several years.

You don't win this thing, she could bolt.

"Maybe it's your fault," he said, talking to the shiny new roaster. He adjusted the knobs one more time. As he straightened, he noticed the old roaster hadn't yet been removed. It had a layer of rust on the outside, and half the knobs needed pliers to work them. "Come on, old lady," he drawled, pushing up his straw cowboy hat as he unplugged the new roaster and plugged in the old one. "Let's try one more dance, for old time's sake."

He fired up the old machine, and it came to life, barely, churning and creaking in protest. The roaster had been on its very last legs two years ago, but Misu had squeezed two more harvests through it. What was one more?

Inexplicably, the roaster's barrel suddenly stopped turning, and Dallas examined the problem: a loose knob. He rigged up a solution with pliers and some wire, praying it would do the job. He had the very last bushels of depulped beans ready to be roasted. It was this batch or nothing. He got to work feeding in the beans, stirring them, checking the temperature. The heat gauge had always been wonky on that old roaster, one of many reasons he'd decided to invest in a new one this year. Midroast, the gauge gave out entirely.

"Dammit!" he cursed, knocking the gauge with his finger, feeling like punching it. How was he going to roast beans if he didn't know how hot the barrel was? He tried to turn down the flame, but it only seemed to get hotter, the knobs controlling the gas flames also malfunctioning. It only took a few minutes for the roast to burn, and suddenly the barn filled with a thick smoke, choking the air with the acrid smell of burned coffee.

Dallas cursed some more, kicked the old roaster as he worked furiously to turn it off. He opened the massive lid in time to see that his last-hope batch had been burned beyond saving. Dallas whipped off his cowboy hat and dumped it on the ground in frustration.

"Whoa! What's going on in here?" Kai limped in, as he surveyed the smoke in the barn. "Are you trying to burn the place down?"

"I'm trying to make award-winning coffee," Dallas muttered. "And failing at the moment."

"I can see that." Kai coughed, waving his hand in front of his face. "Wow, that smells awful."

"I know." Dallas sounded grim, as he turned on a big metal industrial fan in the barn to try to clear the smoke. "This is a disaster."

"What about the other batches?"

"Not good enough. And I don't have enough beans to make another one. If the competition were a month away, maybe we'd have a shot, but as it is… I just don't think we've got the winner here." Dallas put his hands on his hips and surveyed the tin cans of coffee grinds from separate harvests over the past few months, each one labeled by date, lining the worktable. He stared at them as if they were a puzzle to figure out. One was too dark, one was too light, one was too bitter.

"Well, brace yourself for more bad news," Kai said, watching Dallas grab the mug of coffee from the worktable and take another sip. "The mayor is going to announce the judges for this year's competition at the luau Friday. But I had lunch with her today and she let slip who at least one was."

Dallas froze midslurp, coffee mug in the air. "You're not going to tell me…"

Kai nodded slowly, grimacing. "Jennifer Thomas is on the panel."

"Well, hell." Dallas put down his cup and slammed the worktable. "Might as well just not even bother to enter, then. Why her?"

"She's our latest local celebrity, you know that. There's one on the judging panel every year. Last year, it was Miss Hawaii."

"This is no good. No good at all." Dallas paced the small confines of the barn as Kai leaned on his crutch, watching his old friend.

"She's just one judge," Kai reminded him.

"Out of three!" Dallas kicked some black lava dirt with the toe of his cowboy boot. "We'd have to get both the other judges to agree on ours, *and* hope that there's not a unanimous agreement on any of the other coffees, which there could be. I heard Queen's Roast had a great late harvest again this year."

"All you can do is enter and hope for the best," Kai said. "It's like a surf competition. You never know what could happen till the day of. Best not to beat yourself before you even get to the starting line."

Dallas knew his friend was trying to make him feel better, but it wasn't working. "I have to win the competition this year. I just have to. For Misu's sake. For Allie's."

"Allie's?"

"It's important, that's all. You should see how hard she's working for this thing. She's even got some new night cream or something. I don't know. Some spa thing."

Kai laughed out loud. "*You?* In the pampering spa business? I'd never thought I'd see the day."

"I didn't say *I* was doing it. Allie is using some coffee not fit for the contest anyhow. She's into it. You should see the kitchen. It looks like some kind of girl laboratory. She's figuring out how to use yogurt without it going bad." Dallas's mouth curved into a lopsided grin. He was proud of how Allie had dug into the face cream. He liked that she was determined to make something her own. It gave him hope that maybe she'd consider staying when he asked, which he planned to do right after the festival.

Kai coughed, whisking away a bit of smoke still steaming from the old roaster.

"So when are you going to tell her?"

"Allie?" Dallas frowned. "I'm not."

"Dallas," Kai exclaimed. "She has a right to know. The estate is as much hers as it is yours. She'll be livid when she finds out."

"But what good would it do her to know? Best to let her be happy in ignorance awhile longer. There's nothing we can do about it anyway. Unless you have some dirt on the mayor, I'm sure this thing is carved in stone."

"She'll be mad if she knows you knew and didn't tell her."

Dallas shrugged. "Allie's had enough bad news in her life. She doesn't need more right now."

THAT NIGHT, ALLIE and Dallas took a shower together in the outside bathroom, taking turns wiping off the sweat and grime from another day's hard work.

Allie soaped his muscled back, and then took great care scrubbing the thick muscles of his shoulders, moving down to linger along the ridges of his abs. The water sprayed between them, and Dallas stared at her. She hesitated with the loofah at his waist, tempted to explore farther down his body.

"Better not wake the bear," he warned her. "Or you'll be sorry."

"Will I?" she challenged, as she moved the loofah down past his waist to his other bits. They came alive beneath her touch. "Too late. Bear's already awake." She grinned. He growled and pounced, pulling her toward him. She lifted her face to meet his and they kissed, hot water spraying across her cheek as he lashed her tongue with his. He growled once more and then lifted her up, holding her against the shower wall, the hard tiles cool against her back.

"Dallas," she squealed, surprised. "Put me down!"

"I tried to warn you," he groaned as he held her deftly against the wall, her legs wrapped around him, their warm slippery bodies coming together. A red bird flittered across the open expanse of the bathroom, but Allie didn't care—she was too focused on Dallas, on how perfectly they fitted together as he pushed forward into her, finding a delicious rhythm. She gasped, surprised as always by his size. He moaned as he held her, burying his face in her wet neck, the water from her long dark hair dripping, meeting the water from the shower as it slid down her shoulder and down her hip. She came almost instantly, her body rocked with contractions, as he held her. Their eyes met, and she felt as if she could drown in those eyes, and he came, too, in a last thrust of urgent heat. The two shuddered, pressed together in the small shower as the last dregs of climax shivered between them.

"What are you doing to me, woman?" Dallas moaned, pressing his forehead gently against hers as he set her down on shaky legs in the shower.

"I could ask you the same thing," she breathed, feeling deliciously spent. As they finished rinsing, the shower started to sputter.

"It's the pressure again," he muttered. "Hang on. I'll try to see if there's a quick fix. You finish rinsing." He jumped out of the shower, hair dripping, and pulled on swim trunks as he headed from the bathroom and toward the faucet leading to the water tank. Allie stayed. She hummed to herself, happy, happier than she'd been in forever, and she realized she didn't even care she was showering outside. Hell, if Dallas came with every shower, she thought, she'd shower in the middle of the freeway.

She finished rinsing and turned the knobs, stepping out and wrapping herself in a towel. While shaking out her hair, she heard a phone *ping* with an incoming message. She reached for the phone on the bathroom sink, thinking it was hers, before she realized she'd left her phone inside on the kitchen counter.

She didn't intend to snoop. Until she saw the name flash on the screen.

Jennifer.

She read the message without meaning to, as it was short and right there in her face.

R u there?

She put the phone down again on the countertop, wishing she hadn't seen it. She glanced at the door to the bathroom, but it remained solidly shut, no sign of Dallas's return. The phone pinged two more times.

Don't look, she told herself. She had no right to pry, no right to read messages intended for him. And yet…why was Jennifer texting him? After all she'd done to him, why did she reach out now?

Or was this something she did all the time? Allie hadn't seen Dallas preoccupied with his phone. If anything, he tended to forget it, as he did right at that moment. He wasn't like Jason, who had guarded his phone with dear life. No wonder, she thought now, consider he was living a double life.

What if it's something to do with Kayla?

She wondered if she ought to go get Dallas, let him read his messages and find out. She knew on some level that was what she *should* do, but her curiosity simply couldn't wait. She reached out and tipped the phone toward her so she could just see the face. She promised all she wanted to do was see if Kayla was all right. The message was sitting there on the pop-up bubble of his home screen. She didn't even have to open it.

Kayla misses you. She talks about you all the time.

And then…

Times like these make you think about what's important. I miss you, baby. I wish you'd come home so we can be a family again.

The words burned themselves into her brain. She felt woozy for a second, as if she was about to take a long drop off the top of a tall roller coaster.

Suspicion whirled in Allie's brain, and immediately she was right back in Jason's living room, the feel of betrayal hot and sticky at the back of her neck. Was Dallas encouraging this somehow?

The doorknob to the bathroom turned, and Allie almost dropped Dallas's phone in the toilet. She managed to save it at the last minute, putting it down on the sink and quickly running her fingers through her wet hair as if that was what she'd been doing all along.

"Done already?" Dallas asked, sounding a little

disappointed as his eyes took in the white fluffy towel wrapped around her body.

"All done." Her voice sounded too bright, too brittle. But there was no helping it. She watched as Dallas picked up his phone. He moved away from her, out of the bathroom, his eyes intent on the screen.

"Something wrong?" she asked him, trying to sound nonchalant, as she hurried out in just her towel. *Level with me*, she thought. *Just be honest. Don't hide it. There's nothing worse than hiding it.*

That's what Jason would do.

"What?" Dallas looked as if he'd woken up from some kind of dream, distracted and distant. "No. Nothing's wrong." He glanced at his phone again and frowned.

Allie felt her stomach sink. She knew exactly what he was reading. If he didn't have something to hide, why wasn't he sharing it? Part of her worried that it meant he was considering getting back together with Jennifer Thomas. Her stomach flipped, and she couldn't help but think, *I can't trust him, just like I couldn't trust Jason.*

DALLAS FELT THE old fury rising in him at the very sight of Jennifer's name on his phone. Jennifer was like a bad penny, *if* that penny was soaked in toxic waste and dipped in cyanide. Honestly, how could she even *ask* him to get back together?

Why don't you give me the fifty thousand dollars you owe me, and then you can just go to hell was what he felt like texting back to her, but instead, he just deleted her messages and hoped she'd get the meaning from his silence. For all he knew, she'd taken a financial hit during the tsunami and figured he'd be an easy mark. She could think again. He was glad Kayla was all right, and sorry that the girl missed him, but there was no way on God's green earth he'd ever consider getting back with that woman. Not in this lifetime.

Besides, he had Allie now, and the longer he spent with her, the more smitten he got. He found himself thinking about the future in ways he never did with Jennifer, despite being engaged to her. He realized now that he'd proposed to the wrong woman. He didn't feel this way about Jennifer; he never had. It had been a relationship always fraught with problems, and everything about it had been so damn hard. Allie was easy. She just *got* him, and he got her, and there was something really wonderful about that. He'd agonized over proposing to Jennifer. Should he? Or shouldn't he? And in the end he had because of responsibility he felt toward Kayla. Allie was completely different. The way she'd been a seamless partner during the harvest, and frankly, how brave and tenacious she had been during the tsunami, told him she was a keeper.

This was someone he *wanted* to marry, that he wanted to share his life with. He had no doubts.

He watched Allie make her way back inside, holding the towel to her chest, and thought that the only thing stopping him from proposing that afternoon was the fact that she'd probably bolt. He knew a skittish mare when he saw one, and Allie was as easily spooked as they got. Not that he didn't understand. Her ex had done a number on her head. It was no wonder that settling down would be the last thing on her mind. He had to hope that, just like breaking in a fearful horse, that if he gave her time and patience and lots of care, she'd come around. Too much too soon would scare her off for good. Hell, he'd almost blurted out the damn L-word a dozen times in bed only just stopping himself in the nick of time. He would have to be patient and bide his time.

The last thing she needed was to hear about some crazy, delusional ex offering up insanity via text message. Honestly, had Jennifer lost her mind? What on earth made her think he'd ever want to get back with her?

He glanced once more at his phone, shaking his head in disbelief. Jennifer would just have to leave him alone. *Learn to deal with disappointment,* he thought. *It's about time you had your share.*

CHAPTER NINETEEN

ALLIE WANTED TO scream and shout at Dallas, but part of her was just too devastated, too broken-hearted to do it. She knew she'd have to talk to him, but part of her just didn't want to. She wasn't ready for the truth yet. She wasn't ready for a sledgehammer to her heart when she found out it was all true and far worse than she'd imagined. Jason had taught her just how ugly things could get. She sneaked away from the coffee plantation that day. It was time to see her grandmother at the cemetery.

She'd knocked on Kaimana's door and asked if she'd go with her. Kaimana obliged happily. Together, they made the long drive to the eastern side of the island. She knew her grandmother and father were buried at the Alae Cemetery near Hilo. It was where Grandma Misu's father's family had grown up, and where her parents were buried. The cemetery's main feature, a huge rain tree, offered a giant canopy of green for many of the Japanese gravestones. The Pacific Ocean glinted in the distance. The cemetery on the eastern shore had been saved from damage from the tsunami, as had Hilo. Flowers bloomed here, and birds sang.

"Misu will be glad you're here. There was so much she wanted to tell you." Kaimana glanced over the gravestones, her eyes growing misty. "Come. I'll take you to her."

Allie followed Kaimana to the rain tree, stunned by the beautiful edges of it, like an enormous bonsai. The cemetery carried a unique kind of beauty and peace to it, and she had no trouble understanding why her grandmother had wanted her father buried here and why she had chosen to join him. If you had to spend eternity somewhere, might as well be under the shade of a beautiful tree only found in tropical places.

Allie carried a lovely arrangement of Hawaiian flowers: hibiscus, bird of paradise and irises, planning to leave them at her father's and grandmother's gravestones. When she saw that most of the stones had Japanese characters, she was suddenly glad to be following Kaimana through the neatly arranged plots. She stopped in front of a light granite gravestone that held both Japanese and English carvings.

"You know, she never blamed you." Kaimana's voice was so low, Allie almost thought she imagined the words.

"What?"

"For your father's accident. She never blamed you. She worried about you blaming yourself. She was so sad to lose you after she lost her son. It took her a long time to recover, and I'm not sure if she ever really did. She understood why your mother had to go, why you did, too, but she wished you would come back."

Allie felt a zing of guilt. "We never had the money for the flight."

"Misu knew that. It's why...it's why she left you the farm. She had so little when she was alive. She just loved you. She always loved you. Wanted you to be happy."

"I..." Allie wish she'd known that.

"She never abandoned you. Not in here." Kaimana pointed to her own heart. "They're both here with you. Now. I'll give you a minute."

She nodded knowingly and shuffled off, away back through the cemetery and to the parking lot. Allie glanced down at her grandmother's name, and next to it, her father's gravestone. She wanted Kaimana's words to be true. Was she really *not* alone?

"I brought this for you, Grandma and Dad," she said, putting the flowers down, her voice feeling unnaturally loud in this peaceful place. She felt silly for talking out loud but made herself do it anyway.

"I'm working hard to make that winning crop

for you, Grandma," she said and realized she meant it. Somewhere along the way, it had become less about getting Kaimana to sign that paper and more about doing what Grandma Misu wanted. She honestly wanted to win that coffee contest. "And I've even made something else with the coffee we can't use."

Allie brought forth a small plastic container with a screw top. With some help from Teri and Minnie regarding packaging and labels, she'd made special Kona Coffee Estate spa products, which she was almost sure, if she could send any back to Chicago, her old spa would buy by the box load. She put the small white container at the grave, as if her grandmother and father could see it. She wondered how they'd feel about a spa line. Dallas had been excited by the idea. He joked they ought to open up a gift shop on the property. Maybe even start to give tours like some of the bigger farms on the island.

"I'm sorry, Grandma, for not coming to your funeral. I'm sorry for not coming back at all. I..." Tears welled in her eyes and choked the words. "I'm sorry I didn't do more for both of you...when you were here."

She slumped to the ground in front of the gravestones and just cried. After a few minutes, she felt better, lighter. She thought of Kaimana's words. Just because she couldn't see and hear her grandmother or father anymore didn't mean that she couldn't still love them. It didn't mean that she couldn't still choose to feel loved in return. They hadn't abandoned her.

Had Dallas, though?

She cried, worried about him, worried that her heart might be broken once more.

"I don't know if I can do this again," she told her grandmother's gravestone. "I don't know if I can be knocked down one more time and get up again."

She stared at the gravestone, wondering how her grandmother had done it, all those years hanging on to a coffee plantation and barely making ends meet.

"I don't know if I'm strong enough." Could she survive the worst news from Dallas? Could she survive another betrayal? She really didn't know.

The gravestone couldn't answer her. But as she looked at her father's, she realized she was strong and resilient. She'd weathered a lot already in her life, and nothing had killed her yet.

She swiped at her eyes and sniffed. Whatever came, she'd face it.

THE NIGHT OF the luau came quickly. The whole island was abuzz about it. Locals wanted a reason to celebrate. There'd been too much tragedy and loss, and many yearned for a night when they could put the weight of that down, if only to lift up a glass of mai tai and toast what they *did* have. Dallas and Allie arrived together. Dallas wore linen shorts and a button-down floral shirt. Allie had on a simple white linen dress with a matching white flower pinned in her hair. She wore her black hair up in a messy twist, and tendrils hung down her tanned cheeks, looking breathtaking, Dallas thought.

Dallas parked the truck in the overflow parking lot near the beach, which was already crammed with cars. A huge, oversize billboard of Jennifer Thomas's grinning face leered down at them from across the street. Her bright blond hair was like a platinum halo, her green eyes perfectly aligned and her man-made cleavage perky and gravity defying in her plunging neckline. Dallas wished someone would spray paint a mustache on her.

He'd tried to convince Allie not to go to the luau, but she'd insisted. She'd drummed up quite a strong feeling for supporting local causes, and there was no dissuading her from this one. She'd been distant recently, preoccupied. Dallas thought it had to do with her visit to the cemetery, but he hadn't wanted to pry. She didn't seem to want to talk about it, but something was bothering her, he knew that much.

Allie gazed at the billboard worriedly, even as

Dallas pulled her close and laid a delicate kiss on her bare shoulder.

"Have I told you how beautiful you look?" he murmured in her ear. He leaned in to smell her, a wonderful mix of coconut and some tropical flower. She smiled at him weakly. Something was definitely bothering her. "Everything okay?" he asked her.

"Fine," she murmured, and he didn't believe her. She wasn't being honest with him. Something was bothering her. Had she found out that Jennifer was a judge for the coffee festival somehow?

He hadn't told Allie about her texts or the news that she would be a coffee judge. His plan was simple: get her out of there before the big announcement. He wasn't sure he could shield her from the news forever, but he didn't want her to find out at the luau.

Before he could ask more questions, Allie had flipped the handle of the truck door and jumped out. Whatever was bothering her, she didn't want to talk about it. They walked together to the dramatic Punalu'u Black Sand Beach, one of the many one-of-a-kind beaches on the Big Island. Crushed dark lava rock lay out as far as the eye could see, just as pristine and beautiful as any white sand beach, maybe more so because of the rareness of it. Hawaii had the most black sand beaches of anywhere in the world. His flip-flops sank into the black sand, which felt rougher and a little bit bulkier than on other beaches on the island. The dark sand sparkled in the fading sunlight as crystal-blue water came in waves to the shore. Tables were already set up, as were tiki torches, and a local band played surf guitar music. An impressive crowd assembled, as Kai had clearly gotten the word out. The air filled with sounds of socializing and laughter, and the delicious scent of roasted pig hit Allie's nose. A torch marked where the pig had been buried: deep in the hot sand to cook all day. The Hawaiian beach was better than any smoker barbecue pit.

Dallas carried the bag holding Grandma Misu's famous mango salad. He took Allie by the hand and felt immensely proud to have her on his arm. This was the kind of girl a man married, he thought. She bit her lower lip, as if worried.

"Allie?" Dallas saw where she was looking and realized why she was worried: Jennifer stood there mingling with a camera crew, looking buffed and polished. She wore a tightly fitted red dress and wedge sandals, her hair up in an elaborate twist. Dallas put his hand on the small of Allie's back and felt her stiffen. Jennifer's presence seemed to be bothering her even more than him. He wondered why. Maybe she did know she was the judge.

They made their way to the food table. Dallas

put down Misu's teak bowl. It was filled to the brim with mangos and onion and tomato, sitting in a special homemade lime-juice dressing. The fresh ingredients, so plentiful on the island, made the recipe so good.

Teri was there in an instant, removing the saran wrap, and then heaping a big helping on her plate. "This is my all-time favorite," she said and took a big bite. "Mmm," she murmured, closing her eyes to enjoy the salad. "You got this *just* right, Allie. Tastes exactly like Misu's!"

It wasn't long before others had dug in, and Allie beamed at the praise. Dallas could feel Jennifer's eyes on them as they got their own plates of food. Dallas kept a protective hand on Allie, sending a message to Jennifer: *I'm with someone else now.*

As they worked through the line, he glanced up once and saw Jennifer frowning. She could frown all night for all he cared.

Big drums were played, and two high school football players, dressed in traditional Hawaiian warrior garb, went to the spot of the buried pig. Jennifer excused herself from the camera crew and wandered closer to them. Dallas had no intention of talking to her, here or ever.

"It's time for the pig!" Dallas said, and directed Allie away from Jennifer to watch the muscled guys unearth the luau's main course. Dallas had been to a few luaus before, but it never ceased to amaze him. He marveled at how the men removed the pig, first using shovels to remove the sand, then taking off the hot cooking rocks and the banana leaves. Steam wafted up, hitting his nose.

Everyone lined up for their own piece. Dallas and Allie took seats on the beach. They ate and talked and watched the band play. As the sun set, and everyone finished their food, the entertainment began. Dozens of hula dancers from elementary age all the way up through college took turns presenting traditional Hawaiian dances. Dallas applauded each act but kept his eye on the camera crew and Jennifer, who had taken a seat across the performance circle from them, and kept looking in their direction. Dallas couldn't help but think she was plotting a plan of attack.

The last act of the evening was one of Kai's cousins performing an elaborate fire dance, much to the oohs and aahs of the audience. On the moonlit beach, the show was an amazing whirl of floating fire. When he finished, the audience burst into extended applause.

Then the mayor took the stage. A middle-aged Japanese woman, she held the microphone and thanked everyone for coming.

"Maybe we should go," Dallas suggested, not wanting to hear what came next. He'd been planning all along to make an early exit, but Allie had gotten talking to one person and then another. She was too damn nice, saying hello to everyone and chatting up a storm at their table. On a different day, it would have been nice to see her fitting in so well with the locals, but right now all he wanted to do was get her out of there. But she was too intent on hearing the mayor's speech, a snag he hadn't counted on.

"One minute," Allie said, leaning forward and listening, eager to hear what the district's mayor had to say.

"I hope to see everyone at the Kona Coffee Festival, starting tomorrow, and I'd like to introduce our celebrity judge this evening—" The mayor took a deep breath. Dallas grabbed Allie's hand. "Jennifer Thomas."

Allie froze beside him, watching Jennifer stand up and wave to the crowd. The camera crew danced around her, jiggling to get her from the best possible angle.

"Oh, no," Allie breathed. "Dallas…" She glanced at him, face pale with worry as she tightened her grip on his hand.

"It's going to be okay," he said. "She's just one of three judges. We'll still have a shot. We could still win." He thought if he said it often enough, maybe he'd even start to believe it.

"You aren't surprised. You knew." Allie paused and glared at him, a riot of emotion playing out on her face. "You *knew*." She sounded hurt, accusing even. Why was she angry at him? "How did you know?" she spat. "Did Jennifer tell you?"

Dallas frowned, confused. "Why would Jennifer tell me?"

"She texts you, doesn't she?"

Dallas's mind whirled. Jennifer hadn't texted him…except that last one. The one where she'd asked to have him back. Oh, Lord. Allie had seen it. She'd seen it, and she hadn't said anything. All this time, she'd been stewing about it and he hadn't known.

"Allie," Dallas said, but Allie had already moved away from him, gotten up and started walking across the beach. "Allie, wait."

She kept on walking. He had to jog to keep up with her and managed to catch her on the grass near the parking lot. "Allie! Hang on." He took her by the arm, and she whirled on him.

"Why don't you go back to Jennifer? Isn't that what you want?"

"There *is* no me and Jennifer. I *thought* there was a you and me…"

"Dallas. I saw how you were looking at her all night."

"Sure I was. She's a snake, and I don't trust her. I thought she might try to make a scene. I was just trying to be ready for it." Dallas frowned. "Allie, we have to talk." Allie stalked to the pickup truck, and he let her in. He went around to the driver's-side door, thinking that at least in the truck she couldn't go anywhere until they'd finished this conversation. If she could, she would've bolted right there, run away from him, but he was her ride home.

He slid into the truck and fired up the engine. Allie sat next to him with her arms tightly crossed across her chest, her face stubbornly looking away from his out the passenger window. He made his way back to the Kona Coffee Estate, trying to think of how to go about convincing Allie he was telling the truth.

They rode home in silence. He turned into the Kona Coffee Estate, the headlights illuminating the porch of Misu's old house.

Right at that moment, his phone, sitting in the cup holder of his truck pinged an incoming message. The high-pitched sound irked Allie, obviously, and she glared at his phone.

"Who's texting you?" Allie demanded. "Is it Jennifer?"

Dallas put the truck in Park and turned off the engine. He'd never seen Allie like this before: insane with jealousy, completely irrational, hurt and upset. He knew she'd lost control, and all he wanted was to calm her down so he could reason with her, help her see it was all in her head.

"It's no one," Dallas said.

"Your phone. I heard it!" Dallas saw how jealousy grabbed hold of her, illogical and insistent. He knew she couldn't help herself now as the accusations flew out. "Is it Jennifer? I know it is. I know what she's been texting you. I saw the texts."

"Why didn't you say something?" Dallas spread his hands, glaring at her, feeling helpless and frustrated. He wondered why she hadn't just asked him about them. He would've told her then what he planned to tell her now: Jennifer meant nothing to him.

"Why didn't *you*?" Allie countered. "It made me think you were hiding something."

"I *was* hiding something. That I have a crazy ex who is *out of her mind*." Dallas sighed and ran a frustrated hand through his hair. "Allie, I was trying to protect you. I didn't want to upset you. You should know better than anyone that I don't want to be with her. *She's* the one who's hounding me, not the other way around."

"But why would she? Why would she think she even has a chance?"

Dallas shook his head. "I don't know."

"You're encouraging her. Somehow, some way." Dallas could almost see the suspicion thrumming in Allie's brain. He hated it. He could see her reacting to him as if he was Jason, and he was nothing like that asshole. He didn't like sharing the same space in her head with him. "You're hiding something from me."

"Allie, I'm not."

He saw all the insecurities of her old relationship plain on her face. He knew it was hard for her to deprogram the assumption a man was lying to her. This was a knee-jerk reaction to Jason, Dallas knew, and yet he couldn't stop himself from getting angry. He didn't like being accused of things he didn't do. The entire island had done that for the past year with impunity, but he didn't want Allie to fall into the camp. If she couldn't trust him, if she couldn't have faith in him, then he was wasting his time.

He fished his phone out of the cup holder and showed her the face of it. The text had been from Kai. She looked as if she felt silly then, the flare of jealousy fading a bit, the stranglehold of emotion letting go a little.

"You don't love Jennifer?" she asked.

"No, I don't." Dallas ground his teeth. "It's over. I'm never going back to her." He sighed and again ran his hand through his thick blond hair. "But if you can't trust me, then we won't work."

Allie stared at him a long time, the shine of the porch light casting a long shadow across her face.

"You're asking a lot of me," she said. "More than a lot."

"I know what I'm asking. It's hard for me to

do, too, Allie." Dallas stared at her, his blue eyes never leaving hers. She hesitated, unsure.

"I don't know. I just…"

"It's not something you think about. You just know or you don't." Dallas waited, but Allie just couldn't seem to give him what he needed.

"What about tomorrow? What about the competition? We can't win now." Allie deftly changed the subject, clearly not wanting to answer him. Her voice sounded high-pitched and scratchy; he could hear the panic in it.

"I know it means a lot to you. With Jennifer on the panel, I don't know if we can." Dallas already knew what he could do about it. "I could talk to her, I guess."

"No," Allie snapped.

"Maybe I could help her see reason." It had never happened before, but there was always a first time, he thought. He hated the idea of ever asking Jennifer for anything, but for Allie, he would.

"So you can get back with her. Is that why you want to talk?" The anger and jealousy bubbled over in Allie's voice.

Dallas glared at Allie. The woman was making no sense whatsoever. He'd only just told her he wasn't going back to Jennifer. And he was a man of his word. If she didn't know that about him by now, maybe she'd never know it.

Dallas gripped the steering wheel of the parked truck, trying to keep his temper in check. "I know the contest meant a lot to you, and I just want to make sure we had a fair shake, that's all."

A bitter laugh escaped her lips. "That's right. It means a lot to me. You know why?" Her voice vibrated with anger. "We have to win, because that's the only way Kaimana will sign the papers, Dallas. She told me."

Allie might as well have punched Dallas straight in the face. The blow would've been less sudden and painful than her words tumbling into his ears.

"You still want to sell?" He couldn't believe after everything they'd been through, everything they shared, she still had it in her mind to run. He wanted to marry her, but if she was thinking about running, then clearly she didn't feel the same way about him. She was prepared to just throw away the connection they had as if it didn't matter, as if it was something that happened every day.

"I want to keep my options open." Allie glared out the front of the parked truck's windshield, not meeting his eyes.

"Open? So one of your options is to leave the Big Island. To leave me?" Dallas was almost afraid to hear the answer.

Allie hesitated, her gaze flicking back to his.

"I don't know." The truth of her confusion came through in her voice. But Dallas only felt the pain of it. He'd been left by Jennifer. He'd been hurt, too, and for once he wanted a woman who would just stand by him. He wanted the security of knowing that when he needed someone to lean on, she'd be there to offer her shoulder. It was a basic want, yet nobody had been able to give it to him in his whole life. He was used to being on his own, ever since his parents died, but that didn't mean he liked it.

"I can't believe this. Is that why you worked so hard all this time? It wasn't that you even liked the coffee, was it? It was all about making sure you could get the cash at the end. Is that it?" Dallas glanced up at Misu's house, where they'd lived together like a real couple for months. He turned away from the sight, his insides a tumble of emotions: anger, frustration, resentment. If she'd planned to sell, why string him along all this time? Why make him believe they had something special?

"Dallas, that's not what I mean."

"Sounds like it."

"I want *you* to have the plantation. If I do sell, I want to sell to you." She put her hand on his arm, her dark eyes earnest, looking as if this news should somehow make him happy. As if it was a peace offering.

Dallas shook his head, a hoarse laugh escaping his lips. "I can't buy it, Allie," he said.

"Don't you want it?" Allie sounded surprised. The wind off the ocean picked up, whipping her dark hair into her face. She pushed it out.

"Of course I do."

"Then, what's the problem?"

Now was the moment of truth. Dallas couldn't wiggle out of it, and he knew it. He sighed.

"I can't buy it because Jennifer stole most of my savings," he said grimly. "She wiped out my bank account when she left."

Allie blinked fast, trying to process this new bit of information. "She…what?"

"The woman you *thought* I still cared for. She guessed my passwords. She transferred the money into a joint account and then she just drained it. I never went to the police because I didn't want Kayla's mother going to jail. And I didn't say anything to anyone else because I didn't want Kayla being hurt by the rumors."

"Dallas…" Allie's voice trailed off as the enormity of the news sank in. "I'm so sorry."

"Are you?" Dallas asked her, feeling anger well up in his chest. "Are you really? Because it seems to me that your plan all along was just to leave."

Thunder rumbled in the distance. A storm was blowing in off the ocean. "That had always been my plan," she said. "You knew that."

"Yeah, but…I thought… I guess I thought you'd changed your mind."

"Dallas…" Pain ripped through Allie's face. Dallas chose not to see it.

He sighed, frustrated that after all this time, she still wanted to walk away from him, from everything they could be together. "Never mind. If after all this…you *still* want to go… Then nothing I can say even matters."

"But, Dallas…" Her voice sounded bitter and angry. "This is Jason's fault. If he hadn't cheated, I wouldn't be crazed with jealousy. I'm not normally like this. It's just…"

Dallas felt frustration well in him. He didn't know why she was so stubbornly clinging to the past. Why was she looking backward when there was so much potentially ahead of them?

"I'm not Jason." Dallas glanced at her from the driver's side of the truck.

"I know."

Dallas shook his head.

"No, I don't think you're hearing me. I'm not Jason. And I'm not going to have you treat me like Jason."

Allie's eyes brimmed with tears. He was making her cry, but he couldn't help it. He needed to reach her somehow.

"Let that go."

Tears rolled down Allie's face. "What if I can't?"

"Then you'll always be running away from your feelings, and you'll never be happy." Dallas shook his head, refusing to look at her. "I thought I could help you, Allie. I really thought I could, but it's like Jennifer all over again."

He could see the effect of his words on her, like a slap. He knew he should stop, but he couldn't help it.

"I couldn't help her, and I can't help you, either. You've got to do it yourself. I can't fix these problems for you," he said. "Go, then, if that's what you want." He reached across her and opened the passenger-side door.

"It's not what I want," she said, voice thick with tears.

"Then why do you want to sell?"

"I…I…"

The hesitation was enough for Dallas to want to give up. This girl wasn't in it for the long haul, no matter how hard he tried to convince her to stay. He didn't want to argue anymore, didn't want to hear her excuses. How could he trust her when in her mind she always had one foot on a plane? Big drops of rain splashed down on his windshield. The storm had come.

Reluctantly, she slipped out of the cab of the truck, tears glistening on her cheeks. Part of him wanted to wrap her up in his arms, kiss away those tears and tell her it was all going to be okay.

But he couldn't do that. She wanted to leave him, and he had to accept that.

"Are you coming in?" Her voice sounded like a small croak.

"No," he said. He didn't want to look at her. The anger and frustration built up inside. He didn't trust himself to be with her. He'd yell at her or say things he'd regret. He needed to be alone. She shut her door with a defeated-sounding *thunk*.

Dallas turned the ignition and the truck roared to life. He drove blindly in the tropical rainstorm, not even sure where he was going. He found himself on the road by the shoreline, just driving to who knew where. He didn't care. He still felt blindsided by Allie telling him she planned to sell. He couldn't understand why she didn't want to stay put, didn't want to stay with him, after the connection they had; he just didn't understand it. *Maybe she doesn't feel the same way* was all he could think. *Or maybe she's too scared to realize something like this doesn't come along every day. She's too busy hung up on the past; she's never going to be ready for her future.*

Whatever the case, he'd gone and fallen in love with another project, and he was done with fixer-upper women. He should've learned his lesson with Jennifer, and yet here he was again, in the exact same spot. *No, not quite the same*, his memory was quick to remind him. Jennifer was an awful and selfish person who did what she wanted when she wanted. Allie was just misguided, too fearful to trust in the happiness that could be hers.

Not that he blamed her. He'd come to think happiness was pretty much a mirage, too. Just when he thought he had it in his grasp, it always seemed to fade away. Through the hard-pouring rain, the streetlight ahead of Dallas turned yellow and then red. He hit the brakes and hydroplaned to an uneasy stop. The water pooled on the narrow road; the torrential rain flowed down the gutter and made little rivers in the ditches along the roadside. He drove aimlessly until he realized he was headed straight for the tree house. Maybe he could clear his head there.

The light turned green, and he pulled through the intersection, his back tires losing a little grip on the slick road until they found traction again.

What can I do to convince Allie to stay? Or should I even bother? It was up to her now, he knew as he drove through the rain, realizing as he passed a sign that he'd gone halfway around the island already.

Rain poured down from the dark night sky, and his truck's windshield wipers had trouble keeping up. He passed by a big tourist resort. A bright new red sedan, clearly a rental car, swerved out into the road without looking, and Dallas only just missed him, hitting the gas and accelerating.

Drunk tourist, he thought, and decided he'd try to get the license plate and call his friend Lyle to see if the car couldn't be picked up. In his side mirror, he saw the driver throw out an empty beer can. He'd already hit something because the left headlight was cracked and not working. Dallas got a bad feeling then, his heart rate jumping.

The rental sped up, its one headlight bright in Dallas's rearview mirror. He blinked against the brightness.

What's that idiot doing? Dallas thought, even as he moved over to the other lane. The car wove dangerously back and forth across the road, even passing the yellow median marker. *He's going to kill someone.*

The turnoff to the tree house came, and he took it, anxious to get away from the warbling lights. Amazingly, they followed him.

What the hell?

The headlights came to his side mirror again; this time, they were speeding up. Dallas clutched the steering wheel. The drunk driver gained, and Dallas tried to slow down and get out of the way, but the other car sloppily swerved into his lane. The passenger tire of Dallas's truck caught the edge of the road.

This is going to be bad, Dallas thought, his

heart in his throat as his truck skidded off the highway, veering toward a tall palm tree, and he braced for the inevitable impact.

CHAPTER TWENTY

THE NEXT MORNING, the morning of the first day of the Kona Coffee Festival, Allie woke up feeling sick to her stomach. She put her hand on his side of the bed and felt only a cold emptiness. His side of the comforter hadn't been touched the entire night. He'd left her in a chilling silence the night before, and he hadn't come home. Allie hadn't expected him to. Not after the fight they'd had. She didn't even understand it herself.

Last night, it had been the jealousy that had taken over. She'd thought she was over Jason. Sure, she still felt angry anytime she thought of him, but wasn't that just natural? He'd lied to her about everything he'd ever been, and he'd made their whole relationship a lie. It still burned like stomach acid in her throat when she thought about it. But part of her knew Dallas was right. She was holding on to the past, even if it was just by being angry. It was a fatal character flaw, she realized: always looking backward, never forward. She was like a girl in a horror movie, running through the dark woods, stumbling because she was too busy looking backward to find the path ahead.

She glanced at her suitcase in the corner, thinking, *I could pack right now. I could pack up my stuff and head to the airport and get on the first flight out to anywhere.*

What was she doing? Thinking about running… again? God, she was tired of running. She was tired of not trusting anyone. She sniffed, wiping her tears angrily from her face. She was tired of crying. She *liked* it here. She liked the people, too.

And she loved Dallas. She wanted to trust him.

But how? The means escaped her. How was she supposed to do it?

Maybe the key to trusting Dallas was just *deciding* to do it. Maybe it was just that simple.

She called Dallas but got his voice mail. No matter. She'd fix this one way or another.

She might not know what the right thing was to do, but she'd at least try to win that contest. They'd worked too hard to give up now. She wasn't going to let Jennifer take away another one of Dallas's dreams. Not on her watch.

THE KONA COFFEE FESTIVAL banner hung across the main street, which had been blocked off by a police car for pedestrians only. White tents dotted the thoroughfare, and tourists and locals mingled together on the street shaded by huge palm trees. The crowd was big, and Allie knew the locals would be glad. The PR Kai had done with the luau had clearly worked. People on other islands must've seen it and hopped puddle jumpers to get there in time for the festival. She saw lots of T-shirts advertising Maui and Oahu restaurants and bars worn in the crowd. The strong smell of rich Kona coffee filled the air. Allie inhaled, loving the scent.

Allie found the judge's station, a small white tent with a long table. They'd be tallying scores there, but otherwise, they'd be wandering down to each tent, savoring cups of smooth coffee.

Allie just made it to the Kona Coffee Estate tent, which had nothing but a white cover and a table. She hastily set up the coffee machine she'd brought, as well as some bags to sell, and a few jars of her new exfoliating coffee face mask. She put out a sample and a mirror, as well. She'd planned to have a presence here, and hoped Dallas would show up. He'd worked so hard for this, she couldn't imagine he'd just not come.

Maybe that's how badly you hurt him, she thought. *Maybe that's how mad he still is about hearing you want to leave him.*

She watched as the judges, who wore white ribbons, mingled near the judges' tent at the far end of the street. Jennifer stood near her camera crew, which never seemed to leave her side, overdressed as usual. She wore a tight-fitting white sundress and matching espadrilles. She looked her intimidating best: with her ample cleavage on display and a pound of makeup. She carried an expensive designer bag, and suddenly Allie felt angry. Had she spent Dallas's money on the bag? On her brand-new shoes?

Or was that something Dallas had made up? She believed him, or at least she wanted to believe him, but a nagging doubt in her mind dogged her. There was only one way to find out for sure: go talk to the woman. Either she'd find out she was secretly having sex with Dallas, or she'd find out Dallas was telling the truth. Either way, she had to know.

She'd never done anything like this, brazenly confronting a near stranger and accusing them of grand theft. She realized, standing there in the middle of the festival, that she'd run away from conflict her whole life: she'd run away from the car accident, run away from facing Grandma Misu, and she'd run away from Dallas, too.

But flight hadn't worked so well for her in the past. It was time for fight.

She marched through the crowd, abandoning her tent.

"Excuse me," she said as she tapped Jennifer's shoulder. The woman turned, a slow smirk appearing on her face when she saw her.

"Allie Osaka, right?" Jennifer flipped her blond hair off her shoulder. Her makeup was flawless. Allie barely wore any. But she didn't care.

"I need to talk to you. About Dallas McCormick. In private." Allie's heart thumped so loudly in her chest she thought for sure Jennifer would be able to hear it.

"Oh, the whole island knows the way Dallas treated me. Nothing's a secret here." Allie was surprised. If Jennifer really had been having a secret affair with Dallas, she wouldn't still be bad-mouthing him in public. Unless… Unless, she'd never had an affair with him at all. Unless, he'd rejected her and she was still angry about it.

In that instant, Allie knew Dallas had been telling the truth. He'd really ended things with Jennifer and had no intention of getting back with her. The honest hurt and anger on Jennifer's face told Allie everything. She'd been wrong to mistrust Dallas. He'd been true to his word. That meant this woman had stolen money from him, just like he'd said.

"Unless you want the whole island to know what you really did, you'll come with me right now." Allie kept her voice low enough not to be overheard, but Jennifer got the message loud and clear.

Jennifer's face registered shock and then something more—fear. "Not here," she said, and she steered Allie away from her camera crew and back to a more secluded spot between two tents.

"What do you know?" Jennifer asked, her voice low and suddenly not quite as confident as she was just a few minutes ago. Allie looked at Jennifer and saw for the first time the dark rings under her eyes, the way she fidgeted nervously with her cuticles. She'd chewed her nails down the quick. Dallas had been telling the truth. Jennifer had done all he'd said!

"I know you stole fifty thousand dollars that didn't belong to you," Allie began. She was glad her voice sounded calm and even.

"I didn't steal…" Jennifer murmured, but her heart wasn't in her own defense.

"I don't want to hear your side. I want you to stop bad-mouthing Dallas."

"I—I…" Jennifer chewed on one of her cuticles again, anxious. The woman was as guilty as she could be. It was all the proof Allie needed.

"Don't lie to me. You're spreading lies, and they stop now."

"Or?"

"Or I tell the whole town, including the police, what you've done."

Jennifer turned as white as the polished inside of a seashell.

"You wouldn't."

But Jennifer sounded unsure, and she shifted her weight from foot to foot.

"Oh, yes, I will." Allie lowered her voice as a group of tourists sauntered by. "You can do this the easy way, or we can do it the hard way."

"Okay, listen. I think we can work this out, all right?" Jennifer splayed her hands helplessly. It only made Allie angrier. She knew the girlish gesture was all an act.

"Mommy?" Kayla had wandered between the tents, holding her stuffed animal by one paw.

"Sweetie, I told you to stay with Auntie Amy."

"Amy talked to too many grown-ups. It got boring." The girl shifted on one foot and then the other. Jennifer picked up Kayla gently and lovingly kissed her on the cheek. The picture was hard to reconcile: the coldhearted woman who'd drained Dallas's bank account and then the woman who lovingly cared for the little girl.

The scene made her think that maybe Jennifer wasn't 100 percent bad. Like everyone else, she was part good, part bad, doing the best she could with the hand she'd been dealt. Seeing her made Allie rethink Jason a little bit, too. Could he have been both the kind, doting fiancé she'd known and the man who'd cruelly cheated? Were those both *true* parts of him? Maybe the loving fiancé wasn't a lie, but it wasn't the whole truth, either. He was both men. That made it easier to live with somehow.

She hadn't been duped; she'd just not seen all of the truth until the end.

Jennifer held her daughter and sniffed back tears.

"Kayla!" Aunt Amy, apparently, called out for her.

"One minute," Jennifer said, and then she carried her girl out and left her with Amy once more. She beat a hasty return.

"I'm sorry, okay? I know I did a bad thing! I know it." Tears started to well in her pretty green eyes. "I c-c-couldn't help it."

"You couldn't help cheating on Dallas? Or stealing his money? *I* think you could."

"I know I've done bad things." Jennifer sniffed back more tears as she grabbed a tissue from her shoulder bag. She blew her nose indelicately. "But *you're* Dallas's latest prize. You have to know how it feels. Women throwing themselves at him all the time. He's a good man and gorgeous, but how is he supposed to resist that *all* the time? I mean women line up to watch him kayak, for God's sake. *Line up!* There was always someone younger or skinnier than me. Always. How could I compete?"

Allie didn't say a word. She let Jennifer speak, let her get it out. She knew what it felt like to feel as though she didn't measure up. After all, she'd had Jennifer's beaming face on billboards to deal with for the past months.

"I did what I did because I just didn't believe I could keep Dallas. I didn't believe it was possible. I'm just *one* woman. A man like him needs more than one. I know. I've dated plenty of them. They're amazing in bed, and so damn hot, but in the end, they can't be faithful. It's just not in their biology. Men are just men."

Allie couldn't exactly argue. Her experience with Jason told her the same thing.

"Did Dallas ever cheat on you?" Allie felt her stomach tighten, not quite sure she wanted to know the answer or not.

"Not that I know of, but who knows? It could've happened. Probably did." Jennifer wiped her runny nose angrily. "And it *would've*. That's what's important. I slept with a producer because I had to hedge my bets. That's all. I didn't want him to leave me first."

Allie just shook her head, amazed at the twisted logic. Jennifer really believed it was all about self-preservation. Jennifer barreled on, as if Allie could somehow absolve her of her sins.

"I took Dallas's money because he owed me for leaving. He told me he'd take care of me and Kayla. He promised me." Jennifer swiped at her eyes with the balled-up tissue. Allie almost felt sorry for her—almost. "Dallas gave his money away to *everybody* but me. Don't you understand that? He gave it to God knows how many losers on this island. Helping them with this and that, but what about me? What about the promises he made to me?"

Allie shook her head sadly. As she looked at the sniveling, pathetic mess of this girl in front of her, it suddenly hit her that she was on the path to becoming just like her. If she kept believing that all men were Jason, if she kept mistrusting and seeing deception everywhere she looked, she'd be no better than Jennifer.

"Dallas left, too, like they all do in the end. Just like my dad. My high school boyfriend. Everybody leaves." Jennifer started sobbing. And Allie felt more resolved than ever not to become like her. *This was what happens when you become a victim in your own life*, she thought. *Everything spirals out of your control, and you lose the things you love most.*

How long have I let Dad's car crash define who I was? How long would I let Jason's betrayal make me who I am? Those things don't define me. I decide who I am. Everything is a choice. I can choose to be obsessed with the past or I can move forward.

She wasn't about to become like Jennifer, someone who spent her life wondering what bad thing someone was going to do to her next and figuring out how to stick it to them first. And then she realized how she could do it: simply decide *not* to. The answer was amazingly straightforward. She felt freer and lighter. She could be who she wanted to be.

"Jennifer, the past is the past," Allie said, confidence welling in her. "But from here on out, you don't say another word about Dallas."

"And if I do?" she sobbed.

"Then things are about to get a whole lot worse for you."

"Fine," she agreed reluctantly.

Allie glanced up at the white coffee tent in front of her, the aroma of fresh-roasted coffee wafting through the flaps.

"And one more thing," she said. "When it comes to the Kona Coffee Estate, you're going to abstain from voting."

Jennifer raised her eyebrows in surprise. "Abstain? You're not going to twist my arm for a vote?"

"Nope," Allie said. "That wouldn't be fair to everyone else. But you have a history with Dallas, and you should tell the other judges you don't think you can be objective. End of story. You don't vote."

Jennifer frowned as Allie imagined her idea

of twisting the knife once more in Dallas's back evaporated before her eyes. "Okay," she agreed. "Whatever you want. I'll do it."

CHAPTER TWENTY-ONE

ALLIE KEPT EXPECTING Dallas to make a miraculous last-minute arrival at the festival before the judging began at ten, but he was a no-show. Right about then, Allie started to worry. Where was he? As she waited her turn to be judged, festivalgoers came by in droves to sample coffee and to try out the coffee scrub and mask she'd created. Several women bought tubs on the spot.

The judges came to each tent, and when they stopped at Allie's, Jennifer did exactly what she was told. She glanced at Allie anxiously, but she didn't take the mug of coffee sitting on the table. She told the other judges they'd have to decide.

Neither one looked particularly surprised. Both probably had known about her relationship with Dallas. Almost every local knew. As they tasted the coffee and jotted down notes, Allie watched their faces carefully for any sign of approval, but they simply sipped the Kona Coffee Estate mugs with poker faces. Allie's palms felt clammy with nerves. She wished Dallas were here, and couldn't imagine where he could be. Was he that angry that he'd stayed away? She called him multiple times, but each attempt to reach him went straight to voice mail.

As she waited, she got more anxious. Then, when she saw Officer Lyle approach her tent, she knew in her heart something was wrong.

"Allie, right?" Officer Lawson said. "Listen, I know you and Dallas are friends, so…"

She knew that somber expression he wore: police and doctors only wore it when they had bad news to deliver.

"Has something happened?"

"He's been in an accident, miss. Looks as if a drunk driver pushed him off the road. He's at the hospital now."

"Oh, my God." Allie felt her knees go weak, and she nearly fainted. *Please, no. Not Dallas!* Officer Lawson gently grabbed her by the shoulder and steadied her.

"I want to go there. Can you take me there? I have to see him… I…" Her head felt dizzy.

"Of course." Lyle helped her to his police car, parked not too far away. With his lights on, traffic parted, allowing him through. Allie gripped her seat with white knuckles. All she wanted to do was get to that hospital. She couldn't think of anything else. There was so much she wanted to tell him, but most of all, she wanted to apologize for mistrusting him, for thinking the worst. But it might be too late. She felt panic in her throat. Dallas couldn't be taken from her, not now, not when she'd finally figured it all out.

Lyle let his sirens wail as they pulled in and out of traffic, and cars nudged themselves over to the shoulder, out of his way. When he pulled up to the ER entrance, Allie was out of the car, desperate to find out if Dallas was all right. She charged the nurse's station, ready for war. When Lyle approached, too, the nurse had no choice but to give them the information they wanted: Dallas McCormick was resting comfortably down the hall in 112.

Allie had never felt such relief in her life. He was alive! She sprinted down the hallway and burst into his room.

"Allie?" came Dallas's deep voice in surprise. He was sitting up in bed, his head wrapped in a bandage, his arm in a sling, wearing only a striped hospital gown. She couldn't help herself—she threw her body on top of his and cried.

"Ow," he said, and instantly she pulled back.

"I'm sorry! Did I hurt you?"

"The arm is a bit tender," he said. "Doc said I broke it in two places and nearly broke my head, too. I was knocked out cold for hours."

"Are you all right? I…I thought you were mad at me. I had no idea you…"

"I'll be fine, Allie. It was a drunk driver. I

swerved to avoid hitting them and hit a tree instead. I don't know how long I was out, but one of Lyle's buddies who was on patrol saw me and called it in. I've been at this hospital since, but I only just woke up. Once I did, I had Lyle find you. I knew you'd be at the festival, so I sent Lyle to get you and…"

Allie hugged him again, lighter this time. "I was so worried about you. There's so much I have to tell you…I…"

Dallas pulled her in for a kiss, stopping her midsentence. Lyle cleared his throat awkwardly, and the two reluctantly pulled apart.

"Give us a minute, Lyle," Dallas said, sending the patrol officer out of the room.

He squeezed her hand with his good one and smiled.

Her heart thrummed loudly in her ears as she worked up the courage to say what she knew needed to be said.

"Dallas, I am so sorry. I was wrong to want to leave," Allie said. "I didn't get to tell you before, but I should have. I…I…love you."

Dallas's eyes brightened. "You do?" he teased, his voice sounding raw and hoarse.

"Dallas!" Allie felt like punching him in the arm. Now was not the time to joke. She'd just laid her heart on the line! If he didn't say he loved her back, then she was going to be an inconsolable mess. "Don't tease. My heart can't take it."

Dallas grew serious as he pulled her palm up to his lips and kissed it. "Allie, I love you. I've loved you since the moment I laid eyes on you. All I want to do is spend the rest of my life showing you just how much I love you."

Allie leaned down and they kissed, their lips meeting in a tender rush, and Allie felt as if her heart was going to burst with happiness.

Jesse came rushing into the room. "Lyle called us," Jesse breathed, and Allie saw Kai still with a slight limp but the brace gone. "Are you all right?"

"Clearly, word of his demise has been *greatly* exaggerated," Kai joked as Allie scrambled out of the bed, and flattened her wrinkled shirt with the palm of her hand, a blush creeping up her cheek.

"Seriously! You scared us," Jesse said, play swatting Dallas on the arm. "Lyle said a drunk driver hit you! That you hit a tree!"

"I'm tougher than I look, and I have a lot to live for." Dallas squeezed Allie's hand once more, and she felt a warm tingle all the way to her toes.

Jesse and Kai crowded around Dallas's bedside. "We have to stop meeting at hospitals like this," Kai joked, and Dallas let out a reluctant laugh.

"It's a much better visit for me when *you're* in

this bed," Dallas grumbled, but Kai laughed. Dallas joined him, until a fit of coughing cut him off.

"Easy there, guy. I can't whoop your butt surfing if you don't recover." Kai nudged his friend playfully.

"Ha. Ha." Dallas smiled up at his friend.

"By the way, Lyle told us they just picked up the drunk driver," Jesse said. "Some tourist from the mainland. A ranger found him wandering Volcanoes National Park. He's in jail tonight, going to be arraigned tomorrow. He told me to tell you he'll be by tomorrow morning to get your statement."

"Good," Dallas said. "That guy could've killed someone."

"I am very glad he didn't." Allie squeezed Dallas's hand.

"I have even better news," Kai said. "What with all this life-or-death action, you both missed all the excitement at the festival."

Now he had both Allie's and Dallas's attention.

"Don't tell me—Jennifer Thomas tanked our chances." Dallas looked resigned to defeat.

"No, actually," Jesse said. "I heard that she abstained."

"Why would she do that?" Dallas sat up straighter in bed.

Jesse glanced at Allie. "I *heard* Allie might have had something to do with it."

Dallas stared at Allie, who shrugged. "I might have."

"Allie…what did you do?"

"Just a little talk, woman to woman."

Kai laughed. "Was there scratching and hair pulling involved? Tell me you got her good."

"No fighting. But I won anyway." Allie grinned, and Dallas pulled her in for a hug.

"I knew there was an excellent reason I loved you."

"But who won?" Allie could hardly stand to hear what had happened.

"Do you want the bad news or the good news first?" Kai asked, a twinkle in his eye.

"You *mean* the good news or better news," Jesse clarified. Allie felt butterflies tickle her stomach. She could hardly wait to find out.

"Just tell us already!" Dallas couldn't wait, either.

"You got *second* place for your coffee." Kai pulled out a red ribbon from his pocket and handed it to Dallas.

"*That's* not bad news, by the way," Jesse felt the need to say, but Allie could see the disappointment flicker across Dallas's face. He'd been so hoping for a blue ribbon.

"I knew we wouldn't win, but still. I was hoping."

"You *won* second place," Jesse pointed out. "Nothing wrong with that."

"And what's the other news?" Allie asked. She couldn't imagine there was more.

"You *did* win first place for New Coffee Product." Kai produced a blue first-place ribbon and handed it to Allie. "Your coffee spa scrub won."

Allie felt as if she hadn't heard him right. "It... won? But I didn't enter it. How...?"

"I did," Jesse said. "Well, technically, Teri did, but I helped fill out the paperwork."

Allie hugged Jesse. "Thank you," she said, and took the blue ribbon, suddenly feeling very proud. She'd *won*!

She glanced at Dallas, but he didn't look as happy as she felt.

"I guess this means you can sell," Dallas said. "Kaimana didn't say *which* competition you'd have to win. Just that you win."

Allie glanced at the blue ribbon in her hand, her mind already made up. "No, it means that we try again next year for the blue ribbon for coffee."

Hope crossed Dallas's face. "You mean it?"

"I want to stay!" Allie had never felt surer of anything. A joyful grin lit up Dallas's face, even as Kai and Jesse wrapped Allie in a bear hug.

"That's good, because you know we weren't going to let you leave," Kai said.

"We would've shut down the airport," Jesse promised.

"Would you let her go? I need my hug," Dallas complained. Reluctantly, Kai and Jesse released Allie. Dallas pulled her to his side of the bed.

"It took you long enough to decide," he said, and then tugged her down, her face even with his, for a kiss.

EPILOGUE

Two months later, Volcanoes National Park, Big Island

"ARE YOU COMING?" Allie asked, pushing ahead up the trail that would take them to the summit of the island's most active volcano, Kīlauea. Allie couldn't wait to get to the top.

"You're going so fast," Dallas groaned, a bit out of breath as he followed her up the steep, dark trail of the near-barren mountain face. He'd gotten his cast off, but his arm was still tender as he worked to strengthen the muscles.

Black lava rocks sat everywhere, and the landscape looked strangely barren, as if they'd landed on another planet. Yet every so often, a bright green tree or tropical plant would spring up from the dirt, a vibrant reminder that after the burning lava cooled, it healed over to provide some of the richest soil on earth.

He thought it was a lot like life. When someone scorched your heart, sometimes beautiful things could grow there after, even if you thought love could never live there again.

Dallas saw the huge cracks in the earth where rocks had shifted and cooled a long time back. As always, he felt awe at the power of the active volcano that had been erupting since 1983. Mountains of black soil and rock surrounded them as they walked through the trail in the valley. He walked by a single baby green palm tree springing up from a crack in the dirt and shook his head at the miracle.

"Come on, slowpoke," Allie chided. "I finally get you away from tending to the coffee for *one day*. You can't go and waste it by dragging your feet."

"I'm going as fast as I can!" Dallas protested, but grinned. "I'm the one with the broken arm, remember?"

"Are you walking on your hands or what?" she teased, poking his belly. As she led the way, her backpack bounced on her back, her hiking shoes making trails in the dust. "Come on, I've never seen a real live volcano!"

Allie hurried ahead, excited. He smiled, too, feeling glad to see her happy. He sped up and grabbed her by the waist, unable to keep his hands off her a second longer. He kissed her there, on the trail, tasting her tongue, inhaling her sweet scent.

"What was that for?" she asked, a little bit breathless as she pulled away.

"Because I can't help it since you're so beautiful." He grinned. "Plus these might be our last minutes alive on earth. Only you would think it's safe for us to go see a live volcano. Wasn't it good enough we survived a tsunami *and* a drunk driver?"

"The volcano is safe," Allie chided even as she giggled. "See? The eruption predictions today are on the other side of the mountain." Allie waved the ranger's brochures in his face.

"Right. We are disaster prone. You know that."

"That's why we're on the east side today." Allie bounded away from Dallas, picking up her pace along the trail, where a single posted wooden sign told them to head east for a lookout point.

Dallas let her go, watching her bounce forward, thinking he'd never been happier. He slipped his hand in his pockct, looking for the black velvet box he'd hidden there. He didn't feel nervous at all. He wanted to see his ring on her finger more than he'd wanted anything in his life. Unlike with Jennifer, he felt not a single doubt. His only real worry was that she'd say no. He was pretty sure she'd gotten over her fears of putting down roots, but he'd test that today.

He followed her up the trail, and as they climbed up the mountain, she clasped the metal rail along the trail leading upward. When they got to the summit, a little bit out of breath, they were rewarded with an amazing view of the huge crater left by old ash and lava, ringed with bright green trees, and in the far distance, the hint of the blue sparkling Pacific Ocean.

"Oh, Dallas!" she cried, grabbing his hand and holding it tight. "It's beautiful!" A single plume of steam rose up from the hole in the crater in the distance. "Look! There!"

Allie pulled out her binoculars and focused on the steam. "I can't believe we're standing on a live volcano. This is…amazing," she murmured.

"You know this is why our coffee tastes so good," Dallas said. "The lava soil is like no other on earth."

Allie put down her binoculars. "The Big Island amazes me. It does. Where else can you have all this together? I just can't imagine another place on earth this wonderful. You know, Kaimana said Pele lives here."

"Does she, now? What did Kaimana say we should do? Offer up a sacrifice?"

"Yes, as a matter of fact, she did." Allie tugged off her backpack and pulled out a small bottle of gin.

"What on earth?" Dallas couldn't help but laugh. He thought Allie might take a swig straight from the bottle. Instead, she unscrewed the cap and dumped half of it into the dirt near their feet.

"Here's to Pele," Allie said, grinning. "Kaimana said the volcano goddess loves gin."

Dallas just laughed. "Are you sure that's not another one of her tricks?"

Allie shrugged. "Can't hurt, right?" She screwed the cap back on the half-empty bottle and then put it into her backpack.

Dallas twisted and picked Allie up one-handed, holding her by his good arm around her waist.

"Dallas! Put me down!"

He carried her closer to the mouth of the volcano.

"So you *want* me to throw you into the volcano?" His eyes were bright.

"Dallas!" Allie squealed, playfully swinging her legs. On the trail, they came to a wooden sign that said, Caution! Trail Below. Do Not Throw Anything Into the Volcano!

"Oh, well," Dallas said, putting Allie back on her feet. "Guess I can't throw the maiden into the volcano. It's against park rules."

Allie giggled and hit him on his arm. "You are terrible!"

"Am not. Given our luck with natural disasters, I was just trying to be on the safe side." Dallas glanced left, away from the steaming volcano mouth beyond, and saw the lookout he'd been waiting for. It was a beautiful view of the lush tropical rain forest beyond. "Hey, let's go there." Dallas guided Allie to the spot.

"Can you see the tree house?" he asked her, pointing into the thicket of trees below.

"No! Where?" She raised her binoculars, scanning the treetops.

He reached into his pocket and grabbed the velvet box. When she turned around, he knelt before her. Confusion passed across her face until he opened the box in his hand, revealing a bright diamond ring. Tears sprang to her eyes as she covered her mouth with both hands.

"Alani Osaka, I love you. You came into my life at a time when I thought I could never love again. I want to wake up with you every morning, and go to sleep with you every night. You make me want to be my best self, and make me believe anything is possible. You are my sun and my moon, and my everything. We're here on this mountain celebrating the fact that the Big Island is always growing, always changing, and I can't imagine a better life than one with you in it, here, with me. I've always said this is the most beautiful place on earth, but now I realize it wasn't until you got here. Allie, my beautiful love, will you marry me?"

Allie's eyes brimmed with tears as she choked on emotion. She didn't say a word for a beat, and Dallas almost worried that the skittish Allie might return. For the briefest of moments, his heart clenched. Was she going to tell him no? This was why he wanted to marry her and fast—he didn't want her to slip away from him. Not again. Not ever.

"Allie?" Dallas asked her, even as a tear slid down her cheek. She moved her hands from her mouth.

"Yes, yes, a million times, yes!" she blurted, and Dallas felt awash in relief. Nothing could've made him happier than to hear those words.

Dallas took the ring from the box and slipped it on her finger. She gazed at it, tears in her eyes, and then jumped on him as he was trying to rise to his feet. She nearly toppled him, but he found his footing, wrapping her up in his arms. Allie stood on her tiptoes and kissed Dallas furiously, and Dallas returned the favor. Behind them, smoke rose from the volcano in a hissing puff, as if Pele approved.

"I'm never going to let you go, Dallas McCormick," Allie promised.

"I'm counting on it," Dallas drawled, and dipped his head for another kiss.

* * * * *

LARGER-PRINT BOOKS!

HARLEQUIN

Presents®

GET 2 FREE LARGER-PRINT NOVELS PLUS 2 FREE GIFTS!

PASSION
GUARANTEED
SEDUCTION

YES! Please send me 2 FREE LARGER-PRINT Harlequin Presents® novels and my 2 FREE gifts (gifts are worth about $10). After receiving them, if I don't wish to receive any more books, I can return the shipping statement marked "cancel." If I don't cancel, I will receive 6 brand-new novels every month and be billed just $5.30 per book in the U.S. or $5.74 per book in Canada. That's a saving of at least 12% off the cover price! It's quite a bargain! Shipping and handling is just 50¢ per book in the U.S. and 75¢ per book in Canada.* I understand that accepting the 2 free books and gifts places me under no obligation to buy anything. I can always return a shipment and cancel at any time. Even if I never buy another book, the two free books and gifts are mine to keep forever.

176/376 HDN GHVY

Name _____ (PLEASE PRINT)

Address _____ Apt. #

City _____ State/Prov. _____ Zip/Postal Code

Signature (if under 18, a parent or guardian must sign)

Mail to the **Reader Service:**
IN U.S.A.: P.O. Box 1867, Buffalo, NY 14240-1867
IN CANADA: P.O. Box 609, Fort Erie, Ontario L2A 5X3

**Are you a subscriber to Harlequin Presents® books and want to receive the larger-print edition?
Call 1-800-873-8635 today or visit us at www.ReaderService.com.**

* Terms and prices subject to change without notice. Prices do not include applicable taxes. Sales tax applicable in N.Y. Canadian residents will be charged applicable taxes. Offer not valid in Quebec. This offer is limited to one order per household. Not valid for current subscribers to Harlequin Presents Larger-Print books. All orders subject to credit approval. Credit or debit balances in a customer's account(s) may be offset by any other outstanding balance owed by or to the customer. Please allow 4 to 6 weeks for delivery. Offer available while quantities last.

Your Privacy—The Reader Service is committed to protecting your privacy. Our Privacy Policy is available online at www.ReaderService.com or upon request from the Reader Service.

We make a portion of our mailing list available to reputable third parties that offer products we believe may interest you. If you prefer that we not exchange your name with third parties, or if you wish to clarify or modify your communication preferences, please visit us at www.ReaderService.com/consumerschoice or write to us at Reader Service Preference Service, P.O. Box 9062, Buffalo, NY 14240-9062. Include your complete name and address.

HPLP15

LARGER-PRINT BOOKS!

GET 2 FREE LARGER-PRINT NOVELS PLUS
2 FREE GIFTS!

♦ HARLEQUIN®

Romance

From the Heart, For the Heart

YES! Please send me 2 FREE LARGER-PRINT Harlequin® Romance novels and my 2 FREE gifts (gifts are worth about $10). After receiving them, if I don't wish to receive any more books, I can return the shipping statement marked "cancel." If I don't cancel, I will receive 4 brand-new novels every month and be billed just $5.09 per book in the U.S. or $5.49 per book in Canada. That's a savings of at least 15% off the cover price! It's quite a bargain! Shipping and handling is just 50¢ per book in the U.S. and 75¢ per book in Canada.* I understand that accepting the 2 free books and gifts places me under no obligation to buy anything. I can always return a shipment and cancel at any time. Even if I never buy another book, the two free books and gifts are mine to keep forever.

119/319 HDN GHWC

Name	(PLEASE PRINT)

Address	Apt. #

City	State/Prov.	Zip/Postal Code

Signature (if under 18, a parent or guardian must sign)

Mail to the **Reader Service:**
IN U.S.A.: P.O. Box 1867, Buffalo, NY 14240-1867
IN CANADA: P.O. Box 609, Fort Erie, Ontario L2A 5X3

Want to try two free books from another line?
Call 1-800-873-8635 or visit www.ReaderService.com.

* Terms and prices subject to change without notice. Prices do not include applicable taxes. Sales tax applicable in N.Y. Canadian residents will be charged applicable taxes. Offer not valid in Quebec. This offer is limited to one order per household. Not valid for current subscribers to Harlequin Romance Larger-Print books. All orders subject to credit approval. Credit or debit balances in a customer's account(s) may be offset by any other outstanding balance owed by or to the customer. Please allow 4 to 6 weeks for delivery. Offer available while quantities last.

Your Privacy—The Reader Service is committed to protecting your privacy. Our Privacy Policy is available online at www.ReaderService.com or upon request from the Reader Service.

We make a portion of our mailing list available to reputable third parties that offer products we believe may interest you. If you prefer that we not exchange your name with third parties, or if you wish to clarify or modify your communication preferences, please visit us at www.ReaderService.com/consumerschoice or write to us at Reader Service Preference Service, P.O. Box 9062, Buffalo, NY 14240-9062. Include your complete name and address.

HRLP15